J. J. Connington and The Murder Room

**››› This title is part of The Murder Room, our series dedicated to making available out-of-print or hard-to-find titles by classic crime writers.

Crime fiction has always held up a mirror to society. The Victorians were fascinated by sensational murder and the emerging science of detection; now we are obsessed with the forensic detail of violent death. And no other genre has so captivated and enthralled readers.

Vast troves of classic crime writing have for a long time been unavailable to all but the most dedicated frequenters of second-hand bookshops. The advent of digital publishing means that we are now able to bring you the backlists of a huge range of titles by classic and contemporary crime writers, some of which have been out of print for decades.

From the genteel amateur private eyes of the Golden Age and the femmes fatales of pulp fiction, to the morally ambiguous hard-boiled detectives of mid twentieth-century America and their descendants who walk our twenty-first century streets, The Murder Room has it all. ›››**

The Murder Room
Where Criminal Minds Meet

themurderroom.com

J. J. Connington (1880–1947)

Alfred Walter Stewart, who wrote under the pen name J. J. Connington, was born in Glasgow, the youngest of three sons of Reverend Dr Stewart. He graduated from Glasgow University and pursued an academic career as a chemistry professor, working for the Admiralty during the First World War. Known for his ingenious and carefully worked-out puzzles and in-depth character development, he was admired by a host of his better-known contemporaries, including Dorothy L. Sayers and John Dickson Carr, who both paid tribute to his influence on their work. He married Jessie Lily Courts in 1916 and they had one daughter.

By J. J. Connington

Sir Clinton Driffield Mysteries
Murder in the Maze (1927)
Tragedy at Ravensthorpe (1927)
The Case with Nine Solutions (1928)
Mystery at Lynden Sands (1928)
Nemesis at Raynham Parva (1929)
 (a.k.a. Grim Vengenace)
The Boathouse Riddle (1931)
The Sweepstake Murders (1931)
The Castleford Conundrum (1932)
The Ha-Ha Case (1934)
 (a.k.a. The Brandon Case)
In Whose Dim Shadow (1935)
 (a.k.a. The Tau Cross Mystery)
A Minor Operation (1937)
Murder Will Speak (1938)

Truth Comes Limping (1938)
The Twenty-One Clues (1941)
No Past is Dead (1942)
Jack-in-the-Box (1944)
Common Sense Is All You Need (1947)

Supt Ross Mysteries
The Eye in the Museum (1929)
The Two Tickets Puzzle (1930)

Novels
Death at Swaythling Court (1926)
The Dangerfield Talisman (1926)
Tom Tiddler's Island (1933)
 (a.k.a. Gold Brick Island)
The Counsellor (1939)
The Four Defences (1940)

Tom Tiddler's Island

J. J. Connington

An Orion book

Copyright © The Professor A. W. Stewart Deceased Trust 1933, 2013

The right of J. J. Connington to be identified as the author of this work has been
asserted in accordance with the Copyright, Designs and Patents Act 1988.

This edition published by
The Orion Publishing Group Ltd
Orion House
5 Upper St Martin's Lane
London WC2H 9EA

An Hachette UK company
A CIP catalogue record for this book is available from the British Library

ISBN 978 1 4719 0635 0

www.orionbooks.co.uk

CONTENTS

Introduction
by
Curtis Evans

During the Golden Age of the detective novel, in the 1920s and 1930s, J. J. Connington stood with fellow crime writers R. Austin Freeman, Cecil John Charles Street and Freeman Wills Crofts as the foremost practitioner in British mystery fiction of the science of pure detection. I use the word 'science' advisedly, for the man behind J. J. Connington, Alfred Walter Stewart, was an esteemed Scottish-born scientist. A 'small, unassuming, moustached polymath', Stewart was 'a strikingly effective lecturer with an excellent sense of humor, fertile imagination and fantastically retentive memory', qualities that also served him well in his fiction. He held the Chair of Chemistry at Queens University, Belfast for twenty-five years, from 1919 until his retirement in 1944.

During roughly this period, the busy Professor Stewart found time to author a remarkable apocalyptic science fiction tale, *Nordenholt's Million* (1923), a mainstream novel, *Almighty Gold* (1924), a collection of essays, *Alias J. J. Connington* (1947), and, between 1926 and 1947, twenty-four mysteries (all but one tales of detection), many of them sterling examples of the Golden Age puzzle-oriented detective novel at its considerable best. 'For those who ask first of all in a detective story for exact and mathematical accuracy in the construction of the plot', avowed a contemporary *London Daily Mail* reviewer, 'there is no author to equal the distinguished scientist who writes under the name of J. J. Connington.'[1]

Alfred Stewart's background as a man of science is reflected in his fiction, not only in the impressive puzzle plot mechanics he devised for his mysteries but in his choices of themes and depictions of characters. Along with Stanley Nordenholt of *Nordenholt's Million*, a novel about a plutocrat's pitiless efforts to preserve a ruthlessly remolded remnant of human life after a global environmental calamity, Stewart's most notable character is Chief Constable Sir Clinton Driffield, the detective in seventeen of the twenty-four Connington crime novels. Driffield is one of crime fiction's most highhanded investigators, occasionally taking on the functions of judge and jury as well as chief of police.

Absent from Stewart's fiction is the hail-fellow-well-met quality found in John Street's works or the religious ethos suffusing those of Freeman Wills Crofts, not to mention the effervescent novel-of-manners style of the British Golden Age Crime Queens Dorothy L. Sayers, Margery Allingham and Ngaio Marsh. Instead we see an often disdainful cynicism about the human animal and a marked admiration for detached supermen with superior intellects. For this reason, reading a Connington novel can be a challenging experience for modern readers inculcated in gentler social beliefs. Yet Alfred Stewart produced a classic apocalyptic science fiction tale in *Nordenholt's Million* (justly dubbed 'exciting and terrifying reading' by the *Spectator*) as well as superb detective novels boasting well-wrought puzzles, bracing characterization and an occasional leavening of dry humor. Not long after Stewart's death in 1947, the Connington novels fell entirely out of print. The recent embrace of Stewart's fiction by Orion's Murder Room imprint is a welcome event indeed, correcting as it does over sixty years of underserved neglect of an accomplished genre writer.

Born in Glasgow on 5 September 1880, Alfred Stewart had significant exposure to religion in his earlier life. His father was William Stewart, longtime Professor of Divinity and Biblical Criticism at Glasgow University, and he married Lily Coats, a daughter of the Reverend Jervis Coats and member of one of

Scotland's preeminent Baptist families. Religious sensibility is entirely absent from the Connington corpus, however. A confirmed secularist, Stewart once referred to one of his wife's brothers, the Reverend William Holms Coats (1881–1954), principal of the Scottish Baptist College, as his 'mental and spiritual antithesis', bemusedly adding: 'It's quite an education to see what one would look like if one were turned into one's mirror-image.'

Stewart's J. J. Connington pseudonym was derived from a nineteenth-century Oxford Professor of Latin and translator of Horace, indicating that Stewart's literary interests lay not in pietistic writing but rather in the pre-Christian classics ('I prefer the *Odyssey* to *Paradise Lost*,' the author once avowed). Possessing an inquisitive and expansive mind, Stewart was in fact an uncommonly well-read individual, freely ranging over a variety of literary genres. His deep immersion in French literature and supernatural horror fiction, for example, is documented in his lively correspondence with the noted horologist Rupert Thomas Gould.[2]

It thus is not surprising that in the 1920s the intellectually restless Stewart, having achieved a distinguished middle age as a highly regarded man of science, decided to apply his creative energy to a new endeavor, the writing of fiction. After several years he settled, like other gifted men and women of his generation, on the wildly popular mystery genre. Stewart was modest about his accomplishments in this particular field of light fiction, telling Rupert Gould later in life that 'I write these things [what Stewart called tec yarns] because they amuse me in parts when I am putting them together and because they are the only writings of mine that the public will look at. Also, in a minor degree, because I like to think some people get pleasure out of them.' No doubt Stewart's single most impressive literary accomplishment is *Nordenholt's Million*, yet in their time the two dozen J. J. Connington mysteries did indeed give readers in Great Britain, the United States and other countries much diversionary reading pleasure. Today these works constitute an estimable addition to British crime fiction.

After his 'prentice pastiche mystery, *Death at Swaythling Court* (1926), a rural English country-house tale set in the highly traditional village of Fernhurst Parva, Stewart published another, superior country-house affair, *The Dangerfield Talisman* (1926), a novel about the baffling theft of a precious family heirloom, an ancient, jewel-encrusted armlet. This clever, murderless tale, which likely is the one that the author told Rupert Gould he wrote in under six weeks, was praised in *The Bookman* as 'continuously exciting and interesting' and in the *New York Times Book Review* as 'ingeniously fitted together and, what is more, written with a deal of real literary charm'. Despite its virtues, however, *The Dangerfield Talisman* is not fully characteristic of mature Connington detective fiction. The author needed a memorable series sleuth, more representative of his own forceful personality.

It was the next year, 1927, that saw J. J. Connington make his break to the front of the murdermongerer's pack with a third country-house mystery, *Murder in the Maze*, wherein debuted as the author's great series detective the assertive and acerbic Sir Clinton Driffield, along with Sir Clinton's neighbor and 'Watson', the more genial (if much less astute) Squire Wendover. In this much-praised novel, Stewart's detective duo confronts some truly diabolical doings, including slayings by means of curare-tipped darts in the double-centered hedge maze at a country estate, Whistlefield. No less a fan of the genre than T. S. Eliot praised *Murder in the Maze* for its construction ('we are provided early in the story with all the clues which guide the detective') and its liveliness ('The very idea of murder in a box-hedge labyrinth does the author great credit, and he makes full use of its possibilities'). The delighted Eliot concluded that

Murder in the Maze was 'a really first-rate detective story'. For his part, the critic H. C. Harwood declared in *The Outlook* that with the publication of *Murder in the Maze* Connington demanded and deserved 'comparison with the masters'. 'Buy, borrow, or – anyhow – get hold of it', he amusingly advised. Two decades later, in his 1946 critical essay 'The Grandest Game in the World', the great locked-room detective novelist John Dickson Carr echoed Eliot's assessment of the novel's virtuoso setting, writing: 'These 1920s [. . .] thronged with sheer brains. What would be one of the best possible settings for violent death? J. J. Connington found the answer, with *Murder in the Maze*.' Certainly in retrospect *Murder in the Maze* stands as one of the finest English country-house mysteries of the 1920s, cleverly yet fairly clued, imaginatively detailed and often grimly suspenseful. As the great American true-crime writer Edmund Lester Pearson noted in his review of *Murder in the Maze* in *The Outlook*, this Connington novel had everything that one could desire in a detective story: 'A shrubbery maze, a hot day, and somebody potting at you with an air gun loaded with darts covered with a deadly South-American arrow-poison – *there* is a situation to wheedle two dollars out of anybody's pocket.'[3]

Staying with what had worked so well for him to date, Stewart the same year produced yet another country-house mystery, *Tragedy at Ravensthorpe*, an ingenious tale of murders and thefts at the ancestral home of the Chacewaters, old family friends of Sir Clinton Driffield. There is much clever matter in *Ravensthorpe*. Especially fascinating is the author's inspired integration of faerie folklore into his plot. Stewart, who had a lifelong – though skeptical – interest in paranormal phenomena, probably was inspired in this instance by the recent hubbub over the Cottingly Faeries photographs that in the early 1920s had famously duped, among other individuals, Arthur Conan Doyle.[4] As with *Murder in the Maze,* critics raved about this new Connington mystery. In the *Spectator,* for example, a reviewer hailed *Tragedy at Ravensthorpe* in the strongest terms, declaring of the novel: 'This is more than a good detective tale. Alike in plot, characterization, and literary style, it is a work of art.'

In 1928 there appeared two additional Sir Clinton Driffield detective novels, *Mystery at Lynden Sands* and *The Case with Nine Solutions.* Once again there was great praise for the latest Conningtons. H. C. Harwood, the critic who had so much admired *Murder in the Maze,* opined of *Mystery at Lynden Sands* that it 'may just fail of being the detective story of the century', while in the United States author and book reviewer Frederic F. Van de Water expressed nearly as high an opinion of *The Case with Nine Solutions.* 'This book is a thoroughbred of a distinguished lineage that runs back to "The Gold Bug" of [Edgar Allan] Poe,' he avowed. 'It represents the highest type of detective fiction.' In both of these Connington novels, Stewart moved away from his customary country-house milieu, setting *Lynden Sands* at a fashionable beach resort and *Nine Solutions* at a scientific research institute. *Nine Solutions* is of particular interest today, I think, for its relatively frank sexual subject matter and its modern urban setting among science professionals, which rather resembles the locales found in P. D. James' classic detective novels *A Mind to Murder* (1963) and *Shroud for a Nightingale* (1971).

By the end of the 1920s, J. J. Connington's critical reputation had achieved enviable heights indeed. At this time Stewart became one of the charter members of the Detection Club, an assemblage of the finest writers of British detective fiction that included, among other distinguished individuals, Agatha Christie, Dorothy L. Sayers and G. K. Chesterton. Certainly Victor Gollancz, the British publisher of the J. J. Connington mysteries, did not stint praise for the author, informing readers that 'J. J. Connington is now established as, in the opinion of many, the greatest living master of the story of pure detection. He is one of those who, discarding all the superfluities, has made of deductive fiction a genuine minor art, with its own laws and its own conventions.'

Such warm praise for J. J. Connington makes it all the more surprising that at this juncture the esteemed author tinkered with his successful formula by dispensing with his original series detective. In the fifth Clinton Driffield detective novel, *Nemesis at Raynham Parva* (1929), Alfred Walter Stewart, rather like Arthur Conan Doyle before him, seemed with a dramatic dénouement to have devised his popular series detective's permanent exit from the fictional stage (read it and see for yourself). The next two Connington detective novels, *The Eye in the Museum* (1929) and *The Two Tickets Puzzle* (1930), have a different series detective, Superintendent Ross, a rather dull dog of a policeman. While both these mysteries are competently done – the railway material in *The Two Tickets Puzzle* is particularly effective and should have appeal today – the presence of Sir Clinton Driffield (no superfluity he!) is missed.

Probably Stewart detected that the public minded the absence of the brilliant and biting Sir Clinton, for the Chief Constable – accompanied, naturally, by his friend Squire Wendover – triumphantly returned in 1931 in *The Boathouse Riddle*, another well-constructed criminous country-house affair. Later in the year came *The Sweepstake Murders*, which boasts the perennially popular tontine multiple-murder plot, in this case a rapid succession of puzzling suspicious deaths afflicting the members of a sweepstake syndicate that has just won nearly £250,000.[5] Adding piquancy to this plot is the fact that Wendover is one of the imperiled syndicate members. Altogether the novel is, as the late Jacques Barzun and his colleague Wendell Hertig Taylor put it in *A Catalogue of Crime* (1971, 1989), their magisterial survey of detective fiction, 'one of Connington's best conceptions'.

Stewart's productivity as a fiction writer slowed in the 1930s, so that, barring the year 1938, at most only one new Connington appeared annually. However, in 1932 Stewart produced one of the best Connington mysteries, *The Castleford Conundrum*. A classic country-house detective novel, Castleford introduces to readers Stewart's most delightfully unpleasant set of greedy relations and one of his most deserving murderees, Winifred Castleford. Stewart also fashions a wonderfully rich puzzle plot, full of meaty material clues for the reader's delectation. *Castleford* presented critics with no conundrum over its quality. 'In *The Castleford Conundrum* Mr Connington goes to work like an accomplished chess player. The moves in the games his detectives are called on to play are a delight to watch,' raved the reviewer for the *Sunday Times*, adding that 'the clues would have rejoiced Mr. Holmes' heart.' For its part, the *Spectator* concurred in the *Sunday Times*' assessment of the novel's masterfully constructed plot: 'Few detective stories show such sound reasoning as that by which the Chief Constable brings the crime home to the culprit.' Additionally, E. C. Bentley, much admired himself as the author of the landmark detective novel *Trent's Last Case*, took time to praise Connington's purely literary virtues, noting: 'Mr Connington has never written better, or drawn characters more full of life.'

With *Tom Tiddler's Island* in 1933 Stewart produced a different sort of Connington, a criminal-gang mystery in the rather more breathless style of such hugely popular English thriller writers as Sapper, Sax Rohmer, John Buchan and Edgar Wallace (in violation of the strict detective fiction rules of Ronald Knox, there is even a secret passage in the novel). Detailing the startling discoveries made by a newlywed couple honeymooning on a remote Scottish island, *Tom Tiddler's Island* is an atmospheric and entertaining tale, though it is not as mentally stimulating for armchair sleuths as Stewart's true detective novels. The title, incidentally, refers to an ancient British children's game, 'Tom Tiddler's Ground', in which one child tries to hold a height against other children.

After his fictional Scottish excursion into thrillerdom, Stewart returned the next year to his English country-house roots with *The Ha-Ha Case* (1934), his last masterwork in this classic mystery setting (for elucidation of non-British readers, a ha-ha is a sunken wall, placed so as to delineate property boundaries while not obstructing views). Although *The Ha-Ha Case* is not set in Scotland, Stewart drew inspiration for the novel from a notorious Scottish true crime, the 1893 Ardlamont murder case. From the facts of the Ardlamont affair Stewart drew several of the key characters in *The Ha-Ha Case*, as well as the circumstances of the novel's murder (a shooting 'accident' while hunting), though he added complications that take the tale in a new direction.[6]

In newspaper reviews both Dorothy L. Sayers and 'Francis Iles' (crime novelist Anthony Berkeley Cox) highly praised this latest mystery by 'The Clever Mr Connington', as he was now dubbed on book jackets by his new English publisher, Hodder & Stoughton. Sayers particularly noted the effective characterisation in *The Ha-Ha Case*: 'There is no need to say that Mr Connington has given us a sound and interesting plot, very carefully and ingeniously worked out. In addition, there are the three portraits of the three brothers, cleverly and rather subtly characterised, of the [governess], and of Inspector Hinton, whose admirable qualities are counteracted by that besetting sin of the man who has made his own way: a jealousy of delegating responsibility.' The reviewer for the *Times Literary Supplement* detected signs that the sardonic Sir Clinton Driffield had begun mellowing with age: 'Those who have never really liked Sir Clinton's perhaps excessively soldierly manner will be surprised to find that he makes his discovery not only by the pure light of intelligence, but partly as a reward for amiability and tact, qualities in which the Inspector [Hinton] was strikingly deficient.' This is true enough, although the classic Sir Clinton emerges a number of times in the novel, as in his subtly sarcastic recurrent backhanded praise of Inspector Hinton: 'He writes a first class report.'

Clinton Driffield returned the next year in the detective novel *In Whose Dim Shadow* (1935), a tale set in a recently erected English suburb, the denizens of which seem to have committed an impressive number of indiscretions, including sexual ones. The intriguing title of the British edition of the novel is drawn from a poem by the British historian Thomas Babington Macaulay: 'Those trees in whose dim shadow/The ghastly priest doth reign/The priest who slew the slayer/And shall himself be slain.' Stewart's puzzle plot in *In Whose Dim Shadow* is well clued and compelling, the kicker of a closing paragraph is a classic of its kind and, additionally, the author paints some excellent character portraits. I fully concur with the *Sunday Times*' assessment of the tale: 'Quiet domestic murder, full of the neatest detective points [. . .] These are not the detective's stock figures, but fully realised human beings.'[7]

Uncharacteristically for Stewart, nearly twenty months elapsed between the publication of *In Whose Dim Shadow* and his next book, *A Minor Operation* (1937). The reason for the author's delay in production was the onset in 1935–36 of the afflictions of cataracts and heart disease (Stewart ultimately succumbed to heart disease in 1947). Despite these grave health complications, Stewart in late 1936 was able to complete *A Minor Operation*, a first-rate Clinton Driffield story of murder and a most baffling disappearance. A *Times Literary Supplement* reviewer found that *A Minor Operation* treated the reader 'to exactly the right mixture of mystification and clue' and that, in addition to its impressive construction, the novel boasted 'character-drawing above the average' for a detective novel.

Alfred Stewart's final eight mysteries, which appeared between 1938 and 1947, the year of the author's death, are, on the whole, a somewhat weaker group of tales than the sixteen that appeared between 1926 and 1937, yet they are not without interest. In 1938 Stewart for the last time managed to publish two detective novels, *Truth Comes Limping* and *For Murder Will Speak* (also published as *Murder Will Speak*). The latter tale is much the superior of the two, having an interesting suburban setting and a bevy of female characters found to have motives when a contemptible philandering businessman meets with foul play. Sexual neurosis plays a major role in *For Murder Will Speak*, the ever-thorough Stewart obviously having made a study of the subject when writing the novel. The somewhat squeamish reviewer for *Scribner's Magazine* considered the subject matter of *For Murder Will Speak* 'rather unsavory at times', yet this individual conceded that the novel nevertheless made 'first-class reading for those who enjoy a good puzzle intricately worked out'. 'Judge Lynch' in the *Saturday Review* apparently had no such moral reservations about the latest Clinton Driffield murder case, avowing simply of the novel: 'They don't come any better'.

Over the next couple of years Stewart again sent Sir Clinton Driffield temporarily packing, replacing him with a new series detective, a brash radio personality named Mark Brand, in *The Counsellor* (1939) and *The Four Defences* (1940). The better of these two novels is *The Four Defences*, which Stewart based on another notorious British true-crime case, the Alfred Rouse blazing-car murder. (Rouse is believed to have fabricated his death by murdering an unknown man, placing the dead man's body in his car and setting the car on fire, in the hope that the murdered man's body would be taken for his.) Though admittedly a thinly characterised academic exercise in ratiocination, Stewart's *Four Defences* surely is also one of the most complexly plotted Golden Age detective novels and should delight devotees of classical detection. Taking the Rouse blazing-car affair as his theme, Stewart composes from it a stunning set of diabolically ingenious criminal variations. 'This is in the cold-blooded category which [. . .] excites a crossword puzzle kind of interest,' the reviewer for the *Times Literary Supplement* acutely noted of the novel. 'Nothing in the Rouse case would prepare you for these complications upon complications [. . .] What they prove is that Mr Connington has the power of penetrating into the puzzle-corner of the brain. He leaves it dazedly wondering whether in the records of actual crime there can be any dark deed to equal this in its planned convolutions.'

Sir Clinton Driffield returned to action in the remaining four detective novels in the Connington oeuvre, *The Twenty-One Clues* (1941), *No Past is Dead* (1942), *Jack-in-the-Box* (1944) and *Commonsense is All You Need* (1947), all of which were written as Stewart's heart disease steadily worsened and reflect to some extent his diminishing physical and mental energy. Although *The Twenty-One Clues* was inspired by the notorious Hall-Mills double murder case – probably the most publicised murder case in the United States in the 1920s – and the American critic and novelist Anthony Boucher commended *Jack-in-the-Box*, I believe the best of these later mysteries is *No Past Is Dead*, which Stewart partly based on a bizarre French true-crime affair, the 1891 Achet-Lepine murder case.[8] Besides providing an interesting background for the tale, the ailing author managed some virtuoso plot twists, of the sort most associated today with that ingenious Golden Age Queen of Crime, Agatha Christie.

What Stewart with characteristic bluntness referred to as 'my complete crack-up' forced his retirement from Queen's University in 1944. 'I am afraid,' Stewart wrote a friend, the chemist and forensic scientist F. Gerald Tryhorn, in August 1946, eleven months before his death, 'that I shall never be much use again. Very stupidly, I tried for a session to combine a full course of lecturing with angina pectoris; and ended up by establishing that the two are immiscible.' He added that since retiring in 1944, he had been physically 'limited to my house, since even a fifty-yard crawl brings on the usual cramps'. Stewart completed his essay collection and a final novel before he died at his study desk in his Belfast home on 1 July 1947, at the age of sixty-six. When death came to the author he was busy at work, writing.

More than six decades after Alfred Walter Stewart's death, his J. J. Connington fiction is again available to a wider audience of classic-mystery fans, rather than strictly limited to a select company of rare-book collectors with deep pockets. This is fitting for an individual who was one of the finest writers of British genre fiction between the two world wars. 'Heaven forfend that you should imagine I take myself for anything out of the common in the tec yarn stuff,' Stewart once self-deprecatingly declared in a letter to Rupert Gould. Yet, as contemporary critics recognised, as a writer of detective and science fiction Stewart indeed was something out of the common. Now more modern readers can find this out for themselves. They have much good sleuthing in store.

1. For more on Street, Crofts and particularly Stewart, see Curtis Evans, *Masters of the 'Humdrum' Mystery: Cecil John Charles Street, Freeman Wills Crofts, Alfred Walter Stewart and the British Detective Novel, 1920–1961* (Jefferson, NC: McFarland, 2012). On the academic career of Alfred Walter Stewart, see his entry in *Oxford Dictionary of National Biography* (London and New York: Oxford University Press, 2004), vol. 52, 627–628.
2. The Gould-Stewart correspondence is discussed in considerable detail in *Masters of the 'Humdrum' Mystery*. For more on the life of the fascinating Rupert Thomas Gould, see Jonathan Betts, *Time Restored: The Harrison Timekeepers and R. T. Gould, the*

Man Who Knew (Almost) Everything (London and New York: Oxford University Press, 2006) and *Longitude,* the 2000 British film adaptation of Dava Sobel's book *Longitude:The True Story of a Lone Genius Who Solved the Greatest Scientific Problem of His Time* (London: Harper Collins, 1995), which details Gould's restoration of the marine chronometers built by in the eighteenth century by the clockmaker John Harrison.

3. Potential purchasers of *Murder in the Maze* should keep in mind that $2 in 1927 is worth over $26 today.

4. In a 1920 article in *The Strand Magazine,* Arthur Conan Doyle endorsed as real prank photographs of purported fairies taken by two English girls in the garden of a house in the village of Cottingley. In the aftermath of the Great War Doyle had become a fervent believer in Spiritualism and other paranormal phenomena. Especially embarrassing to Doyle's admirers today, he also published *The Coming of the Faeries* (1922), wherein he argued that these mystical creatures genuinely existed. 'When the spirits came in, the common sense oozed out,' Stewart once wrote bluntly to his friend Rupert Gould of the creator of Sherlock Holmes. Like Gould, however, Stewart had an intense interest in the subject of the Loch Ness Monster, believing that he, his wife and daughter had sighted a large marine creature of some sort in Loch Ness in 1935. A year earlier Gould had authored *The Loch Ness Monster and Others,* and it was this book that led Stewart, after he made his 'Nessie' sighting, to initiate correspondence with Gould.

5. A tontine is a financial arrangement wherein shareowners in a common fund receive annuities that increase in value with the death of each participant, with the entire amount of the fund going to the last survivor. The impetus that the tontine provided to the deadly creative imaginations of Golden Age mystery writers should be sufficiently obvious.

6. At Ardlamont, a large country estate in Argyll, Cecil Hambrough died from a gunshot wound while hunting. Cecil's tutor, Alfred John Monson, and another man, both of whom were out hunting with Cecil, claimed that Cecil had accidentally shot himself, but Monson was arrested and tried for Cecil's murder. The verdict delivered was 'not proven', but Monson was then – and is today – considered almost certain to have been guilty of the murder. On the Ardlamont case, see William Roughead, *Classic Crimes* (1951; repr., New York: New York Review Books Classics, 2000), 378–464.

7. For the genesis of the title, see Macaulay's 'The Battle of the Lake

Regillus', from his narrative poem collection *Lays of Ancient Rome*. In this poem Macaulay alludes to the ancient cult of Diana Nemorensis, which elevated its priests through trial by combat. Study of the practices of the Diana Nemorensis cult influenced Sir James George Frazer's cultural interpretation of religion in his most renowned work, *The Golden Bough: A Study in Magic and Religion*. As with *Tom Tiddler's Island* and *The Ha-Ha Case* the title *In Whose Dim Shadow* proved too esoteric for Connington's American publishers, Little, Brown and Co., who altered it to the more prosaic *The Tau Cross Mystery*.

8. Stewart analysed the Achet-Lepine case in detail in 'The Mystery of Chantelle', one of the best essays in his 1947 collection *Alias J. J. Connington*.

CHAPTER I

THE tiny motor-boat, piled with suit-cases in the bow, had left the coast and turned its nose towards the bank of heat-haze which screened its destination. Soon the mainland shore faded into the mist. Except for an inquisitive gull overhead, the little vessel seemed alone on a wide expanse of waveless sea which merged, without a horizon-line, into the fleckless sky of a late afternoon.

The girl in the stern gave a little sigh of content as she trailed her finger-tips in the water. Too young and fit to be physically tired, she was conscious of a certain lassitude. There had been the second half of a long railway journey, ending up, after several changes, at a little wayside station on the moorland. The only available car in the neighbourhood—a decrepit and springless vehicle with a taciturn driver—had bumped for miles and miles over roads hardly better than cart-tracks, jolting and shaking its passengers like peas in a cup. After that it was a relief to get some refreshment at Stornadale, though the inn seemed more a pot-house than an hotel, the tea was treacle-dark, and the bread and butter cut unappetisingly thick.

But after that all had gone like clockwork. A middle-aged man with a sympathetic smile and twinkling eyes had introduced himself to her husband as Dinnet, Mr. Craigmore's factotum at Wester Voe. He had the quiet manner of a good servant, coupled with a certain natural friendliness which gained him Jean's liking almost at first sight. Their luggage was taken down to the motor-boat; Dinnet, without fuss, saw to it that her cushions were comfortably placed; the engine was started; and with Dinnet at the helm they put out on a sea so smooth that the little village behind them was reflected almost as clearly as in a lake. For a while they skirted the coast; then, getting his sailing-marks, Dinnet turned the boat's head towards the mist beyond which lay Ruffa.

For a while Jean was content to enjoy the smoothness of the transit, all the more pleasant after the vibration of the car which had brought them to Stornadale. She looked astern, watching the long triangle of the wake spreading its furrows outward until they were lost in the haze towards the invisible land. Then, abruptly she sat up as though something had crossed her mind.

"Colin! I've just remembered I didn't send Dorothy's bracelet back to her."

Her husband's face showed that he failed to catch her meaning. She glanced rather shyly at Dinnet; then, apparently reassured by his expression she made the matter clearer.

"You know the old superstition, Colin. You've got to be married in

'Something old and something new,
Something borrowed and something blue.'

And when I got to the very church-door, I found I'd forgotten the 'something borrowed.' So

Dorothy lent me a bracelet. You know the one she wears, with a swastika on it for luck. It seemed just the thing. And in the hurry of going away, I forgot to give it back to her. And I've been remembering it and forgetting it for the last three weeks. I must post it to her at once."

She turned to Dinnet in the stern.

" Is there a post office on Ruffa ? "

The suggestion amused Dinnet, but he was too courteous to allow that to appear in his face.

" No, mem, I'm sorry. There iss no post office on the island," he explained. " But if it iss important, I can easily take the boat across to Stornadale. It iss only a run of ten miles. It iss no trouble at all."

Dinnet's slight drawl, his faint touch of the local pronunciation, and his obvious desire to be obliging and to the smooth the way for the visitors, all tended to complete his conquest of Jean's liking. " I wonder what he means when he says he's Mr. Craigmore's ' fac-to-tum,' " she mused, mimicking his intonation in her mind. " Is he a bailiff, or what ? " She glanced at his hand on the tiller. It was scrupulously clean, but it was the hand of a man used to rough work. Not caring to put a direct question, she made a flank attack to gain information.

" Are there many people on Ruffa ? It's quite a small island ? "

" It iss quite small, mem, as you say. About a mile long, perhaps, and half a mile broad, it iss. And there are not many people on it. Mrs. Dinnet and I look after Wester Voe. When

Mr. Craigmore comes, he brings his man, of course. Then at Heather Lodge, across the bay, there iss—let me see—Mr. Arrow, and his niece, Miss Arrow, and the man who looks after them, and two other men."

"What sort of people are they?" Jean demanded, curious to know what new neighbours she might expect during her short stay on the island.

"Miss Arrow iss a very nice young leddy," Dinnet assured her, evading the more general inquiry. "And besides them," he continued rather hastily, "there iss Mr. Northfleet. He iss interested in birds, he says, and Mr. Craigmore has made him free of a little shieling down near the shore on this side of the island. He lives there all alone, and I get him his supplies when I go across to Stornadale for ours. You will be sure to see him, mem. He iss always going about with a note-book—making notes about the birds and their habits, he explained to me, once."

Colin Trent pricked up his ears at the name of Northfleet.

"Used to know a man called Northfleet," he interjected. "What's his first name, d'you know?"

"His initial iss C, sir," Dinnet explained. "I collect his letters for him at Stornadale, and I have noticed some of them were addressed to Mr. C. Northfleet."

"H'm! My man was Cyril Northfleet. Might be the same. But when I knew him, he'd no interest in birds."

"I do not think that he has a very great

knowledge of birds, sir," Dinnet volunteered cautiously.

" No ? "

" No, sir. I have seen him mistake a solan goose for a gull in the twilight. It was too far off to see the shape, of course ; but it was quite easy to see the beat of the bird's wings. Nobody who knew birds well could have taken the one for the other, sir, as probably you know."

" Solan flaps faster than a gull, you mean ? " Colin suggested, airing one of his few scraps of ornithological lore.

" That iss one difference, sir," Dinnet conceded.

Jean made a gesture to attract her husband's attention.

" Look, Colin ! Isn't that pretty ? You'd almost think these boats were sailing in the air."

On their port bow a score of light-brown hulls with steeply-raked masts were emerging from the haze ; and the lack of a visible horizon lent them the appearance of hanging midway between sea and sky. Beyond them, phantom-like in the mist, a grey-painted vessel clung on the fleet's flank.

" What funny pillar-things they've got on them, Colin. What are they for ? I can't see them clearly in this haze."

" Never seen a herring-fleet before, dear ? Now you know where the bloaters and finnan-haddies come from. Smoke-boxes, these things are. Modern speeding-up, you know. Catch your herring, smoke 'em in these fitments on the way back to port, and dump 'em on the quay, all cured and ready for market. See ? "

But by this time one of the fleet was near enough for Jean to see the contents of the towers.

" Thanks, dear. And I suppose that man at the wheel is turning them round in the smoke to cure them all over," Jean said ironically. " What are those black rings along the boat's side ? "

" Lifebuoys," said Colin, promptly. " Must have two lifebuoys for each man in the crew. Government regulation, so that if everybody falls overboard on one side they don't have the trouble of swimming round the boat for a lifebuoy. That's why they're hung at the waterline, of course."

Jean scanned the nearest craft. At a distance the things had looked like lifebuoys, but a nearer view proved them to be old motor-tyres.

" Now I know what they are. They're fenders to prevent the boats bumping into each other. Aren't they ? " she demanded, turning to Dinnet.

" Yes, mem. In harbour the boats are sometimes tightly packed."

" And what's the grey ship beyond them ? "

" Fishery protection boat," Colin suggested. " She dodges up and down the coast to see they don't use more than one hook on a line."

" I can see the nets on deck, dear, thank you."

She turned and interrogated Dinnet with a glance.

" Mr. Trent iss quite right about the boat, mem. She iss a Government boat to look after the fisheries. But what her exact duty iss I am not just sure," he concluded, diplomatically.

Then, apparently glad to have escaped from a direct contradiction of Colin's outrageous assertion, he pointed to where a low, dim shape was emerging from the haze.

"That iss Ruffa, mem. We shall soon be in now."

As the little motor-boat throbbed onward, Jean turned eagerly to examine the island. Soon she could make out a coast of low cliffs against which the tide washed languidly. Above them rose slopes of grass and heather in bloom, broken here and there by dark patches of bare rock.

"Are these white spots sheep ? " she asked.

"Yes, mem. Mr. Craigmore has some very good sheep on Ruffa."

"So we won't starve, eh ? Even if communication with the mainland breaks down ? " Colin suggested.

"No, sir. You are quite safe, so long as you can eat mutton. And it iss not altogether a joke, either. We have often very sudden storms here ; and this little boat would not be safe in them. We have been cut off completely, whiles. But Mr. Craigmore makes us keep a big stock of tinned things, and we have always mutton to fall back on."

"What about milk and butter ? " demanded Colin, who was not uninterested in food.

"We have some cows, sir, as well as the sheep. Mrs. Dinnet and I look after them and make the butter."

7

" It must surely be very lonely in the winter-time," Jean put in. " But perhaps you don't stay here all the year round ? "

" It is rather lonely, as you say, mem. Most of the winter we are quite cut off from the mainland. But we prefer to stay on Ruffa. And the wireless is great company for us, too. Mr. Craigmore has put in a very good set indeed, and he allows us to use it when there iss no one staying at Wester Voe. He ordered fresh batteries for it so as to be ready for your coming, mem, and I coupled them in this morning."

" Mr. Craigmore seems to have thought of everything to make us comfortable," Jean answered. " It was very kind of him to lend us Wester Voe while he's away. But where *is* the house ? I don't see it."

" It iss on the far side of the island, mem. There iss no landing-place on this side. It iss all rocks here. The house is beyond that hill that you see on your right, and the pier iss just below it. We have to round the point, yonder, and then you will see it, mem."

A faint breath of wind broke the mirror of the sea. The heat-haze drifted before it ; and by the time they had turned the point the island was clear from end to end. Slightly inland, on a little plateau a hundred feet above the water, a low, roomy house appeared. Spacious loggias faced south and west fronting a broad expanse of garden. Behind rose gentle heather-clad slopes ; but between the garden and the sea stretched a belt of blue.

8

"What a lovely place," Jean cried, enthusiastically. "I *am* going to enjoy it, every bit of it. What's that gorgeous stretch of blue, there ? "

"That iss an experiment of Mr. Craigmore's, mem," Dinnet explained. "He is wanting to clear that slope of heather, and he iss planting wild lupins to fight down the heather and make the ground fit for good grass. It has been quite a success, so far, mem."

Colin's attention had been attracted by something nearer at hand.

"Nasty skerry, this, that we're coming to."

Dinnet nodded.

"It iss, indeed, a nasty skerry, as you say, sir. It lies just off the bay where we land, and in rough weather the passage iss rather difficult. In fact, I do not care to try it with this little boat if the wind gets up. It iss safer not to."

He pointed to one black fang of rock which rose abruptly within the horns of the little bay for which they were heading.

"One of the galleons of the Great Armada was wrecked on the ' Wolf's Tooth,' there, sir. Mr. Craigmore brought divers, a while back, and made an investigation of the spot. They found two cannon-balls and the gold hilt of a sword wedged in the rocks. You will see them up in Wester Voe now, sir. But that was all they got for their trouble. And once I picked up a gold coin on the beach myself, washed in by the tide after a big storm."

"Nasty place," Colin pursued. "You'll need to give me the sailing-marks some time, if I'm to take the boat in and out easily."

" I shall be very pleased to do it, sir, any time you wish," Dinnet agreed readily. Then, seeing that Jean was still admiring the house, he volunteered further information. " Wester Voe, mem, was built on the site of an old castle that used to stand there a long while ago. Over yonder, on the other side of the bay, you can see Heather Lodge. Mr. Craigmore has rented it to Mr. Arrow, just now, as I was telling you."

" How do they get their supplies in ? " demanded the practical Colin. " Got a motor-boat of their own, or do you help them out ? "

Dinnet shook his head.

" No, sir. They have just that little pleasure-boat you see there on the beach. A big motor-boat calls in now and again, and brings them supplies from the mainland. And they buy some of our mutton."

He volunteered no further information, and Colin felt a suspicion that Dinnet did not altogether approve of the company at Heather Lodge. Something in the man's manner suggested that, without leaving anything definite to fasten upon.

Jean reluctantly took her eyes from the house and examined the cove which they were now entering.

" This is just perfect, Colin," she declared. " Look at that sand. And that pier to dive from. Is it deep ? " she demanded, turning to Dinnet.

" You can dive from the end of the pier at any time, mem. The beach shelves very sharply. And it iss sand for a long way out and not many weeds."

" Just think of it, Colin. Undress in the house ; a run down through these lovely lupins ; a dip ; and a perfect beach for sun-bathing afterwards. Three weeks of it will turn me mahogany colour, and I've often wanted to see what I'd look like then."

Dinnet shut off the engine while there was sufficient way on the boat to bring her alongside the steps of the pier. Colin jumped out and helped his wife to land. She ran quickly up the little stair and stood on the pier-head, looking round eagerly at her new surroundings.

On the other side of the cove lay a trim little pleasure-boat with bright cushions in the stern. Nearer the pier was a long concrete slip with rollers and tackle, evidently used for pulling the motor-boat up on the beach out of range in stormy weather. From the shore end of the pier a flight of rude steps led upward to the path through the lupin field, and so to Wester Voe. Seaward there was clear water for a space, and then the black serrations of the skerry pushed above the surface, whilst here and there faint disturbances of the texture showed the presence of submerged reefs.

" If you will just go on to the house, mem," Dinnet's voice suggested, " I will bring up the suit-cases immediately. Mrs. Dinnet will have seen the boat come in. She will be ready to show you over the house."

" Come on, then, Colin. I'm just dying to see if the inside's as nice as the outside. And I want to have a look at the garden too."

Followed by her husband, she ran lightly up

11

the rude stairway and emerged on the gentle slope which led to Wester Voe.

"*Look* at these lupins, Colin. Did you ever see such a stretch of colour ? I've never seen anything like it before. Isn't it lovely we're to have it all to ourselves for the next month or so ? "

" Sure you won't find it a bit dull ? " Colin inquired, with a shade of doubt in his tone.

" With you, darling ? " Jean returned in a tone which was only half ironical. " No, not a bit of it. You know, Colin, I've just loved these last three weeks, every second of them ; but I was beginning to get enough of it all. These big hotels, and the crowds of new people, and the everlasting chatter and noise, and the continual shifting from one place to another, and the feeling that nobody there had any roots, somehow, and that we hadn't any roots either. We were just birds of passage like the rest, and nobody cared tuppence about us except the waiters, and they wanted us to move on so that they could get our tips. It wasn't restful, somehow, although I did enjoy it immensely."

Colin nodded sympathetically.

" I know. Humanity in the mass is never at its best."

" And the ' young bride ' business. I just revelled in it at first ; but after a bit it began to pall. You know what I mean, Colin. The way the strangers at the next table look at you covertly when they think you don't see them. ' That's a young bride on her honeymoon.' And the middle-aged women looking you up and down, half-envious and half-superior. And the middle-aged men staring at me and envying you —oh, yes, I know they did," asserted Jean, who had a very fair appreciation of her own good looks. " And that whole atmosphere of benevolent curiosity—you know what I mean ? The edge was beginning to go off it all. I want a change, something quieter and more soothing, without that perpetual racket in the background. I was beginning to get tired of it."

She clung to her husband's arm as they walked up through the field of lupins.

" Quiet enough here, certainly," Colin admitted, looking over the empty landscape. " No jabbering humanity, no racket, no one to stare at you, bar Dinnet."

" That ' fac-to-tum ' man's a priceless dear," Jean confessed. " So diplomatic, isn't he ? I thought I'd cornered him into contradicting you over the fishery boat, but he slid out of it gracefully, without so much as a smile."

" Seems a decent sort," Colin assented.

" I wonder what the girl at the other house is like," Jean went on after a pause. " What's her name ? Arrow, or something. We might have them across for bridge, now and again, Colin, if you're afraid of being dull. The ' fac-to-tum ' seem impressed in her favour, didn't he ? That looks as if she might be nice."

" Great judge of character, Dinnet," her husband confirmed. " You saw the way he took to me on the spot, didn't you ? Knows sterling worth when he sees it, evidently."

" Well, you're rather nice on the outside,"

Jean retorted in a mock-judicial tone, stepping back a pace as though to examine him critically. "I've often wondered how you'd sound over the wireless. 'Missing from his home, etc., Colin Trent, age twenty-seven, five feet nine in height, clean-shaven, fair hair, blue eyes, dressed in nondescript plus-four suit with one button loose through his habit of fiddling with it. This man is of weak intellect and makes feeble jokes continually.' That's what I shall send to the B.B.C. if ever you go astray."

"That's mine, is it?" Colin responded. "Well, here's yours. 'Missing, and so forth, Jean Trent, age twenty-three, five feet seven, brown hair, brown eyes, brown face, brown shoes and stockings. Dressed in the fashion before last. This woman chatters continually, and may be accompanied by a husband wearing cotton-wool in his ears.' That ticks *you* off, my dear. Enough of this foolery ! Brace yourself to encounter the housekeeper. Much may depend on the first impression you make, and your tact in the matter of menus. After what we've heard, you'd better not pitch your demands too high. This isn't the Ritz, but it'll be gruesome if we have to live on fried eggs thrice a day because she can't cook anything else. Can you cook, by the way. I forgot to ask you before. Funny how these important things get overlooked."

"Well, I can boil the eggs for you, if you want a change. That should cheer you up, Colin. Now stop being an ass. There she is at the door, waiting for us. She looks rather nice : just the

sort of wife I'd have expected the ' fac-to-tum '
to marry."

On closer approach, Mrs. Dinnet proved to be
a small, brisk person with rosy cheeks and
prematurely whitened hair. She gave them a
welcome in which cordiality was nicely blended
with respect.

" Dinner will be ready in half an hour,
ma'am," she explained. " Dinnet will be bringing your luggage up from the boat immediately.
Perhaps, after that long journey, you'd like a
hot bath, ma'am ? "

" Thanks, I should," Jean agreed. " I expect
you feel rather grimy, too, Colin. But I'd like
to see round the house first, if there's time."

Mrs. Dinnet's manner suggested that this proposal had her warm approval. It was clear that
she took an almost possessive pride in Wester
Voe and preferred that they should make its
acquaintance under her guidance.

" Certainly, ma'am. Dinner can be put back
a quarter of an hour, if you like. If you will just
come with me. . . . This is the dining-room,"
she explained, throwing open a door to the right
of the entrance hall.

She ushered them into a broad, low-ceiling
room with windows on the east and south looking
out over the cove. The table, with its shining
silver and crystal, reassured Colin as to the probable quality of his future meals.

" That is the service-door, sir," Mrs. Dinnet
explained, as he showed some signs of investi-
gating the premises beyond it. " Here is the
cellar-book, sir. Perhaps you will choose what

you would like this evening, and Dinnet will see to it if you will tell him. Mr. Craigmore left particular instructions that you were to please yourselves."

Jean had gone over to the table and was examining the chairs with the air of an expert. Old furniture was one of her idols, though finance constrained her to worship from afar. Mrs. Dinnet watched her with approval.

"Yes, ma'am," she explained, as though in answer to an unvoiced question, "these chairs are Hepplewhite's. Mr. Craigmore prefers old furniture. Except for the lounge, and the bath-room, there's hardly anything in the house less than a hundred years old."

She led the way across the hall into a drawing-room which further roused Jean's ungratifiable cravings.

"This room is not much used, ma'am, except when ladies come here. Gentlemen prefer the lounge, which is next door."

She stood aside again to let them pass out; but Jean had gone across to the windows and was looking down over the gardens which stretched out to the west.

"Come here, Colin. Just look at these roses on the pergolas, and those masses of flowers. And all these mysterious little paths leading away into the background. It's like the Alice-Through-the-Looking-glass garden: you never know what you're coming to next. I'd love to have a walk round it. Have we time now, Colin? Think not? Well, after dinner, then. It'll be light enough to see something of it, even in the dusk."

Then the vista of clean-mown lawns prompted another question.

"Who keeps all this in order?"

"There are four gardeners, ma'am," Mrs. Dinnet explained. "It keeps them very busy most of the year, for there is a large kitchen-garden as well, round towards the right, out of sight behind that high hedge."

"Where do the gardeners live?" Colin inquired, remembering that they had not been included in Dinnet's catalogue of the inhabitants of Ruffa.

"They live in Stornadale, sir. Dinnet brings them over in the boat in the morning, and takes them back after their work is done. Mr. Craigmore prefers it that way. He does not want too many people settled on the island; and of course they all have families."

She ushered them next into the lounge, with its huge windows overlooking the gardens. But the big saddle-bag chairs and cane glass-topped tables failed to interest Jean, who began to feel that they were running time very close for the dinner-hour.

"The gun-room is beyond, there," Mrs. Dinnet explained, pointing to its door. "But that would not interest you, ma'am. Mr. Craigmore left word, sir, that you were to take your choice of the rods and guns, if you wished. He has stocked a small loch with trout, and there is a punt on it, if you would like to fish. And of course there is some sea-fishing as well, but it is mostly lythe. There are hares on the island, and Mr. Craigmore likes them kept down, if you would care to take out a gun, sir. And there are some duck, too, if you are a duck-shooter. Dinnet can tell you all about these matters. The billiard-room is over there," she added, without entering it.

She led the way back to the hall, where Colin's eye was caught by two ancient cannon-balls placed on stands.

" These from the Armada wreck ? " he inquired.

" Yes, sir. They say she was one of the treasure-ships; but the divers didn't find the gold. Mr. Craigmore kept these as curiosities."

Colin's attention was attracted by a glass-fronted case in which several bundles of large rockets were stacked.

" You're looking at the rockets, sir ? " Mrs. Dinnet went on. " Mr. Craigmore was afraid that in the winter Dinnet and I might get into difficulties, possibly, and need help from the mainland. If the worst came to the worst, we could use the rockets to attract the attention of the people at Stornadale. We've never had to use them; but they give us confidence. It's very awkward being cut off from the mainland when the sea's too rough for the motor-boat; and it's nice to know we can get help from far-ther along the coast if we need it, even though there's no boat in Stornadale itself."

" Sound idea," Colin agreed. " I'd just been wondering what would happen if one of you fell seriously ill when you're alone on the island."

Mrs. Dinnet, with a faintly mysterious air, led him to a particular place in the panelling of the hall close to the rocket-case.

" You don't see anything funny about that part of the wall, sir ? There's an old secret passage comes out there."

" Where does it lead to ? " Jean demanded, all eagerness.

" It doesn't lead anywhere now, ma'am," was the disappointing reply. " Mr. Craigmore had the far end of it bricked up a while ago. He didn't like the idea of it being open, I think. If you'll come here, sir, and press down that bit of the carving, and then push sideways on this part, you'll find the door opens."

Colin did as he was bid ; and, as part of the panelling slid aside, he found himself looking into a dark recess in which a flight of ancient stone steps vanished downward in the gloom.

" Ugh ! I don't think I quite like the look of it," Jean ejaculated as she looked over her husband's shoulder. " It's probably full of spiders and earwigs and things. Shut the door, Colin."

Colin examined the interior fastening thoughtfully for a moment, and then obeyed.

" You've been down it, I suppose ? " he asked Mrs. Dinnet.

" I, sir ? No. I don't like the look of it, sir. And Dinnet hasn't been down there either. It's part of the old house—Mr. Craigmore rebuilt most of Wester Voe to suit himself a while ago. Dinnet often wanted to go down there and take a look round, but I was afraid the roof might be dangerous, it being so old, and I made him promise he wouldn't go exploring. They say the place was used after the '45 to hide the Chief until he could get away over to France.

But likely that's just the clash of the country-side, sir, and with nothing in it at all."

It was quite evident that although she approved of the secret passage as a means of impressing visitors, she had a strong distaste for the thing in itself.

" If you will come upstairs, ma'am, I'll show you the bedrooms. I've prepared the east room. It gets the morning sun. And the south room, next it. But if you would rather have one of the others instead, ma'am, you've only to say so. It's no trouble to change, ma'am, none whatever."

Jean followed her upstairs, leaving Colin examining the entry to the secret passage, which seemed to have fascinated him. In a few minutes Mrs. Dinnet came down again, and Jean, from the top of the staircase, summoned her husband.

" This is our room, Colin," she explained. " It faces east. You can have the south-facing one, just next door, over the front part of the dining-room, for your dressing-room. Dinner will be ready in half an hour. I'm going to take this bathroom, next our room. You can have that one—that's its door, yonder. If you're not ready in half an hour to the tick, I give you warning that I'll start dinner without waiting for you. I'm far hungrier than I thought— simply ravenous. And I want to explore that garden while the light lasts, after dinner."

" I could pick a bit myself," Colin admitted. " That sea-crossing in the motor-boat seems to have coaxed me into a faint appetite. I must say, when old Craigmore offered us this place I hadn't a notion he did things on this scale. I thought it would be about the size of a small villa, with surroundings to match. You're pleased with it, darling?"

"I just love it! And the Dinnets are prize specimens. She doesn't seem to think anything a trouble. She just says: 'Of course, ma'am,' or 'It's not a bit of trouble, ma'am,' or 'Would you like so-and-so, ma'am?' or 'Of course, ma'am, if you'd rather" and so on. And yet she does it all quite naturally, so that it doesn't sound fussy in the least. How those two between them manage to look after cows and hens and baking and sheep and the house—it's like a new pin, but you wouldn't notice that of course—and the electric light plant—did you notice the switches?—well, it's a miracle."

Colin looked at his watch.

"Time's on the wing. I'm off. See you when the gong goes."

CHAPTER II

AFTER a postprandial interview with Mrs. Dinnet, Jean insisted on Colin accompanying her on a tour of the grounds. They visited in succession the kitchen-garden, the greenhouses, the tennis-courts, the fruit-garden, the rosary, the rock-garden with its lily-pond, and the long petal-strewn arcades of the pergolas. The young bride displayed all the enthusiasm of a new proprietor going over a freshly-acquired estate. At the gate leading into the little pine-spinney, she was forced to call a halt; and with a glance at her slippers, she turned reluctantly back towards the house.

"We'll have to keep that for another time, Colin. It looks a bit wet underfoot, in there. Let's go and sit in that arbour we saw—the one that looks over the lawn with the sun-dial on it."

Colin raised no objection, and they wandered back through the twilight. Except for the distant hiss of the waves on the shore and the occasional shrill squeak of a bat flittering overhead there was nothing to break the stillness. Unable to enter into Jean's ecstasies, Colin was still haunted by misgivings about their stay on the island.

"Sure you won't find it dull here, darling?" he demanded anxiously as they sat watching the early stars growing brighter in the sky.

"*Please* don't ask me again, Colin. This is

the fifth time you've said that since dinner. You make me think I've married a gramophone. It won't be dull—not a scrap. Why, ever since we landed I've been trying to persuade myself that Ruffa's our own island and we can stay as long as we like, instead of having to turn out in a week or two. That's how I feel about it, Colin."

"Well, that's a relief," Colin confessed, also for the fifth time.

He was a person of strong feelings but limited in expression, so that the same form of words with him had to serve to indicate a whole series of finer shades of feeling.

"Everything's just providentially arranged," Jean declared to reassure him. "If we'd been stranded here alone we'd have hungered for some bridge at nights. We won't even have to go without that. I've been making tactful inquiries from Mrs. Dinnet—I'm a marvel of tact when I set about it—and the results are most encouraging, though a bit rough on my vanity."

Colin made a non-committal sound as she paused.

"I thought I was the only pebble on the beach," Jean went on, "until she began to talk about this girl, Hazel Arrow at Heath Lodge. She's evidently the bill-topper where the Dinnet family's concerned. 'Such a nice young leddy ma'am. . . . Makes you feel as if you'd known her for years the very first time you meet her.' So she's evidently got the gift of being natural. So few people are, at first sight. And she's evidently got some sense of humour, of sorts.

One day she was caught in the rain and got her hair simply soaked. 'There goes my five-guinea wave,' she said to Mrs. Dinnet, and Mrs. Dinnet was terribly distressed. 'But it was only a joke, ma'am. Next day it was just as wavy as ever—lovely chestnut hair, she's got, ma'am.' So evidently it's a natural wave. I wish mine was, Colin. This sea-air's sure to play the deuce with it, and then you'll be disgusted. That's one drawback to Ruffa, worse luck."

Colin reassured her on the point before allowing her to continue.

"Well, according to Mrs. Dinnet, this girl's got 'beautifully arched eyebrows, ma'am, and such a nice smile,' and so on. I can't remember half of it; but she went on describing the wretched girl until I was nearly bursting with envy—I really was. The only flaw, from the Dinnet point of view, was that she's a bit modern in her costume. The Dinnets haven't quite got educated up to hiker's kit, I gather."

"Meaning riding-breeches, puttees, and huge boots?" Colin interjected. "Doesn't sound over-attractive to me, either."

"No," Jean dissented ruminatively. "I don't think it's that. Mrs. Dinnet qualified her carp by adding in a hurry: 'Not that she doesn't look nice in it, ma'am.' I don't think big boots can come into it. Anyhow, we'll see her for ourselves soon enough. Mrs. Dinnet says she spends her time roaming about the island."

"What about the rest of the crew at Heather Lodge?" Colin demanded.

" Not quite so popular in the Dinnet circle,"
Jean decided in a thoughtful tone. " At least,
that's the impression I got, somehow. The
uncle, Mr. Arthur Arrow, just comes up to pass-
mark because Mr. Craigmore let Heather Lodge
to him ; and anything Mr. Craigmore does is
right, in the eyes of the Dinnets. But when I
fished for information about the rest of them,
Mrs. Dinnet drew in her horns and got so reserved that I could see she didn't fancy them
much. So of course I said no more."

" H'm ! " said Colin, reflectively. " Got the
same impression from Dinnet's manner myself.
Funny ! Something's set both their backs up,
one'd think. Wonder what it was. And what
about the Northfleet bloke, or cove, as the case
may be ? "

" Mrs. Dinnet seems to like him," Jean assured
him. " He's well known to Mr. Craigmore, and
that naturally gives him a pull here. Like a
recommendation from Providence. ' He's very
nice, ma'am. . . . Not shy, but reserved, rather.'
One or two other things she said about him
sounded well, but I can't remember them. Anyhow, he and the girl seem good sorts. So if we get
bored with each other's company, we can ask
the two of them over to dinner, or for bridge, or
for tennis. We don't need to have them unless
we want them. I'd rather like to get to know
the girl, unless the Dinnets are exaggerating."

" Bound to come across 'em both in our walks
abroad," Colin pointed out. " We can look 'em
over and ask 'em here later on, if we take to 'em.
I'm not going to give 'em the run of the house,

though, unless they happen to take my fancy. Not inhospitable, of course, but one doesn't want people bursting in on our *tête-à-tête* at all hours of the day, just at present. So keep your gregarious instincts in check at first, or we may find ourselves saddled with a couple of bores."

"Oh, I'm sure they'll be all right," said Jean, who was an optimist by nature. "And perhaps this will turn out to be the Northfleet you used to know. Did you know him well, Colin?"

Colin shook his head.

"Sat next to him in a Maths. class one year at U.C.L. Met him in the Union now and again. He was Science and I was Arts, so we didn't see much of each other."

"What sort of a person was he?" Jean persisted.

"Oh, clever devil, but no side, I remember. Quite affable if he wanted to be. Could keep his thumb on anything that it didn't suit him to talk about, though."

"'Not shy—reserved rather.' That was what Mrs. Dinnet said. It must be the same man, surely."

Colin rubbed his nose thoughtfully.

"It's this interest in birds that makes me think it's hardly likely. My Northfleet hadn't the faintest interest in Zoology. Maths., Chemistry and Physics were his subjects. Must be another fellow of the same name, I think."

"Well, probably we'll come across him to-morrow—we can't miss him on an island the size of Ruffa if he walks about after his birds—

26

so it's no good wondering any more about him now."

Colin seemed to be considering some puzzling point, but when he spoke it was clear that he had put Northfleet's identity out of his mind.

"Seen any dogs about the place, dear? Haven't set eyes on one myself. And yet they must have one at least for the sheep, one'd think."

"Quite correct, old Sherlock Holmes. They had one, Mrs. Dinnet told me, but it took collywobbles or something just the other day and died of them. Dinnet's hunting for a successor, but he hasn't found one to his liking yet."

Jean yawned delicately behind her hand.

"Just one turn more round the garden, Colin, and then I'm going up to bed. I've still got some unpacking to do. Mrs. Dinnet offered to look after it for me, but I told her I'd do it myself. It seems to me the Dinnets have enough on their hands already, in the way of work."

She rose and moved out of the arbour. Colin joined her and took her arm.

"Better stick to the paths," he suggested. "Dew's fallen, and the lawns would soak your slippers, darling."

They strolled down one path and then up another, which brought them out on a tiny terrace overlooking the bay.

"Listen! What's that, Colin?"

Faint through the flower-perfumed dusk came the distant tinkle of a guitar, and then soft notes of a girl's voice singing.

"Somebody out yonder in a boat," said Colin,

peering into the dim seascape. " Sound carries well over water."

" It must be that girl," Jean whispered, " there's nobody else it could be. What a nice voice she has, Colin. Listen ! "

> *As I went down to Shrewsbury Town,*
> *I came by luck on a silver crown :*
> *" And what shall I buy with that," said I,*
> *" What shall I buy in Shrewsbury Town ? "*

sang the fresh young voice ; and at the end of the verse the guitar continued alone as though it crooned to itself in the night.

" I like her choice in songs, anyhow," Jean declared when the music fell silent. " That isn't hackneyed stuff. And now, Colin, I'm positively going to bed. It must be the sea-air, or something, for I'm half-asleep already. Come up later on ; and please don't wake me. I'm sure I'd turn peevish or fractious or something, and most likely I'd bite in my sleep if I were disturbed. You can amuse yourself for a while, can't you ? "

" Oh, I expect I'll find something to fill in with. I can turn on the wireless. Won't worry you, will it, darling ? "

" Not if you put it to my ear, I'm so sleepy. That unpacking will just have to stand over till to-morrow, and things can get crushed for all I care."

Colin accompanied her back to the house.

" Mrs. Dinnet was quite right," Jean said as she kissed her husband good night at the foot of the stairs. " She said this air made you sleep like a log. She and the 'fac-to-tum' wouldn't wake from their slumbers to take notice of an earthquake, by her way of it. So you needn't worry about your wireless disturbing them, especially as they're away at the back of the house. Night-night, Colin. If I stay longer, I'll be crawling upstairs on all fours."

"If you want to, don't mind me," Colin rejoined. "Come on, I'll lead you up."

Half in fun, he took her arm and made a pretence of assisting her to climb the stairs. At the bedroom door he kissed her good night again, switched on her light, and then went down to the ground floor. The wireless, he remembered, was in the lounge.

Alongside the normal set he found a short-wave converter; but for a time he contented himself with running over some stations on the long and medium waves, merely to test the selectivity of the set. After a while, finding nothing to interest him in the programmes, he jacked in the converter and set himself to the more delicate task of picking up the short-wave transmissions. Once he became engrossed in this he lost all count of time.

Someone had evidently taken the trouble to calibrate the set, for a framed series of graphs hung on the wall and made it fairly simple to identify the principal broadcasting stations. But it was an exceptionally bad night for short-wave work. There were some atmospherics, but the main drawback was an almost incessant fading which prevented him from obtaining anything but disjointed excerpts from the programmes.

He tried station after station with an almost uniform lack of satisfactory results; and at last he fell back on the telegraphy transmissions, which, at any rate, were clear and continuous. He had a fair grip of the Morse code and could follow messages if the speed was not too great. Defeated once or twice, he began to range over the dial in search of something easy.

Suddenly, as he turned the knob, he came upon a strong carrier-wave; and merely out of curiosity he tuned in the transmission. A voice began speaking, a clear, loud signal, free from the fading which had hitherto exasperated him.

". . . Hello! Hello, London!" said the voice. "Attention! I am calling and testing . . . testing and calling. I shall repeat this message night by night at ten, eleven, and twelve o'clock. Hello! I am testing. I shall repeat this message each night. Attention!"

Then in fairly slow and carefully-transmitted Morse, the transmission continued:

"Teiil lfilh tcetu fdhso oenpr yyugo . . ."

Colin, disgusted by his earlier failures that night, picked up a note-book which was lying on the table beside the set—evidently a rough wireless log—and began to jot down the incomprehensible series of letters, merely for the sake of practice. The man at the transmitter was sending with such deliberation that even Colin, rusty as he was, had no difficulty in following him:

". . . hngof lovtu gchan noatn aehat isuwe etfst gscad . . ." the message continued; and Colin jotted it down, letter by letter, until between three and four hundred characters had been transmitted. Then the Morse broke off, and the clear voice spoke again :

"Hello, London ! Before closing down I shall put on a gramophone record."

In a few seconds " Ramona " came from the loud speaker. Colin listened to it appreciatively. He remembered dancing with Jean to that tune, in the days before she promised to marry him ; and the music brought with it all kinds of memories. Jolly little kid she was then. And she'd grown a lot prettier since. Funny to think of her sleeping there, upstairs. Marriage still had its first freshness for Colin.

The record ended with the click of the gramophone brake. Evidently the man at the transmitter didn't bother much about refinements in his sending. Then the voice spoke again :

"Hello, London ! This is HSI-314, calling and testing. I am now closing down for the night. I shall repeat the message at ten o'clock, eleven o'clock, and midnight to-morrow. Hello ! This is HSI-314. Good night ! "

Almost immediately the faint hiss of the carrier wave died out and the loud-speaker went dead.

Colin switched off the battery of the converter, yawned unaffectedly, and glanced at his watch. It was far later than he had supposed—after midnight. The curious fascination of the short waves had thrown its spell over him and kept him up far longer than he had intended. He glanced from the converter dial to the calibration chart which hung in front of him and noted that, as he had expected, the signal had come in on the amateur wave-band. Then, as he rose from his chair, his eye caught a big square pamphlet on the table near the set : a blue-bound volume with a cover-design of Pegasus galloping across the globe.

" *Radio Amateur Call Book Magazine*," Colin read. " H'm ! Craigmore seems to have everything on tap," he added, half in admiration and half in envy. " Wonder who HSI–314 is."

Glancing rather incuriously over the pages, he came upon a heading " INTERNATIONAL CALL LETTERS " ; and running his eye down the list, he found the entry " HSA–HSZ—Siam." A note at the foot explained that " International amateur prefixes of one or two letters are to be assigned from the above."

Colin was no short-wave expert. Still, he knew enough to be able to tell if the ether was " alive " or not ; and the word " Siam " made him lift his eyebrows slightly. On this particular evening, the Heaviside layer had been in such a condition as to make the set feel " dead " when he moved the dial. The American stations had been almost inaudible, and even the Zeesen short-wave transmitter had been unsatisfactory. Still, a long-distance fluke was always a possibility.

He passed to the following page of the Call Book, which was headed " WHO'S WHO ON THE SHORT WAVES " ; and using his dial reading and the kilo-cycle calibration graph as guides, he attempted to identify HSI–314. Drawing blank by this method, he turned back to an earlier part of the volume, where he found an alphabetical arrangement of call letters grouped under their respective countries. Here, however, there were but two cognate entries : one referring to a station controlled by the Siamese Navy and another giving the call sign HS1HH, with the Bangkok Post Office address. Nothing corresponding to HSI–314 could he discover. And, on reflection, he began to doubt if HSI–314 was a proper form of call sign at all.

" Rum start," he mused. " No mistake about what I heard. It was clear enough ; and the beggar spoke English as well as I do myself. May be some cove talking to a pal in London and using a prearranged private call sign of his own to prevent people butting in with QSLL demands for postcard acknowledgments. That's it, most likely."

Dismissing the matter from his thoughts, he turned away from the wireless and prepared to go up to bed. Then a question suggested itself to him. Should one lock up the front door ? It seemed an absurd precaution to take on this lonely island, but perhaps it was the custom at Wester Voe. He had forgotten to ask Dinnet about it. Best be on the safe side, he decided eventually ; locking the door could do no harm. He switched off the lights in the lounge and went out into the hall. Before locking up, he opened the front door and stepped to the edge of the loggia to see what sort of a night it was.

Clouds had gathered swiftly since he and Jean

re-entered the house ; and now only a few stars were to be seen, appearing and vanishing through the slowly-moving rifts. A faint wind stirred the unseen lupins beyond the garden, and their rustling mingled with the low plash of the waves on the shore below. Except for that the night was silent. No lights shone in the windows of Heather Lodge, across the bay. Ruffa, with its little group of inhabitants, seemed fast asleep in the loneliness of the sea. Colin, feeling the effect of the unaccustomed island air, yawned expansively and turned back towards the open door.

But as he did so his quick ear caught a new sound in the night, and he halted, rigid, listening for a recurrence.

THE sound came from beyond the gate of the garden, and as Colin listened he heard it again : a low scuffing noise such as a man might make as he shuffled along painfully in the last stages of exhaustion. Then it ceased, and Colin thought he heard a stumble, a soft thud of a body falling to the ground. Silence again. Then, distinctly, a short, low moan of pain.

Colin raced down the garden path to the gate and gazed out into the dark. He could see nothing, and for some moments he stared hither and thither, trying to pierce the night.

" Who's there ? " he demanded. " Are you badly hurt ? "

There was no answer for a moment or two, then he heard another low groan from somewhere on his left, among the lupins. He hurried in the direction of the sound ; but the darkness and the high-growing stems hindered his search, and he had to halt and listen again. Once more the dull sound of pain guided him ; and, striding through the lupins, he almost tripped over a prostrate figure.

Colin knelt down, fumbled hurriedly in his pocket, found his matchbox and, struck a light. It lasted only a moment, for a puff of wind blew it out almost as soon as it flared up. In its brief illumination, Colin caught a glimpse of a flat, brutal face with a hare-lip. From among the

35

roots of the coarse black hair a trickle of blood had flowed down on to the temple.

" Fallen and cut your head on a rock ? " Colin inquired sympathetically as the match went out.

The invisible figure shifted slightly in an effort to sit up, and the movement drew from it another inarticulate sound of pain. Colin hastily lit another match, which shared the fate of the first. In its evanescent gleam, he saw a dark lounge suit which would have consorted with city pavements better than with the rock-strewn heather of Ruffa. Rubber-soled tennis shoes seemed equally unsuitable for the time and place.

" Feel pretty bad ? " Colin asked kindly, as he put his arm round the man's shoulders to support him.

There was no reply. The momentary glimpse of that brutish countenance had repelled Colin ; but as he knelt with his arm about the figure of his protégé, his natural sympathies got the better of his distaste. Whatever the fellow might be, he was a badly-hurt man needing careful handling. And suddenly Colin felt the full weight of the body against his arm.

" Hullo ! The beggar's fainted," he ejaculated to himself as he lowered the unconscious head to the ground.

Fainting was a new phenomenon to Colin. In his circle people simply did not faint. It wasn't done. Consequently, he was at a loss to know what to do with his patient. What *did* one do to bring a man back to consciousness ? If it had been a girl the proper treatment, Colin supposed, would be to splash water over her until she came to her senses. Or did one burn feathers under her nose ? Anyhow, this was a man ; and most likely the best thing for him was a stiff drink—whiskey neat. If it made him cough, he'd wake up all the quicker, probably.

Leaving the stranger lying among the lupins, Colin stepped back to the path and hurried up to the house. At dinner-time he had noticed a whiskey decanter on the sideboard, with a soda-siphon beside it. He went into the dining-room, switched on the lights, and was relieved to find that Dinnet had not removed the decanter. A hurried search through the cupboards of the sideboard secured a tumbler, into which Colin splashed a lavish allowance of whiskey. On second thoughts, after a doubtful glance at it, he tempered the dose with some soda. Then, with the restorative in his hand, he hastened back to the relief of the injured man.

But in the darkness he now found it impossible to retrace his course among the tall flowers. He vainly struck match after match in a search for the alley he had made on his previous journey. The wind had risen higher, and his lights were extinguished before they could serve his purpose. He called at intervals, but elicited no reply. The man had ceased to moan ; for Colin, when he stood still to listen, could hear nothing except the rustling of the lupins in the gentle breeze.

Abandoning his attempt to retrace his steps, Colin began to seek at random around the spot where he supposed the man must be lying. He tramped hither and thither among the swishing stems in the gloom, stooping, peering in the shadows, and occasionally feeling hopefully with his hands when he thought he had struck the right place. For many minutes, this hit-or-miss method yielded no results ; but at last, by sheer chance, he managed to blunder upon the very spot he had last seen his quarry. By the flash of a match he recognised the place beyond doubt, with the stems crushed and broken where the man had fallen.

But the short-lived gleam of the match showed something else. No human figure lay among the lupins. The stranger had vanished.

This was the last thing Colin had anticipated. The man had all the look of being badly hurt and unable to move. How had he got away ? With his superfluous tumbler in his hand, Colin stood for a while, striving to find some explanation of this disappearance. He could only suppose that the fellow had regained consciousness, and that, in a bemused attempt to seek assistance, he had crawled farther into the lupin field, and then fainted once more. Putting his unneeded tumbler on the ground, Colin set himself to search the immediate neighbourhood ; but he expended the remainder of his matches without result. There was no trace of the missing man, nor was there the slightest response to Colin's encouraging calls.

He rose to his feet after some fruitless groping and considered the situation. In the dark it was hopeless to persevere. The man might have crawled for a considerable distance ; and the searching of that great belt of high stems would have been a task for a large party armed with storm-lanterns. Even if he roused Dinnet now, the pair of them could be successful only by a stroke of sheer luck. He glanced at his wrist-watch and the illuminated dial gave him a suggestion. In an hour or two the dawn would break ; and then it would be a simple matter to run the man down. He must have left a plain trail through the lupins as he crawled away. That trail could be followed up in daylight without the slightest trouble, though in the dark the task was beset with difficulties owing to Colin's own manœuvres having left track after track around the starting-point. And, after all, what was a couple of hours ? The first flush of Colin's humanitarian feelings was passing off, and he felt his aversion to the unknown man increasing. That slab of brutish face appeared in his mind's eye and dispelled a good deal of his sympathy. A wrong 'un, that chap, if Colin was any judge. Anyhow, he would come to no harm in a matter of a couple of hours. He wasn't much of a tender plant, by the look of him. Colin, though not quite comfortable in his conscience, decided to abandon his search for the present and await the dawn.

He remembered the tumbler which he had set down, and he began to grope round in the hope of coming upon it. Instead of the glass, his hand encountered a smooth, weighty, metallic object about the size of a small cake of soap. He fingered it in the dark, but could make nothing of it. From its massiveness, he took it be a lump of lead cast in a mould ; no other common metal would have weighed as much for its size. On the face of things it must have some connection with the stranger. When they got hold of the fellow they could return it to him in case it was of importance. Colin slipped it carelessly into his pocket and resumed his gropings after the missing tumbler.

He came upon it at last, knocking it over and spilling its contents on the ground. Picking it up, he began to move towards the house. Then, to quieten his conscience, which still pricked him, he made several casts at random on the offchance of coming upon the stranger. Failing in his rather perfunctory attempt, he called once or twice and halted to listen for a reply. Then, still rather uncomfortable, but plying himself with counter-arguments, he walked back to Wester Voe to await the coming of the dawn.

Dew had been falling heavily that night, and among the lupins he had got himself rather wet. The tumbler in his hand suggested the advisability of a drink, if he was going to sit about for an hour or two. He went into the dining-room, mixed himself a stiff glass of whiskey and soda, and then betook himself to the lounge, where he dropped thankfully into one of the big saddle-bag chairs.

The whiskey had aroused him mentally ; and, having nothing to occupy him until the imminent dawn made renewed searchings feasible, he began to turn over the whole incident in his mind.

Who was this mysterious wanderer in the night ? Whoever he might be, Colin decided, he didn't correspond to Mrs. Dinnet's account of

the man Northfleet. She had described Northfleet as "very nice." Colin still had a vivid
recollection of that blackguardly face, on which
an expression of dull ruthlessness persisted even
in spite of the man's pain. Nobody would call
that "very nice." Northfleet could be eliminated
from the list of possibles.

That left only the people at Heather Lodge ;
and here Colin felt he was on the right track.
The Dinnets, without saying much, had managed
to convey the impression that some of the
Heather Lodge lot were not to their taste. Well,
if what he had seen to-night was a specimen, the
Dinnets were fully justified. No wonder they
didn't like that type.

Colin's reasoning took him a step further in
the elimination. The man he had glimpsed
could hardly be Arthur Arrow himself. Arrow,
if he was an acquaintance of Craigmore's, must
be a gentleman. Craigmore would never associate with an obvious "tough" of the most brutal
type. That excluded Arrow from the list; and the
only remaining " possibles " were the three hang-
ers-on at Heather Lodge. It must be one of them.

At this point Colin found himself floundering
among problems to which he could find no
solutions. If this fellow was one of the Heather
Lodge brigade, what took him abroad long after
midnight ? Ruffa was hardly the place for late
evening calls, Colin reflected whimsically. The
only places the man could have visited were
Wester Voe and Northfleet's shieling. Considering the Dinnets' views, a visit to them was
improbable ; and the shieling, Colin had gathered,

was on the other side of Ruffa, away from the bay. If the man had been at the shieling and had got hurt on the way back to Heather Lodge he would never have come near the lupin field.

" Perhaps he saw the lights on here and was sneaking round the place, spying on us," Colin mused, none too amiably. " I don't see how else he could have got to where he was."

It seemed possible, but not very probable at that hour of the morning.

Then another question suggested itself to Colin. If this was one of the Heather Lodge lot, how had he managed to blunder into trouble ? Ruffa was hardly more than an islet. A man who had lived on it for any length of time ought to know it like the palm of his hand— quite well enough, at least, to keep clear of dangerous ground even in the dark. And yet it looked as though the fellow had fallen over some drop among the rocks. It would take a fair amount to knock out a tough of that type. His head was bleeding, too ; and that looked as though he'd had a bad smash.

That brought Colin up against a further mystery. From what he had seen of the man, he had got the impression that the fellow was pretty far through—completely done up. And yet, within a few minutes, he must have pulled himself together and done a very smart bit of crawling if he got far enough away to evade Colin's search. That seemed the fishiest part of the business to Colin. Why should an injured man creep away into the darkness when he knew that help was coming ?

At the back of Colin's mind the affair was beginning to take on an unpleasant aspect. For one thing, there was Jean to be considered. Of course he would always be about with her if she roamed over the island. There was nothing in it, really, he assured himself. Still, he had a very distinct feeling that neighbours of this kind were hardly what he would have chosen on the strength of their looks. A fellow like the one he had seen wasn't the kind who would stick at much. And the mere look of him would give Jean the creeps. She was a nervous girl in some ways.

"Nuisance, having a crew of that sort on the island," he reflected uncomfortably, before dismissing the matter from his mind.

As he shifted in his chair, something pressed against his side; and he suddenly remembered the piece of metal which he had picked up when hunting for the tumbler. It had slipped from his memory until that moment. He put his hand into his pocket and pulled it out—a roughly rectangular block of some material which looked like phosphor-bronze.

Colin stared at it for some seconds, completely at a loss to know what to make of it. It had evidently been crudely cast, and he turned it over to see if it bore any inscription. There was nothing of the sort on the surface; it seemed to be just a block of metal.

"It must be lead by the weight," Colin inferred, as he mechanically hefted it. "But what the deuce is it gold-plated for?"

Then a grin twisted his mouth as a ludicrous notion shot into his mind.

43

" It's a gold brick, by Jove ! " he ejaculated in amusement at his own jest. " That poor bloke must have been hurrying across hot-foot to sell me it, as soon as he heard the innocents had arrived in town—in such a flurry that he tripped over his own feet on the way. Must be a devil of a competition in the trade, here on Ruffa, if he was in such a sweat to get in first. Moderate-minded cove, too, one'd think, if he was offering a thing of this size. The usual gold brick's as big as a bar of soap, they say. Evidently he didn't want to try us too high."

Much entertained by his simple conceit, he sat turning the little block over and over in his hands ; and as he did so he grew more puzzled by the nature of the thing. For what honest purpose could one gold-plate a lump of lead ? And the skin of the thing certainly had all the look of gold-leaf. If this was the sort of thing that the gold-brick swindlers used, it was quite good enough to take in a not over-bright client, especially if the patter was plausible.

The more he looked at the thing the less wild his idea began to appear. He examined the ingot more and more carefully, looking for a flaw ; but the longer he did so the more difficult he found it to discover any straightforward explanation for its manufacture. Why on earth should anyone go to the trouble of making a thing like that ? It could serve no purpose as an ornament. Lead didn't need a protective coating to keep it from corroding. Baffled, Colin scratched his head mechanically.

" Damn it, I believe it's really the gold-brick

swindle in some shape. Can't be anything else, on the face of things. Well, I'll spoil the beggar's market for him, anyhow."

Pulling out his pocket-knife, he crossed the room to get under the brightest lamp. Then with the blade he made a broad score on the block, intending to scrape off the film of gold and disclose the underlying lead. His first attempt was unsatisfactory, and he tried a second time.

" Well, I'm damned ! "

There was no surface film, such as he had expected. His two abraded streaks were as yellow as the rest. A third and much deeper incision yielded the same result. Whatever the material was, the block was homogeneous.

Colin rubbed his hand on his forehead in bewilderment. He had almost convinced himself that the thing was a sham. Certainly the idea that it was a real gold ingot had never occurred to him. And yet, if it wasn't gold, what was the stuff ? Brass or bronze wouldn't have anything like that density, and he could think of no other alloy which would fit the case.

Still incredulous, Colin approached the affair from a fresh angle. Assuming that the stuff *was* gold, what would the brick be worth ? Gold, he supposed, was worth roughly five pounds per ounce troy. He held the ingot out, trying to gauge its weight, but he found it difficult to estimate.

" Say a couple of pounds. No use bothering about the fourteen ounce troy business. Two pounds is thirty-two ounces, and at five pounds the ounce, that's a hundred and sixty pounds. Phew! And it's more than two pounds, if anything. By Jove! I can hardly believe it. It can't be gold. The thing's absurd. It must be some new alloy or other."

Colin belonged to a generation to whom a coined sovereign is a mere curiosity. Gold ornaments he knew; but he had never associated them with purchasing power. Now, as he stared at the ingot in his hand—a thing hardly bigger than his box of vestas—he came suddenly to realise the concentration of financial power in raw gold. A hundred and sixty pounds and more, all condensed in this heavy little thing on his palm! Made you think, that did! For to Colin a hundred and sixty pounds was a good round sum.

He thrust the ingot back into his pocket and fell into a brown study. This new notion of gold led him on to speculation after speculation. Gradually they grew vaguer. His head began to nod, then slipped down against the chair-back. After a brief effort to wake up, he let himself go and fell asleep.

When he awoke again he found that the sun was up; and a glance at his wrist-watch showed him that it was half-past four. He got out of his chair, feeling cramped through having fallen asleep in an awkward position, and he took a few steps up and down the room to ease his muscles. Then he listened to see if anyone else was afoot. Nobody was astir in the house. Evidently nothing had happened to arouse the others.

In this fresh dawn the events of the night took

on a faintly incredible aspect ; but the weight of
the gold brick in his pocket showed him that the
affair had not been a mere dream. He pulled
out the ingot and examined it once more in daylight, lest he had been deceived by that quality
of electric lamps which makes them treacherous
when tints have to be matched. No, there was
no mistake. The deep scores of his knife-blade
showed the same golden hue as the rest of the
block. This was no gilded lump of lead that he
had in his hand.

That would keep till later, he thought. More
urgent affairs claimed his attention at the
moment. He went out of the house and down
the path towards the pier. In the clear morning
light the traces of his nocturnal doings were
plain enough among the lupins. Even from the
path he could see the swaths where he had
trampled down the stems in his blind wanderings
to and fro.

He made his way among the flowers, and soon
came upon the spot where he had discovered the
stranger. It was easy enough to identify, for all
around it was a maze of channels in the high
stems, Colin's own trails made while he was
searching for the missing man. But in addition
to these, broad and plain, there was another
track.

"I never made that one," Colin assured
himself.

A few steps brought him into it, and he
hurried along the little corridor which opened up
among the plants. This was certainly none of
his making, for it led in an almost straight line,

whereas his own movements had been irregular, like those of a dog trying to pick up a lost scent. With the feeling that he was hot on the trail, he hastened on through the lupin field. The track trended downward, and then abruptly Colin emerged from it at the head of the little flight of steps leading down to the pier. There was no second opening in the lupins. Whoever came this way must have gone down the steps into the bay.

Colin stood at the head of the stairway and gazed down over the pier and the stretch of sand below him. The motor-boat was still moored in the lee of the jetty. Across the bay the Heather Lodge pleasure-boat had been hauled up above high-tide mark. Except for these two things the bay was empty, and the pier was bare. Nowhere was there the slightest trace of the missing man.

"Must have scrambled down to the pier and then gone home across the sands. Tide would wash out his footmarks."

Colin's explanation hardly satisfied him. It demanded quick movement on the part of the man, since he must have got well away before Colin recommenced his search after returning from the house. That fellow was in no condition to walk, or even to creep at any speed. And yet, there were the facts. He had got away, however it had been managed.

"Damn funny!" was Colin's rather unhappy summary of the case.

He glanced down at the little bay; and the sight of the Heather Lodge pleasure-boat, by

some curious association, brought into his mind
the words that the girl had sung last night :

As I went down to Shrewsbury Town,
I came by luck on a silver crown . . .

Colin gave a faint chuckle as he recalled them.
"Wonder what sort of song the cove would
have made of it if he'd come by luck on a golden
brick, like me ? " he reflected. "What the devil
am I to do with the thing, anyway ? One can't
pocket a hundred quids' worth of gold and say
nothing about it. I'll have to hunt the beggar
up and hand it back to him. Then he'll have to
explain the whole affair."

As he turned away from the bay a fresh
thought struck him and he retraced his steps to
the spot where he had found the injured man.

"That track was the way he left," he mused.
"But he must have made another track through
the lupins, getting here. Let's have a look for
it."

This second track he did at last manage to
discover. It was much less conspicuous than the
alley down to the pier, and Colin had overlooked
it in his excitement at finding the plainer route.
The new trail led him through the lupins in the
direction of Heather Lodge ; and when it came
out from among the stems, it was lost in the rocks
and heather which fringed the low slope of the
bay.

But now Colin had some second thoughts.
All that the facts showed was the presence of
two trails. So far as that went, the man might
have come along the sands and returned by the

cliff-top to Heather Lodge. There was no proof that he had left via the pier stairs.

The sun was well above the horizon now, and Colin glanced again at his watch, as he turned back towards Wester Voe. Could he creep up to bed without waking Jean ? And that mental inquiry turned his thoughts in a fresh direction. Should he say anything about this affair to Jean ? She certainly wouldn't relish the idea of people sneaking about Wester Voe in the dark. It would make her nervous, spoil some of her pleasure in the place, probably. Much better to keep his thumb on the business, say nothing about it at all, unless something forced his hand. No need to worry Jean with it. And when he returned the gold brick to its owner he could give the fellow a straight tip not to come skulking about Wester Voe in the dark again. But probably the lesson he'd had already would have cured him of that, Colin decided grimly.

CHAPTER IV

REFRESHED by an unbroken night's sleep, Jean came downstairs to find, as a pleasant surprise, that the breakfast table had been set in the south loggia, overlooking the bay. The clouds had passed in the early morning; overhead the sky was fleckless, and a light haze on the sea gave promise of a brilliant day. Jean crossed the loggia and, leaning on the balustrade, looked out at the flickering of the sunlight on the wave-crests. In her case, second impressions of Ruffa were even happier than the first ones. Already she was setting to work to plan out her day : an exploration of the islet in the morning, a cruise in the motor-boat in the afternoon, and a quiet evening in the garden. Then she would have seen her new kingdom from all points of view.

Colin made his appearance almost immedi-ately. Jean's quick glance, piercing his pretence of briskness, detected the underlying lethargy due to his vigil in the small hours.

" I slept like a log last night, Colin. You don't look as if you had, somehow. What was wrong ? "

Colin shrugged his shoulders to dismiss the point.

" Excitement following on our arrival," he said truthfully, but with enough irony in his tone to make his remark misleading. " Not used to that sort of thing, you know."

" When did you get to bed ? " Jean demanded suspiciously.

" Don't know, really," Colin confessed, sticking to the literal truth. " Got interested in the wireless."

Jean nodded. The explanation apparently satisfied her.

" Well, come on. Let's start breakfast, Colin. I feel simply famished. It must be the sea-air, I suppose. Isn't it nice having breakfast out here in the open. The Dinnets seem to know just what one would like."

Breakfast over, Jean wandered again to the balustrade and gazed out over the wave-ridged expanse. Colin gravitated to her side, filling his pipe as he went.

" Now, I'll tell you what we're going to do, Colin. First of all, I've got to finish my un-packing or the things will be crushed beyond hope. Then I've got to interview Mrs. Dinnet about one or two things. That won't take long. Then we can have a look at the garden till the dew dries up. And after that we'll go and ex-plore Ruffa till lunch-time. Perhaps we'll come across some of the inhabitants."

" Suits me," Colin approved.

" All right, then. I'll go upstairs now. I shan't be long, really."

She went in through the French window of the dining-room, leaving her husband temporarily to his own devices. Colin lounged for a time in the loggia, gazing out over the empty waters below him. Suddenly, round the point came the little motor-boat belonging to Wester Voe, with

Dinnet at the helm and four other figures aboard.

"Bringing the gardeners over, likely," Colin surmised.

As the tiny vessel swung round to enter the channel, he descended from the loggia and walked down towards the landing-place. He watched the boat come alongside. The four men got out and came up the path, greeting him with rough courtesy as they passed. Dinnet had remained behind to moor the boat, and Colin reached the pier as this was finished. Dinnet wished him good morning with his habitual quiet politeness. Colin acknowledged the salutation and made this the opening for an aimless talk on the weather prospects.

"By the way," he edged in, as if by an afterthought. "What's Mr. Arrow like ? To look at, I mean. I may come across him on the island. Save bother if I know him when I meet him."

"That would be convenient, as you say, sir," Dinnet paraphrased in concurrence.

He paused for a moment or two, as though trying to crystallise his recollections.

"Mr. Arrow, sir," he went on, "iss rather striking-looking. He iss tall, and rather thin. His hair iss iron-grey, or greyer than that ; but his eyebrows are quite dark, and they tilt up a little at the outer ends. You could recognise him from that alone, sir. And he has a well-marked nose, too. But most likely you will not meet him just yet, sir. He does not seem to bother much about exercise."

53

" Bit of a recluse, eh ? "

" You might call him that, sir. He iss some sort of scientific man, and perhaps his work keeps him indoors a lot. I do not see him very often myself."

" H'm ! " Colin's tone did not sound enthusiastic. " And what about the three men he employs ? What do they look like ? "

Dinnet again pondered for a few moments before answering.

" One of them wears spectacles, sir. He does the cooking and helps Mr. Arrow with his scientific work, too. So Mrs. Dinnet gathered from a chance remark Miss Arrow made to her, once. Then there iss a big, burly man with a brown moustache. He iss some sort of a foreigner, I think. And there iss a little red-haired man with a face like a ferret and the same kind of eyes. He may be a foreigner, too, for I have not spoken to him. The big man speaks English, sir, but he cannot pronounce ' th ' well."

He paused for a moment and Colin had a fleeting impression from his manner that he was going to add some warning. If this were so, Dinnet evidently thought better of it, for he ended lamely :

" That iss all I can do to describe them, sir."

" Quite clear enough," Colin acknowledged. " By the way, Dinnet, could you give me a small sheet of paper and some twine ? I want to wrap up a parcel—a thing about the size of your fist," he added, to give Dinnet an idea of the paper required.

" Very good, sir. You shall have it at once."

"Oh, by the way, Dinnet," Colin added in what he hoped was an indifferent tone, "has the spectacled man a hare-lip, by any chance. You know the thing I mean?"

Dinnet seemed slightly mystified by the question.

"A hare-lip, sir? I did not notice it; and none of the others iss hare-lipped, either, I am sure."

Colin was momentarily nonplussed. He had seen that hare-lip too clearly to be mistaken. Then he hit on an explanation which seemed to fit the case. The Dinnets, obviously, were not in close touch with Heather Lodge, and a fifth man might have joined Arrow's establishment within the last day or two without attracting their attention. Such a person, new to the island, might easily have blundered into danger after dark.

"I will get you the paper and string for your parcel, sir," Dinnet suggested, seeing that Colin had no further questions to ask.

Colin followed him to Wester Voe, secured the materials, and made a neat package of the gold brick, which he slipped into his pocket. Finding nothing else to do, he wandered aimlessly about the premises until Jean reappeared.

"No letters, and no newspapers, until Dinnet brings them over from Stornadale, when he takes the gardeners back in the evening," she announced. "It makes one feel really at the Back o' Beyond, doesn't it? Now, I'll tell you what we'll do, Colin. These gardeners are working all over the place, so I think we'll give the garden a miss this morning. First of all, we'll make a tour of the island, and see what's what and who's who. That'll take us some little time. Then, when we get back here, we'll have a bathe off the pier. Lunch will be about half-past one, if that suits you."

"O.K.," Colin assured her. "What about getting your feet wet? Wait till the sun dries the dew?"

Jean glanced down at her neat brogues.

"I'd go even if it were raining cats and dogs. It may surprise you, Colin, but I've got more than one pair of shoes. Come along."

As they walked to the gate, Jean decided that they had better explore the northern shore of the island first of all, since they had already seen some of the southern side from Wester Voe. With this aim, they climbed the rising ground behind the house and dropped down a steep slant on the farther side. As they descended the slope and rounded a corner, Jean caught sight of a white spot farther along the coast.

"That must be the shieling where the celebrated Mr. Northfleet resides, Colin. I believe I can see a figure moving about there. We'll be able to drop in on him on our way round. That'll break the ice naturally. If we waited for him to make a formal call he mightn't come at all, being 'reserved, rather' as Mrs. Dinnet says."

At the edge of the cliffs fringing the northern coast of Ruffa a belt of springy turf made easy walking. Jean seemed in no haste. She preferred to go slowly and examine each stretch as she came to it She was in a mood to be delighted with everything she saw : a quaint natural arch with the waves washing through it ; the effortless flight of the gulls ; a hare startled in its form and racing off to cover ; the aerial acrobatics of the golden plovers ; a sleek otter basking confidently below them ; the swarms of rock-pigeons on the cliff faces ; and the sudden appearance, beyond a flock of swimming coots, of a round, dark object which Colin assured her was the head of a seal.

" I don't wonder this Northfleet man comes here to study birds," she exclaimed at last. " The place is simply alive with them, Colin. What's that, there ? I've never seen one like it before."

" Heron," Colin explained, with a wave of his pipe-stem. " They sometimes nest on the cliffs when no trees are handy. Not many of them about, though, I'd imagine."

They topped a little rise and came suddenly upon the shieling, a tiny little building with whitewashed walls and a thatched roof. Beside the door of it a man was sitting at a camp-table, engrossed in some papers outspread before him.

" My man, after all," Colin said in an undertone to Jean. Then, as they advanced, he hailed.

" Hullo, Northfleet ! Remember me, by any chance ? Trent. U.C.L. in your day."

Colin's rather incoherent greeting seemed to be sufficient. Northfleet got up from his chair, and Jean saw a clean-shaven, hard-bitten man, an inch or two taller than Colin. The two were much of an age, but this stranger had something about him which made Colin seem rather boyish by comparison. Jean could not quite define what it was. " Gravity " wasn't the word, neither was " sternness."

" He looks the sort of person who could see a thing through if he took it up," was her almost unconscious summing-up in her mind. " But he's not like Colin. You can't tell what he's thinking, from his face."

Perhaps that was what Mrs. Dinnet meant by " reserved, rather."

Something in Northfleet's attitude when he caught sight of them had suggested, though only for an instant, that they had interrupted him at an inopportune moment. But nothing of this showed in his expression as he came forward with a gesture of greeting.

" Mr. Northfleet, Jean. This is my wife," Colin added, with that mixture of pride and diffidence which marks some newly-married husbands.

" My husband and I have been wondering about you, since we heard your name," Jean explained candidly. " I was quite sure, somehow, that you'd turn out to be the right person and not a total stranger."

Northfleet did not seem anxious to follow up this opening.

" You're staying at Wester Voe, I suppose. A nice place. My own quarters "—he nodded towards the shieling—" are hardly so palatial. If you go inside and face south, you're in the bedroom. Face to the west, where the fireplace is, and you're in the kitchen. Turn to the south, and you're in the dining-room, because the table's there under the window. There are no stairs or passages to confuse one. The architect evidently made no provision for entertaining visitors."

If there was an intention behind the last words, Northfleet took care not to underline it by his facial expression.

" It serves my purpose," he added carelessly.

" You're interested in birds, aren't you, Mr. Northfleet ? " Jean asked. " You must find plenty here, on the island."

" Yes, I'm interested in birds," Northfleet confirmed.

But he did not seem the voluble type of enthusiast, for he made no attempt to develop Jean's topic.

Colin did not take the hint.

" Ornithology's a new line for you, Northfleet, surely. You used to be rather down on the birds-beasts-and-fishes business in the old days."

" I don't know much about it, even now," Northfleet admitted with apparent frankness.

Then a fresh thought seemed to strike him, and he turned to Jean.

" Are you making a long stay on Ruffa, Mrs. Trent ? "

" Three weeks or so," Jean explained. " Isn't it a lovely place ? We're just exploring it for the first time this morning."

Northfleet seemed to consider for a moment, as though making some mental calculation before answering.

"I've made a very crude map of Ruffa," he volunteered. "The Dinnets helped me with the place-names for it. If it's of any interest to you, I'll make a second copy and leave it for you at Wester Voe."

"I should like it very much indeed," Jean said gratefully. "It makes things more interesting when one knows the real names of places, doesn't it?"

"Must have taken a bit of work to draw it up," Colin commented.

Northfleet made a careless gesture.

"One must fill in one's time somehow on a place like this," he said, in what seemed deprecation of his work. "It's not even a plane-table survey, you know; I only used a prismatic compass for the bearings, and worked the thing out roughly."

"I'd have thought the birds would have kept your hands full," Colin suggested.

"The birds? Oh, that's a regular routine. I go about, with a note-book, over the island at more or less fixed times and jot down what seems interesting. There's a meadow-pipit up yonder which changes its ground once or twice a week for some reason that I haven't discovered. And I'm interested in a couple of owls."

"Isn't it rather lonely for you?" Jean demanded, with the idea of paving the way to an invitation.

"Lonely? It was at first. One gets used to it."

"Of course, there are the people up at Heather Lodge," Jean suggested.

"Yes, of course," Northfleet agreed, with a touch of dryness in his tone.

Jean's eyes caught some birds on a cliff near at hand.

"Look at these, Colin, the way they're sitting, two by two, as if they were getting ready to go into the Ark. There's one just flown away. See how graceful it is : it seems to fly without troubling to move its wings. What sort of gull is it, Mr. Northfleet ? "

Northfleet glanced in the direction to which she pointed.

"Oh, a herring-gull," he said, carelessly. "You'll see them all along the coast."

Jean dismissed the subject, since it did not seem to lead further. She was becoming faintly piqued by Northfleet's manner. "Reserved, rather" seemed to err on the mild side as a description of him.

"We're rather interested to know what sort of neighbours we've got," she explained frankly. "You know Mr. Arrow, don't you ? What sort of person is he ? Is he sociable ? Would he care to play bridge ? "

Northfleet met candour with candour, apparently.

"I know Mr. Arrow by sight, but I've never spoken to him, so I've no idea what his tastes may be. But Miss Arrow will be here in a few minutes, I expect. There's a good bathing-pool just below here and she comes down every morning about this time. You can ask her, if you like. She's his niece. I suppose the Dinnets told you that ? "

" Yes, I knew that," Jean admitted. " Do you play ' Contract,' Mr. Northfleet ? "

" Moderately," Northfleet replied, in a tone which somehow suggested that he meant what he said, neither more nor less.

" And tennis ? "

" Fairly well."

" And would you join us, if we can get a fourth ? "

For the first time Jean detected a faint hesitation in Northfleet's manner. He seemed to be weighing two things against each other in his mind before he answered ; but when he accepted her invitation there was no sign of any afterthought in his tone.

" I shall be very glad if you want me. Only, sometimes I'm not free, you understand. This work of mine keeps me tied by the leg and I couldn't get away. But any other time I shall be delighted to come."

" Is Miss Arrow a bridge-player ? "

" I've never played with her," Northfleet said cautiously. " But you can ask her."

" She must find it rather lonely here," Jean suggested sympathetically.

" Possibly," Northfleet concurred.

Jean thought she noticed a faint stiffening of his reserve as he answered, and she tactfully dropped the subject of the Heather Lodge party.

" Are you staying long on Ruffa ? " she asked.

Northfleet seemed disinclined to give a definite answer to this.

" Oh, for some time yet."

" And are you quite comfortable here ? Is there anything we could do . . . ? "

" Nothing whatever, I'm afraid. It's not a palace, but at least it's weathertight," he explained, with a nod towards the shieling. " We've had one or two bad gales since I came, but the place has been quite snug. It's as well, for the wind springs up very quick hereabouts, and it blows hard while it lasts. If you go out in that motor-boat, be sure to run for safety if there's the least sign of a heavy blow. It's not a nice coast in a high wind."

" Dinnet said much the same," Colin acknowledged.

" He knows what he's talking about."

Jean, recollecting that they had interrupted Northfleet in some work, began to fear that they were outstaying their welcome.

" I think we must be moving on, Mr. Northfleet. We've still got a lot of exploring to do before lunch, you know."

Northfleet glanced at his watch.

" Miss Arrow should be here almost immediately," he said. " Could you stay for a few minutes ? "

" If you're sure she'll come," Jean agreed elliptically. " But we mustn't stay long, Colin, or we'll be keeping her from her bathe."

Northfleet had been scanning the hillside, and now he made a gesture to draw Jean's attention.

" There she is."

Jean followed his indication and saw a figure topping a slope a couple of hundred yards away. Behind it, appearing and disappearing among the bents, was a grey dot. Northfleet drew out his pocket-handkerchief and began to wave to the girl, while Colin watched him with a broadening grin. The girl had halted, with the dog scampering round her ; and when Northfleet finished his waving, she made a graceful gesture in reply.

" I understand Morse," Colin explained, as Northfleet turned and caught him with the smile on his face.

" Oh, you do ? " Northfleet returned, without showing the slightest embarrassment.

Colin saw no reason why Jean should not share the joke.

" He's taken you at your word, Jean. His signal was : ' The Trents. They won't stay long '."

" Well, there's no harm in that, is there ? " Jean pointed out, lest Northfleet should think she was offended. " It's just what I said myself a minute or two ago."

Northfleet evidently thought it wisest not to excuse himself in any way, and Jean tacitly approved of his decision. " He'd only have tied himself up in knots if he'd tried," she reflected. " Much more sensible to let well alone, when he saw we weren't offended. And I like the way he smiled when Colin caught him out." Then another idea crossed her mind. " He must know that girl pretty well, I should think. He wouldn't have done that if she'd been a semi-stranger."

Jean had not a trace of the pettiness which refuses to recognise excellence in others. Secure in her own good-looks, she never troubled to consider whether another girl outshone her or not. She could admire without a touch of jealousy—a virtue which had earned her a well-deserved popularity with her own sex.

She turned slightly to make an unobtrusive survey of the approaching stranger. At a distance, in her grey shorts and pull-over, Hazel Arrow looked like a slim-built boy ; but on a nearer view she turned out to be one of those girls who suit hiker's kit and look just as feminine in it as in an evening-frock. She picked her way adroitly down a slight rocky declivity, and a glimpse of slim ankles and neat tennis-shoes made Jean smile to herself as she recalled Colin's dismal prophecy about monstrous boots. At the foot of the little descent Hazel Arrow called her dog to heel and came forward to meet them with a shy friendliness which went straight to Jean's heart.

" I'm sure I'm going to like this girl," Jean decided, without further ado.

For a few moments after Northfleet had introduced them they exchanged the usual remarks which serve to bridge the gap between strangers. Then Hazel's dog—a nondescript animal which had apparently decided to be an Airedale and then suddenly changed its mind—came up and sniffed inquiringly at the hem of Jean's skirt.

" He's quite safe," Hazel hastened to reassure her. " He isn't much to look at, but he's very, *very* wise, and he never mistakes a friend. He's taken to you at once. That'll do, Peter. Heel ! "

" Isn't Ruffa a lovely place ? " Jean demanded, feeling sure of her ground.

" Yes," Hazel agreed, without enthusiasm.

Then, catching Jean's rather surprised look, she added :

" I'm not running it down on its merits ; but I expect even the Garden of Eden would grow hateful it you couldn't get out of it when you wanted to. That sounds like dreadful grousing, doesn't it ? " she admitted with a smile. " But just think of months and months and months of it. No bridge, no golf, no badminton, no shops, no newspaper in the morning, and no one to talk to except Peter, and that's a one-sided business. I thought it was perfect at first, but after a bit the novelty wore off and I've felt a perfect Robinson Crusoe except that I'd no parrot to throw in a remark now and again."

Then, apparently ashamed of having let herself go so freely, she laughed at her own complaints.

" It's really all right. Only, I'm over the first enthusiasm."

Jean had enough imagination to fill in the picture for herself. Evidently Mr. Arrow was so wrapped up in his scientific work that he spared no time to his niece. The other three men were not of the same class. It must have been a deadly monotonous existence for a girl, month after month. Cyril Northfleet's arrival on the island must have been a perfect godsend.

" It must have been awfully dull," she admitted sympathetically. " I hadn't thought of it like that. And I know how one misses bridge. Would you care to make up for lost time ? We'll be delighted if you'll come over for a rubber now and again."

" Oh, I should like to," Hazel accepted, eagerly. " It's good of you to take pity on me."

"Mr. Northfleet will make a fourth," Jean explained, rather unnecessarily.

Then she remembered the roadless condition of the island.

"Don't dress," she stipulated, turning to Hazel. "I don't suppose there's a taxi on Ruffa, and you'd ruin a frock if you came over these paths in it. Wear anything you like," she suggested vaguely. "And we don't expect you to put on a stiff shirt, Mr. Northfleet, even if you've only got to turn to the east to be in your dressing-room in there."

Northfleet smiled at the way in which she had taken up his jest about the accommodation in the shieling.

"I might turn to the east and pray for long enough," he admitted ruefully, "but I couldn't conjure up a dinner-jacket from my luggage. A dinner-party will be something I never expected to see on Ruffa."

"Well, that's that," Jean declared in a business-like tone. "To-morrow night? Half-past seven? That'll give us plenty of time for bridge afterwards. And now we mustn't stay long."

She shot a mischievous glance at Northfleet, who received the thrust imperturbably.

"We've got the rest of the island to explore before lunch. I suppose you're going to bathe?" she added, turning to Hazel.

"Yes, there's a good pool down yonder. It's a change from the bay."

"Well, then, to-morrow at half-past seven, if we don't see each other before then. Come along, Colin."

CHAPTER V

"THEY'RE a nice pair, aren't they, Colin ? " said Jean, when they had walked well out of earshot of the shieling. " I like that Northfleet man. He's got nice grey eyes. Why haven't you got grey eyes, Colin, instead of these blue-green things ? It would improve your looks. And I like his mouth, too. You can guess he's got a sense of humour, without his having to guffaw to show you he sees a joke."

" Never noticed his eyes, and I've known him longer than you have," Colin admitted, placidly. " They can't be so wonderful, after all."

" Don't be jealous. What I like about him is that he looks so—well, so dependable."

Colin halted to re-light his pipe.

" I shouldn't depend much on his ornithology, anyhow," he grunted, between puffs. " Doesn't know the difference between a fulmar petrel and a herring-gull. Not much of a birdist, evidently, and a poor bluffer on a weak hand."

" He said he didn't know much about it himself," Jean retorted in triumph. " I don't call that bluffing."

Colin put his matches back in his pocket and moved on again at her side.

" This bird-watching game is all my eye, if you ask me," he pronounced oracularly.

" Then what's he doing here on Ruffa ? " Jean demanded, with the air of having posed an unanswerable question. " He must be all right, or

Mr. Craigmore wouldn't have had him on the island. You aren't going queer in the head, Colin, taking fancies and what not ? "

" Well, what's he doing here ? " Colin repeated the question with a slightly different inflexion. " Look at it this way, Jean. He's no birdologist. He's a consulting chemist nowadays, unless my memory's all wrong."

" Do you mean he keeps a shop and makes up prescriptions ? "

Jean's enthusiasm was slightly damped. She tried to imagine Northfleet, in a white apron, selling drugs over a counter. Somehow it seemed incongruous.

" Yes, of course," Colin agreed, with a grin. " And if you've got a pain in the pinny, he advises you what to take for it. That's why he's called a consulting chemist. It's a superior brand."

The grin dissipated Jean's doubts.

" What does he do really, Colin ? "

Colin decided that it was of no use trying to carry the joke further.

" It's like this, dear. Suppose you run some factory where the process turns partly on chemistry. Something goes wrong. You can't make out what it is. You whistle in an expert like Northfleet to go into the whole affair and find out what's amiss. That sort of thing."

" I don't see anything strange in his being a consulting chemist," said Jean stoutly.

" No more do I. It's his way of making a living. But what I don't see is what he's doing on Ruffa, mistaking solans and fulmars for gulls to pass the time. Rum, I'd call it. What's a consulting chemist doing up here, so far from his little home, if you can tell me ? Unless—" he paused abruptly as a fresh idea came into his mind—" unless there's some dashed valuable mineral on Ruffa and he's been sent up on the quiet to look into it. *That* might account for all this camouflage of studying our feathered friends."

He stopped short and began to think out this new explanation ; but before he had readjusted his mind in the fresh bearings, Jean began to laugh so unrestrainedly that she speedily had to control herself and wipe her eyes.

" Well, what's the joke ? " Colin demanded, with a shade of testiness. " You'll get a fit of the hiccups if you don't look out."

Jean put away her handkerchief and composed herself with an effort.

" It serves you right for trying to pull my leg, Colin. Why, you poor old blind bat, anyone else could guess what brings him up here. You stood in front of her not five minutes ago."

Colin, rather resentful at Jean's finding a simpler explanation than his own one, seemed somewhat critical.

" H'm ! Engaged, you think ? "

Jean shook her head.

" Not yet, I imagine. She wasn't wearing a ring, at any rate."

" Proves a lot, that, considering the dearth of jewellers' shops on Ruffa."

" Well, they didn't meet for the first time to-day. I could see that."

"No, that's so," Colin conceded. "I follow your line. He went on like a tic-tac man at the races as soon as she hove in sight; that argues previous acquaintance. He knew just when she would turn up; that implies prearrangement and the plot thickens. Finally, she had no bathing-dress or towel over her arm and yet she was going swimming; that suggests that she knows him well enough to leave her things in his hut. Do I follow you, Watson."

"You're really quite a clever old dear," Jean retorted, mockingly. "But my methods are more intricate. I just watched him. That face of his doesn't give much away, but it gave away *that* thing as plain as print. And, what's more, I'll bet you a pair of gloves—six and elevenpenny ones barred—that he hasn't asked her yet."

"Well, why doesn't he?" demanded the mystified Colin. "She's a dashed pretty girl, and he wouldn't have much difficulty in finding a quiet corner on this island where he could get to grips with the question without interruption. I didn't spend much time in backing and filling in my day, I know."

"It puzzles me," Jean confessed. "But there it is. I'm sure I'm right."

"Well, but——" said Colin doubtfully. "What's happening to his practice all this time? He's been here for weeks. Seems to have settled down on a long lease. Dash it, Jean. I believe there's something in my notion, after all, whether you're right or wrong about the girl. It would——"

He broke off abruptly to avoid betraying the

first secret he had kept from his wife. A valuable mineral deposit on Ruffa ? Then what about this gold brick in his pocket at that very moment ? Colin had a considerable store of information, most of it disjointed and useless for any practical purpose ; but now from that dump of casually-acquired knowledge he dug up something else which seemed to fit in. Gold *had* been found in the North before this. Deposits had been discovered in the Leadhills district and at Glencoich in Perthshire. It wasn't in paying quantities in either case ; but at any rate it was there. And there might well be a richer vein on Ruffa.

But this merely opened up a further field of speculation to Colin. Suppose somebody had found gold in paying quantities on the island. What was the need for all this mystery-mongering—unless Jean was right and Northfleet's presence on Ruffa was a purely private affair ? Then there drifted up out of Colin's memory two words : " Mine Royal." He had a vague idea that the Crown could step in somehow in the case of gold or silver deposits. But, try as he would, he could recollect no more than the two words. They refused to link themselves up with any useful and definite information. Mine Royal ! If the Excise people came into the matter, then Colin could see a very sound reason why an unscrupulous prospector should keep his finds dark.

Jean broke into his preoccupation.

" There's one thing I don't understand, Colin. If he's an old friend of that girl, why doesn't he go to Heather Lodge ? They could have put him up there comfortably, instead of letting him pig it in that awful little shieling."

Colin waked up suddenly from his fruitless speculations.

"Because he isn't an old friend of the family. You heard him say he hadn't met old Arrow. Knew him by sight, that was all."

"Well, I'm right about one thing, anyhow," said Jean, obstinately. "And I hope it comes off, too. They're both nice."

"Burning to have a finger in the pie, eh? You miserable little matchmaker!"

"Well, I like being married myself. Did you look at that girl, Colin? What's her name? Hazel, isn't it? Well, she's got that extra inch or two of height that I've always wished I had myself. And she sunburns to that sort of golden tan that shows a flush through it. I burn Hindoo-colour myself, worse luck."

"Fishing for compliments? Sorry. Out of stock. Used 'em all up when I was engaged."

Jean paid no attention to him.

"Do you know, Colin," she went on. "I don't care much for her uncle, from what we've heard about him. He sounds like an old pig, if you ask me. Look at the way he's brought that girl away up here, and left her to amuse herself as best she can. She must have had a miserably dull time of it."

"On your adored island?"

"*Alone* on my adored island," Jean corrected. "I don't know whether I'd like Ruffa so much if you weren't here—even if that makes you conceited. Anyhow, I'm going to be nice to her."

"Meaning you're going to hang round her neck and leave me in the lurch?" protested Colin, indignantly. "Thank you!"

"No, of course not. But there's a half-way house between that and ignoring her entirely. Besides, it'll do you good to miss me, now and again."

"Oh, all right, then," Colin acquiesced. "If you want it, you must have it. Now let's push on a bit faster or we won't be back in time for a bathe."

They continued their way to the eastern tip of the island. In the clear air they could make out the white cottages of Stornadale village on the mainland, and beyond them the smoke of a steamer, hull-down on the horizon.

"Not much traffic hereabouts," Colin observed as he gazed out over the empty sea. "That's the Fishery protection boat, most likely. I expect the fishing fleet's somewhere round the corner."

"Sniff hard and perhaps you'll smell the smoking of the herrings on board," suggested Jean, who had not forgotten how he had tried to impose on her. "And when you've had your fill of that, suppose we turn home? We'll keep along the coast, past Heather Lodge, and then we'll have seen almost the whole of the shore."

As they strolled along a rough path through the heather, there appeared over a ridge ahead a heavily-built man holding in leash an enormous hound, wiry-haired and grey. Jean started at the sight of it and moved closer to Colin.

"Oh, Colin! Look at that dreadful creature!" she exclaimed nervously. "It's as big as a baby donkey. What is it? Is it safe?"

74

" Let's run ! " Colin proposed, in mock panic.
Then to reassure her, he explained : " Irish
wolf-hound, by the look of it. Nothing to worry
about, dear. Gentle as lambs, really, though
they look fearsome brutes. But I shouldn't like
to have one set on me. Immensely strong beasts,
able to tackle a wolf single-handed, they say.
Knock a man over as easy as look at him."

" Well, I hope it won't take a dislike to me
as we pass it. Wouldn't it be better to go off
the track a bit till it's gone by, Colin ? I don't
really like the look of it."

" Nonsense ! The last time I saw one of that
breed it was being led down the street by a little
girl, a kiddy not half the size of the hound. You
mustn't let yourself get into a funk about it."

" I suppose it must be one they keep at
Heather Lodge," said Jean, still eyeing the
hound mistrustfully.

She found her fears quite groundless when
the hound and its keeper came abreast of them.
Colin, determined to satisfy her, hailed the man
as he drew near.

" Nice dog you've got there."

The man stared at him intently for a few
seconds before replying. Evidently he had
noticed Jean's momentary panic.

" It would not hurt anybody. Ze lady can
feel quite safe. Zere is no danger from it," he
explained genially.

Colin had no difficulty in fitting Dinnet's
description to this stranger. This was the
" big, burly man with the brown moustache."
Although his words were quite correct and his

pronunciation was good, he gave himself away by those modulations of the voice and a slight misplacement of those stresses which form traps for anyone speaking a foreign language. One glance had satisfied Colin of one thing : this was not the stranger of the previous night.

Encouraged by her husband, Jean nervously made an attempt to grow friendly with the gigantic hound. It showed no hostility, only a gentle indifference to her advances ; but at least she became convinced that it was nothing to be afraid of. The keeper watched her performance in moody silence. He was evidently a person of few words and with no gift for enlivening casual meetings. When they at last moved on, his relief was more obvious than polite. He led the hound on down the path, and Jean turned to watch it as it went.

" I was rather a fool to be afraid of it," she admitted at last. " But there was some excuse for me. Anyhow, I'm glad I met it first in broad daylight, Colin. Fancy seeing that great grisly brute loom up on you out of the dusk, if you weren't expecting it ! It would have scared me stiff. Like *The Hound of the Baskervilles*. I wonder if they let it loose at night," she concluded, rather nervously.

" Shouldn't think so. Ask your girl-friend. She ought to know. It wouldn't hurt you, anyway."

In a short time they reached Heather Lodge.

" A walled garden ! " Jean exclaimed as they came up to it. " I didn't expect that, somehow."

"Well, old Arrow evidently means to keep it to himself," Colin pointed out. "Broken glass on top of an eight-foot wall. Fairly fresh, too, by the look of the mortar it's fixed on with. No road this way, that's clear. Let's have a squint at the front of the house."

They passed along the side-wall, and Colin was the first to turn the corner. The wall was continuous, except for a small gateway which gave admission to the garden. Beside this gateway, on a wooden chair, sat a small figure in riding-breeches and leggings ; and Colin had no difficulty in identifying him as Dinnet's "red-haired, ferret-faced man."

At the first glimpse of Colin he sprang to his feet and faced round in their direction with a cat-like swiftness. He made a sudden movement rather like the Japanese salutation, crouching slightly and bringing his hands down to his thighs. Then, as Jean appeared, he relaxed again and seemed to have realised a mistake.

As he straightened up once more, Colin was amazed by his accoutrement. Down the side of each thigh ran a great flap of leather, depending from a belt, and at the lower tip of this a second flap was sewn to the first, forming a huge holster. In that peculiar movement the man's hands had gone down into the holsters with automatic accuracy, but, to Colin's relief, they had come out again empty.

"By jove !" Colin reflected in surprised admiration, "that's a cute notion. You can't miss an opening that size to start with, and as soon as your hand's in the holster the narrowing of the pocket guides you straight to the pistol-butt. And in a holster of that size you couldn't get your gun tangled up: it would come straight out with a jerk when you wanted it."

Then the extraordinary incongruity of such paraphernalia on an island like Ruffa struck him in its full force. Jean, fortunately, had not seen the hostile movement; but as she came forward she stared with frank curiosity at the holsters.

Colin thought it advisable to go forward at once. Evidently this person's suspicions, if he had any, should be allayed as soon as possible.

" Can I see Mr. Arrow ? " he asked, resolutely ignoring the peculiarities of the situation. " My name's Trent. I'm staying at Wester Voe over yonder."

The ferret-faced man examined him with a pair of gimlet eyes before replying.

" Mr. Arrow is busy," he said succinctly.

Again Colin had the impression of a man speaking a foreign language. The bluntness with which he had been repulsed roused his obstinacy.

" Mrs. Trent would like to see the garden. May we go in and look round ? "

" No."

" Surely that can't do any harm ? " Colin persisted, feeling that he was not showing up very well before Jean.

" It is not permitted."

Then, as a concession, the ferret-faced man added an explanatory sentence.

" It is a dangerous process that Mr. Arrow is working on."

"So you're put on guard here to warn people off, eh?"

"That is so."

"And you're so anxious for their safety that you carry a brace of pistols to persuade them to move on," was Colin's inward comment.

"Would you and the lady please go now?" the ferret-faced man suggested, politely enough but with a distinctly unfriendly note in his tone. "It is best not to come too near when Mr. Arrow is working."

"I'll go in a minute," Colin conceded. "I just want to ask one thing. If the hare-lipped man's in, just now, I'd like to have a word or two with him."

"Hare-lipped? I do not understand."

"Hare-lipped," repeated Colin, and then tried to elucidate his meaning partly by a gesture. "Split lip. As if he'd got his lip cut open with a knife and it hadn't healed right. A cleft in it. Is that clear?"

"*Ach! mit einer Hasenscharte?*" the red-haired man exclaimed. His eyes lighted up for a moment and then turned sullenly suspicious.

"No, there is no such man in this house. I know nothing about him."

"But I'll bet you do," Colin commented to himself. "You gave yourself away that time, my gunman friend."

Aloud, however, he accepted the statement.

"Oh, very well. It's nothing important."

He turned away with Jean, leaving the guard staring after them in obvious doubt and perplexity.

" What was that you said about a hare-lipped man, Colin ? " Jean demanded as soon as they were out of earshot.

Colin saw that he had betrayed himself, but he recovered his ground instantaneously.

" I was just trying to find out if he was a Mason," he explained glibly.

" Oh, so that's one of your pass-words, is it ? I'll try it on the next Freemason I come across and give him a start. Perhaps Mr. Northfleet's one. I'll try it on him. Colin," she went on seriously, " that man had two huge pistols in these holsters. Did you see that ? What on earth could he want with them on Ruffa ? It doesn't look—well, quite what one would expect here. I don't half like the look of that, Colin."

But Colin, once launched into deceit, found his path unexpectedly smooth. He was more than a little disturbed himself by what he had seen, but he was determined to quieten Jean's doubts.

" You don't suppose he means to shoot people with them, do you ? " he said derisively. " Who is there to shoot on a place like this ? You, or me, or the Dinnets, or Northfleet, perhaps. You've got too vivid an imagination, that's what's wrong with you, dear. Look at the fuss you made over a harmless hound. And now you get all sorts of blood-and-thunder Deadwood Dick notions because a man happens to have a revolver. I expect he brought them out to prac-tise with, to while away the time when he's on guard there. And if old Arrow is brewing some dangerous explosive or something of that sort, it seems to me only decent of him to put a fellow on point-duty to warn us off. You're on the wrong track again."

"Well, you may be right," Jean admitted rather hesitatingly. "I don't see myself who he could want to shoot hereabouts. Still—it's queer, Colin. It's no wonder the Dinnets don't like those men at Heather Lodge. That was a nasty little creature at the gate; and the other man wasn't very friendly either."

"If we don't hurry up we'll get no bathe before lunch," Colin pointed out, abruptly closuring the discussion. "Come along—as you're always saying to me."

But as he walked on by Jean's side Colin began to find that his soothing explanation raised awkward questions in his own mind. For, after all, he had been sound enough, so far as he went. There was nobody on Ruffa who was likely to need an armed guard to keep them away from the gate of Heather Lodge in broad daylight. And yet, there the guard was—and obviously very much on the alert, too. Colin had a vivid recollection of that threatening gesture as he hove in sight round the corner.

"These fellows are afraid of something," he inferred easily enough. "And that hound points in the same direction. If they wanted a dog as a pet, they've got Miss Arrow's mongrel already on the premises. That wolf-hound is meant for serious business."

Then in his mind Jean's passing reference to *The Hound of the Baskervilles* acted like a seed-crystal in a supersaturated solution. A whole series of previously isolated thoughts suddenly fitted themselves together into a pattern, and in Colin's mental theatre a sinister drama began to unfold itself. He saw a stranger with a hare-lip landing on the island ; a stealthy figure slinking under the wall of Heather Lodge in the darkness ; some drugged meat thrown over to silence the hound, perhaps, or else an entry which evaded the beast ; a burglar's visit to the house ; an alarm ; a flight into the heather. The penultimate picture showed him a hare-lipped man stumbling through the night with that grisly monster on his heels, flying blindly to avoid his pursuer ; then a sharp dip on the hillside, a fall, a crash on the rock, and a wounded man crawling for safety towards the lights of Wester Voe, while the hound, perhaps bemused by the drug, failed to follow up the trail. The next picture needed only memory, for he himself had been an actor. But what had happened after he left the man ? That seemed more mysterious than ever, in spite of Colin's efforts to account for the vanishing of the stranger.

"Wonder if I shouldn't try to talk it over with Northfleet ? " he speculated. " Something damned queer going on here, that's plain. I don't like it. And Northfleet's always another man on hand, if anything does turn up."

Then the recollection of Northfleet's ornithological camouflage crossed his mind and made him hesitate.

" He's another dark horse in the business. Between the lot of them, I don't know where I stand. Better go cautious, perhaps. See how things develop."

CHAPTER VI

JEAN sipped her coffee contentedly, assured that her little dinner-party had proved a complete success. It was the first time she had played hostess ; for in her own home there were elder sisters who had taken the upper end of the table when her mother was absent.

Beforehand, she had been just a little doubtful of Colin's attitude, for quite obviously he had not wholly welcomed the incursion of strangers so soon after their arrival at Wester Voe. In the event, however, her forebodings had proved baseless. Her own vivacity, Hazel's gift of naturalness and appreciation of Colin's little jokes, Northfleet's rather more cynical turn of humour : all had contributed to keep the conversation not only alive but nimble. The two guests seemed to have acquired almost immediately the status of old friends with whom there is no need to stand upon formality. Colin, completely reassured, had even taken the initiative in making plans for tennis.

" Please switch on the lights, Colin," Jean requested.

" That's one thing I envy you," Hazel declared, as Colin rose to comply. " I never realised what a convenience electric light really is until I came up here and had to do without it. Lamps give one a nice soft light in the evenings, but they have their drawbacks. They make a room so frightfully hot in weather like this."

An association of ideas carried Colin to a fresh subject.

"Must be a bit of a job getting your coal up to Heather Lodge," he surmised. "Not like toting it straight up from the pier to this place."

"There's a simple way round that difficulty," Hazel pointed out. "Do without coal. We don't use any."

"Then how do you manage about cooking ?" Jean demanded, rather aghast at the idea of tinned meats in perpetuity.

"Oh, there's no bother about that," Hazel assured her. "You see, my uncle put in a benzene-gas plant. Is that what they call it ?" she interjected, turning to Northfleet. "He needed it for his work—to run Bunsen burners and a furnace in the laboratory ; and it feeds a stove in the kitchen as well. I'm not accustomed to it myself ; but Beeston—that's my uncle's assistant—gets splendid results from it. Beeston ought to have been a chef, really. He simply loves cooking, so I've let him take over that side of things entirely. I can cook if I'm put to it, but I can't take the sort of fatherly interest in a roast that Beeston does. So the arrangement suits both of us ; and we get far better meals that way, I'm sure."

"Take up a lot of his time, one'd think," Colin suggested. "Doesn't Mr. Arrow object ?"

"Oh, no. Beeston seems to have plenty of time on his hands. He and my uncle work in spurts. They're very busy for a while, and then they seem to have very little to do for a bit.

I expect they've got to wait at some stages in the process, whatever it is."

"Aren't you nervous, living in a house with all this risky work going on ?" Jean inquired.

Hazel lifted her arched eyebrows slightly.

"Risky ? I don't know about it being risky. My uncle never said anything of the sort to me."

"The man at your gate told us," Jean explained. "He warned us off the premises. He certainly said that Mr. Arrow was in the middle of a dangerous bit of work and that we oughtn't to linger about the place."

Hazel laughed, but to Colin's ear there seemed to be just a trace of embarrassment mingled with her amusement.

"Oh, you came across the Bogey Man ?" she asked. "I ought to have warned you about him yesterday, but I forgot you'd be passing Heather Lodge. I'm awfully sorry. You must have got a bit of a shock, coming on him suddenly, with all his war-paint on. Which of them was it ?"

"It was a small, red-haired man," Jean particularised.

"That's Natorp. Zelensky's the other one— a big, heavily-built man with a moustache."

"Saw him too, out with your wolf-hound," Colin volunteered.

"Oh, you saw the wolf-hound too ?"

Hazel seemed to ponder for a moment or two. Then, taking some definite decision, she went on, though in a rather hesitating tone :

"I hate to pull the family skeleton out of its cupboard and rattle its bones at you like this ;

but my uncle, Mr. Arthur Arrow, has brought it on himself, with all this absurd business, and I expect Natorp must have looked a queer creature to find in a place like this."

Colin, intently interested, caught a peculiarity in her tone when she mentioned her uncle's name. There was almost a touch of amused contempt in the way she drawled out the syllables, as though she had made some obscure joke which did not altogether please her.

" If I said nothing," Hazel continued, rather reluctantly, as though she now regretted that she had begun, " you might feel—well, mystified, and perhaps a trifle worried by the look of things. There's nothing to worry about, really. It's just a kind of kink my uncle's got."

At this point Colin's ear detected less amusement and more vexation in her tone.

" There's no madness in our family," Hazel assured them ironically. " But in the last few years my uncle seems to have got a sort of quirk. It started with his fitting our house in London with burglar-alarms. Then more burglar-alarms, until locking up for the night became a regular toil, what with pulling this bolt and pushing that button, and setting something else. And, of course, they all had to be taken off before one could open a window or a door. It was about as complicated as escaping from the Bastille, if one wanted to go out in the morning."

She shrugged her shoulders in thinly-veiled contempt.

" Then he imported Beeston to live in the house—to give him more confidence, I suppose.

And a while after that, Zelensky was taken on as a night-watchman. And now we've got Natorp, and on top of him the wolf-hound. I wish my jewellery justified all the fuss! It doesn't, worse luck. My own impression is that it all started with a little fussiness on my uncle's part, and it's grown and grown, just by thinking about it. Anyhow, you needn't worry. Zelensky and Natorp are no company, but there's no harm in them. They're just there so that my uncle can sleep quietly in his bed."

A thought seemed to cross her mind and she laughed gently.

"It is a nuisance, though," she admitted rather ruefully. "The night before last we had a full-dress rehearsal: everybody waking up and rushing about in the middle of the night, doors banging, the wolf-hound loosed, my uncle in a fearful state brandishing a revolver and telling me to stay in my room. Poor Peter completely bewildered by it all and determined to lay down his life to protect me—such growls! And then, in the morning, it all turns out to be a false alarm. Nothing in it at all. But it unsettled my uncle thoroughly; and as a result he posted Natorp at the gate."

"'Most disturbing,' as Jeeves says," Colin commented in what he hoped was a light tone.

Hazel Arrow had evidently swallowed the tale of a false alarm without the slightest suspicion; but Colin knew too much about the night before last to be taken in so readily. This new evidence hinged too neatly on to what he had learned independently ; the false alarm notion was clever enough, but it cut no ice with Colin.

His glance flickered momentarily to North-fleet's face, but he could read nothing there. Northfleet seemed intent on the girl opposite him, and at the close of her tale he nodded slightly, as though he entirely shared her views about the affair.

" Well, that's the family skeleton," Hazel concluded. " I hope it's made your flesh creep. Honestly, you mustn't let yourselves think any more about it. It's just my uncle's silliness. And quite likely that false alarm was a put-up job on the part of our two Bogey Men. They may have wanted to give my uncle a run for his money and suggest that they were really earning their pay by facing awful dangers. I wouldn't put it past them."

Much to Colin's relief, Jean evidently accepted Hazel's view of the affair.

" It sounds like something straight from Hollywood, doesn't it ? " she suggested, lightly. " I'm glad you told me all about it, for I was really just a wee bit taken aback by the reception we got at Heather Lodge that morning. It didn't err on the side of effusive hospitality, to put it plainly. But it's all right now that one knows what's what. I'm nervous myself, at times, and I've got a fellow-feeling for your uncle about his precautions. Unless I knew our front door was locked at night I wouldn't be able to sleep a wink. I'd be imagining all sorts of things. Why, it's silly, but I'd hate to sleep on the ground floor. Somehow it seems safer to be upstairs. Anyhow, after this, I shan't worry even if one of your Bogey Men springs up from behind a rock and shouts : ' Hands up ! ' or ' Stand and deliver,' or whatever it is that they do say."

Hazel seemed relieved that Jean had taken the matter in this way.

" My uncle is really right over the score," she admitted frankly. " But so long as his fads don't worry you, it's all right, I suppose."

" Well, you may have armed guards and so forth," Jean retorted, " but Wester Voe can keep its end up too. We've got a secret passage on the premises. Did you know that ? "

" Have you ? "

Northfleet seemed more interested than Colin had expected.

" Oh, yes," Jean assured him. " Colin will let you see it some time. He knows how to work the spring that opens it. I don't. But it's really rather dull. Just a dark hole with some steps going down into it."

" I'd like to see it, some time," Northfleet suggested, though without any particular eagerness.

An idea seemed to cross Jean's mind, making her smile mischievously.

" Have you met the hare-lipped man, Mr. Northfleet ? "

Northfleet's face showed only puzzlement at the question.

" Hare-lipped man ? " he repeated. " No, I can't say I have. Who is he ? I thought I knew everybody by sight on Ruffa."

89

"Perhaps I've got the words wrong," Jean hazarded, rather put out that her joke had missed fire. "Are you a Freemason?"

"No, I'm not," Northfleet replied, still with a puzzled look. "Why?"

"Oh, nothing," Jean rejoined hastily.

Then, to escape from the situation, she turned to Hazel.

"Suppose we leave them here to finish their smoke, while we go out and take a turn round the garden before starting bridge. Would you care to?"

Hazel acquiesced at once.

"That's another thing I envy you here," she said as she rose from the table. "At Heather Lodge everything's been allowed to run to seed and the garden's just a wilderness. Your gardens are simply lovely, I know. Mrs. Dinnet used to let me wander about in them any time I chose, and it was a real treat, after the rack and ruin up yonder."

Colin opened the door, and the two girls passed out. As he returned to his seat, Colin again hesitated over the problem of taking Northfleet into his confidence. This tale of the "false alarm" had made it clear to him that his surmises had not been far out. The hare-lipped stranger had really been prowling round Heather Lodge that night. Arthur Arrow's precautions had not been quite so superfluous as Hazel imagined. Still, he wavered in his mind over Northfleet, for Northfleet was also a dark horse as far as Colin was concerned. Perhaps the best thing to do was to feel his ground a little more before coming to plain talk. He thought he saw his way to one step further, but that could be delayed until later in the evening. In the meanwhile there were one or two things he wanted to find out.

"You hadn't heard about this secret passage before?" he inquired with apparent casualness, helping himself to a fresh cigarette.

Northfleet shook his head.

"No. This is the first time I've been inside Wester Voe. I don't know Craigmore personally. Some friends of mine tackled him and got me permission to stay on Ruffa for a while. And when you don't know a man it seems rather cheeky to pry into his house. The Dinnets would have shown me over, and probably told me about this passage, but I didn't encourage the idea, you understand."

Colin sympathised with this point of view. He hated people who took an ell when you gave them an inch. And he was rather relieved by what Northfleet had said. Evidently he would come to Wester Voe when he got a special invitation, but he wasn't the sort who would take liberties and imagine that he had the run of the premises merely because he had been asked there once.

"That lot at Heather Lodge don't seem to be very good mixers," he said tentatively.

Northfleet did not rise to the bait.

"I've never spoken to any of them," he explained, with apparent frankness. "Miss Arrow I came across casually on the island. One was bound to meet her going about, just as you did. But the rest I've only seen in the distance."

Colin ruminated over the implications of this. " One point cleared up, anyhow," he reflected. " Jean's all off the mark. He didn't come here on the girl's account. So it's my notion or nothing. Better go cautiously."

" Interested in this secret passage ? " he asked, in order to lead the talk into another channel. " I'll let you see the opening of it, if you'd care to look at it."

" Where does it come out at the other end ? " Northfleet inquired. " I'm not sure I'd care about a thing of that sort. I don't suffer from Arrow's persecution-mania "—he smiled at the words—" but I'd rather not run the risk of some fellow creeping into my abode without permission."

" Craigmore evidently felt the same," Colin explained. " Bricked up t'other end of it. So the Dinnets say. Quite right, too."

" Oh, then it goes a fair length ? "

" No notion about that, myself. Never been into it. Come out into the hall and I'll let you see the start of it."

He led Northfleet out of the dining-room and showed him the panelling behind which the passage started.

" Nothing to show, is there ? " he demanded, stepping aside to let Northfleet examine the woodwork. " Nobody'd suspect anything amiss there. Good bit of work. Now, look. You press down that bit, and then you shove this projection sideways, and whoop she goes ! "

The door opened under his hand as he spoke, and Northfleet peered into the dark recess.

"H'm ! Most ingenious. Let's see it again, will you ? "

Colin closed the door and repeated the opening process.

"Mind if I try it myself ? " Northfleet asked, and taking consent for granted, he tested the mechanism once or twice. "The catch at the back is in plain sight, of course," he commented, opening the door to verify this. "Well, I wonder where it ends up. I'd rather like to go down there sometime. That sort of mysterious gloryhole always had an attraction for me."

"I'll go down with you, some time, if you like," Colin suggested. "Interesting to know where it leads to, before you come to the bricked up bit. It's an old affair. Wester Voe's built on the site of an extinct castle, the Dinnets say, and most likely this thing dates from the castle period."

"It may go a good distance, then," Northfleet surmised. "Labour was cheap in the old days."

He snapped the door back into place as the two girls appeared coming up the steps from the garden.

They settled down to bridge in the drawing-room and the time passed swiftly.

Hazel was the first to realise how late it was growing.

"After we finish this rubber I must really go," she intimated firmly at last.

"Afraid the Bogey Man'll catch you ? " Colin asked feebly.

" Not quite. But it's getting late and I've a walk in the dark."

" There ought to be a moon, if that's the trouble."

The rubber ended more speedily than they had anticipated, but Jean was loath to let Hazel go.

" Stay for just a little longer. It's really not late yet. Colin, Miss Arrow and I have lots to talk about which you're too young to hear."

" Tact. Trent brand. New model," Colin explained. " She thinks a whiskey and soda would brighten us up. If you'll come into the lounge—— "

He stood aside to allow Northfleet to leave the room. Jean quite unwittingly had played into his hands, and he meant to try an experiment. A glance at his watch had assured him that the time was ripe for it.

After pouring out whiskey and soda, Colin drew Northfleet's attention to the wireless.

" Ever do anything with the short waves ? " he asked.

Northfleet shook his head.

" Never bothered with them. Is it any good ? "

This was the lead Colin had wanted. He switched on the set.

" You read Morse," he said over his shoulder as he began to search. " Unless one does, short-wave work's a bit limited. There ! Listen to that."

Northfleet gave his attention to the signals for a few moments.

" It's not over-thrilling," he confessed.

"What's it all about ? I can hear him repeating the same thing time after time : '*GKT de GFWV*. *QTC5*.' It doesn't excite me much."

"It's the *Majestic* calling up the Portishead station and saying she's got five telegrams to transmit," Colin explained, with modest pride in his knowledge.

He glanced at his watch and fell to adjusting the dials afresh until the hiss of a carrier-wave came from the loud-speaker.

"Just hold on a jiffy . . . Ah, there's something plainer."

Suddenly the clear voice spoke as on the previous night, and Colin, having adjusted the dials, swung round to watch the effect of the message on Northfleet.

"Hello ! Hello, London ! Attention ! I am calling and testing . . . testing and calling. I shall repeat this message night by night at ten, eleven, and twelve o'clock. Hello ! I am testing. I shall repeat this message each night. Attention ! "

Then once more the slow Morse transmission began :

"Teiil lfilh tcetu fdhso . . . ."

Northfleet's habitual control over his features had failed him when the voice began to speak. It was the merest flicker of an expression ; yet Colin saw something which made him suspect that his companion had been startled by that message out of the void. But as the succession of Morse letters came into the signal, Colin guessed that they conveyed no more to Northfleet than they did to himself.

" Rum things on the short waves at times," he commented as he switched off abruptly in the middle of the message. " He repeats that, just as you heard it, night after night. Took a copy of it myself, just for practice. Must be testing his transmission with some pal, I expect, just as he says at the start."

Whatever the message had conveyed to Northfleet, he made no effort to share his information with Colin.

" It seems a queer enough jumble," he said in an indifferent tone. " How does it look when you get it down on paper ? "

Colin was acute enough to see that Northfleet, despite his assumed incuriosity, was angling for the transcription of the message. But if North-fleet could hold back information, so could Colin. He checked his movement towards the note-book containing his copy.

" Oh, just as weird as when you hear it," he said carelessly. " No meaning in it at all. Expect he's just transmitting letters at random to make a decent length of signal."

If Northfleet was disappointed at a failure to secure the transcript, he betrayed no sign of it in his expression.

" I don't know anything about the short waves," he admitted, " but that sounded a fairly powerful signal."

" It is," Colin agreed. " In fact, the other night, when general conditions were pretty bad, it came through as clear as a bell. He gives the call-sign HSI–314, at the tail-end, if that suggests anything to you."

" No—nothing whatever," said Northfleet promptly.

Colin began to feel that he had done well in not being too ready to consult Northfleet. This little episode, which he had planned as an experiment, had revealed one thing very plainly : Northfleet did not intend to put his cards on the table for the asking. He had spotted something in that short-wave message which Colin himself had missed, for some reason or other ; and yet he had shut up as tight as an oyster about it, didn't even admit that he'd heard anything to interest him. But for that flicker of interest on his face at the opening words, Colin would never have guessed that the message meant anything to him at all. Not that it had meant so very much after all, apparently. Colin guessed that the jumble of Morse conveyed as little to Northfleet as it did to himself. The man's attitude had given that away, although he had kept his face straight. The whole pose of his body had betrayed his alertness when the message began, but there had been an obvious slackening of attention when the incomprehensible portion was reached. And he had made no complaint when Colin switched off—of malice aforethought —in the very middle of the transmission. If he had been able to read the stuff and understand it as he went along, he'd have wanted to hear the lot, Colin conjectured. And yet he was interested in it, or he wouldn't have tried to get a look at the copy. Well, if he wanted that, he'd have to put some of his cards on the table. Nothing for nothing was going to be Colin's motto in this affair. The Northfleet method had uncovered a streak of obstinacy in Colin's character.

"Here we are," Jean said, as she opened the door of the lounge. "Miss Arrow won't stay a minute longer, she says. We've arranged to bathe off the pier before breakfast, Colin, if you can creep out of bed early enough. And perhaps you'll come too, Mr. Northfleet? Or is it too much trouble to come across the island? Anyway, we shall expect you if we see you."

She turned to Hazel, who had followed her into the room.

"Are you sure you won't need a wrap to go home in? I can let you have one, if it's any use."

Hazel shook her head.

"It's quite a warm night, thanks. Now I must really go," she protested. "You can't imagine how I've enjoyed myself this evening. And I'm looking forward to some tennis, Mr. Trent. You've got perfect courts here. After all these months on Ruffa, I'm beginning to feel quite civilised again, now that Mrs. Trent can tell me something about shops, and theatres, and concerts."

From the loggia Jean and Colin watched their guests disappear down the garden path and then returned to the drawing-room.

"It was nice of you to ask them to tennis, Colin," Jean said approvingly. "You're not half such an old bear as you pretend to be. And you know, Colin, that girl must have had a ghastly dull time of it here. She wasn't grousing about it to me; she isn't the grousing sort ; but she let slip one or two things that made me realise what it's been like. It might not be so bad for a man ; but just think how deadly lonely it must have been for a girl like that, week after week, with no one to talk to except the Dinnets, until your Northfleet man turned up."

" Well, he didn't turn up here on her account," said Colin triumphantly. " So your intricate methods were off the mark there, my dear Watson. He'd never met her until he came here."

" Score to you ? Well, I can tell you something I *was* right in. They're not engaged, just as I told you. Candidly, Colin, I think your man Northfleet's a bit of an ass. They're just made for each other ; and why the idiot hasn't asked her to marry him, I can't conceive."

" He might have had a dash at it, certainly," Colin agreed. " One of the slow-but-sure brigade, evidently."

" What I can't make out is why he and she didn't play tennis occasionally to pass the time," Jean went on. " The courts were there for them and there was nobody at Wester Voe. I'm sure the Dinnets wouldn't have objected."

"Northfleet's got moral scruples about pushing in without an invitation—thank goodness ! " Colin explained. " That's probably why. He's not a friend of Craigmore's, it seems, so perhaps he felt it would be going over the score to use the courts without express permission."

" Is he still the same as he was when you knew him before," Jean demanded. " You said he was tight-lipped, or something. Didn't talk much. Well, to-night at dinner he kept up his end of the conversation well enough, surely."

" Yes," Colin rejoined. " And how much did you learn about him from it all ? He's just the same as he used to be—tells you just as much as he wants to, and not a scrap more."

" That's true," Jean admitted in a reflective tone. " He didn't get autobiographical. I was rather dreading that he might, Colin, and then you and he would have started off talking about dear old friends that I never heard of, and ruined the evening. He didn't do that, sensible man."

" Neither did I," protested Colin. " You give him all the credit, of course. Off you go to bed. I'll come up in a minute or two when I've locked up the door."

Jean lingered for a moment or two before going.

" That old Mr. Arrow must be a weirdish bird," she ruminated aloud. " I'm glad Hazel explained things. I was getting a bit worried about that lot at Heather Lodge. But I can quite understand the old boy's feelings. See that you make that front door fast, Colin."

CHAPTER VII

" MAY I offer anybody some more tea ? " Jean inquired, as she put her own cup on the garden table. " You're not supposed to accept, for there's no more hot water in the kettle ; but it sounds polite to ask you. Cigarettes, Colin."

" Aren't you going to start again ? " Colin asked, with a nod towards the courts in front of them.

" I don't think I care about another set just immediately," Jean decided. " I'd rather sit here quietly for a while before tackling violent exercise."

" Boa constrictors feel much the same, at times," Colin commented darkly.

Indignantly Jean sat up and called her guests to witness.

" You're not suggesting that I've over-eaten myself on the strength of two bits of bread-and-butter, one rock-cake, and a potato scone, are you ? That's all I've had for tea ; and I can bring two credible witnesses to swear to it, if necessary. No, I just feel lazy. If you're desperately energetic, Colin, can't you run away and find something to amuse you : fish for tittle-bats in the lily-pond or widen your education by reading the labels of the flower-beds ? "

Then a more acceptable suggestion occurred to her.

" Didn't you promise to show Mr. Northfleet that secret passage ? "

" Go down there in flannels ? " Colin inquired protestingly.

" Flannels can be washed, even on Ruffa," Jean pointed out. " And besides, there's no need to rub yourself against the walls all the way along, is there ? "

Northfleet gave a silent vote in favour of Jean's proposal by rising from his chair.

" You see, Colin ? " Jean quoted maliciously, "*Everyone says, 'Run along, there's a little darling.*' Take the hint, dear. Hazel and I have heaps to talk about. In fact, I don't think I want to play any more tennis before dinner ; so you can fill in the time till then for yourself."

Colin shrugged his shoulders in mock resignation.

" Very well. If I don't come to the surface again—No Flowers, By Request."

" Colin ! You don't think it's dangerous ? " Jean demanded with a faint disquiet.

" There'll be lots of spiders," Colin prophesied gloomily. " But cheer up ! If any spider dares to gnash its teeth at me, I'll make it rue the day. What I'm really afraid of is one of them dropping down my neck and biting me in the spinal cord. I'm almost sure these brutes never brush their teeth—haven't a tooth-brush amongst the lot. Bite's sure to be septic."

Jean shivered instinctively.

" That's quite enough, Colin. You know I simply loathe spiders, and you're making me feel creepy all over with that sort of talk."

" Spiders ! " said Colin resentfully. " I once lived in an old country house where they used to march downstairs and bark in your face, they were so mettlesome. I'm accustomed to spiders. Lead me to them."

And with the air of a martyr preparing to face the lions he rose from the tea-table. When they reached the house, Northfleet procured a small parcel which he had brought with him that afternoon.

" I don't mind confessing I meant to keep you to your promise about showing me this place," he explained as he untied the packet. " I'd have asked you, even if Mrs. Trent hadn't suggested it. So I brought along a flash-lamp, a prismatic compass, and one or two other odds and ends that might be useful."

" Going to make a survey ? " Colin asked, in some surprise.

" One may as well enter the thing up on the map I made," Northfleet explained. " That is, if the tunnel extends any distance before we come to the block in it."

" No harm in that," Colin assented, leading the way to the entrance to the secret passage.

Northfleet's attention was attracted by the glass case containing the rockets.

" For signalling to the mainland in case of trouble, eh ? "

" So Mrs. Dinnet says," Colin confirmed. " Seems a sound idea."

Northfleet inspected the rockets thoughtfully.

" Craigmore evidently believes in doing things thoroughly," was his verdict. " These things would carry a life-line to a wreck, at a pinch, to judge by the size of them. And now, let's see if I've remembered how to work this spring, without hints from you."

His recollection was sound, for the door opened at his first attempt. Colin stepped forward, but a gesture from Northfleet restrained him.

"Wait a bit. No harm in seeing if the air down there's all right before we go into it. We'd better have some newspaper, if there's any handy. Is Dinnet about?"

"Gone over to the mainland in the motor-boat, I expect. To get the newspapers and letters," Colin explained. "I'll get some paper."

He procured a few sheets of newspaper; and Northfleet, after tearing off a piece, crumpled it slightly, and lit it with a match. When he threw it down the stairway it burned quite freely.

"Seems all right; but we'd better try it from time to time as we go along. If the tunnel's blocked at the other end, there can't be much free circulation, and we might strike a bad patch."

He led the way cautiously down the rude, uneven steps, repeating his test from time to time during the descent. At the foot, he waited until Colin joined him.

"Fifty-seven steps. Say they're eight inches high. That puts us about forty feet below ground-level, now. Evidently they took no risks of coming near the surface when they built this place."

Northfleet flashed his light about him. The stair ended in a cell, twenty feet by ten. On their right was a doorway about four feet broad; and when Colin stepped through this he found himself in a six-foot passage running parallel to the stairway. The stonework of walls and roof was rude, but a glance was enough to show that it had stood the test of time. As Northfleet followed him through the doorway Colin saw by the light of the flash-lamp that the straight part of the corridor was only some forty feet long. At each end it bent at right angles out of sight.

"Hadn't bargained for more than one passage," Colin commented, glancing first at one end and then at the other. "Complicates things, this. Won't do to get lost down here, if the thing starts branching out in all directions, like the Catacombs. Better be cautious, eh?"

Then another piece of casually-acquired information surged up in his memory and served to reassure him.

"Safe enough, though, if we keep one hand on the wall all the way along. That takes you through any maze. And to get back, you just turn round and keep the other hand on the same wall. That brings you back to where you started."

"So some people say," Northfleet returned, rather dryly. "I believe in making sure, myself; so I'll just fasten this thread here and pay it out as we go along. I've an extra reel or two in my pocket, if the first one isn't enough. Now you take the flash-light, Trent, and go ahead with your stunt. I'll pay out the thread behind us. Just a moment! I want to take the bearing of of this corridor before we start."

He fished out his prismatic compass, took a reading, and made a jotting in a note-book.

"I'm going to count my paces," he explained

as he put his compass back into his pocket, " so
we'd better not talk except when we stop at a
turn in the passage, if you don't mind. Now you
can go ahead."

Colin set off briskly along the short stretch of
straight path, keeping his hand on the wall as
he went. The flash-light lit up the passage
brilliantly, and he could not help being impressed
by the thought of the labour which had gone
to the excavating of this burrow, when every
spadeful of earth must have been carried up to
the surface as it was dug out. At the corner he
halted, while Northfleet entered up his figures in
the note-book. (See page 121.)

" There's no need to take a fresh bearing,
Trent. It's a right-angled turn. Go ahead. It's
only a few yards to the next corner."

The new turn was also towards the right and
at an angle of ninety degrees.

" Easier than I expected," Northfleet declared
thankfully. " If it's all rectangular like this,
we'll only need to take a bearing now and again
as a check. Go ahead."

When they turned the corner, the wall on
their right continued unbroken; but half-way
along the other wall Colin caught sight of the
entrance to a new corridor. Northfleet halted
and jotted down a note.

" Seems a regular maze," said Colin, with less
enthusiasm in his tone. " Still, we can't go far
wrong with that thread of yours."

" Ten paces," Northfleet noted, as they came
to yet another turn to the right.

The new stretch was only a few yards long;

then came another right-hand turn ; and almost immediately Colin found himself back at the doorway leading to the staircase.

" Your method certainly brings you back to where you started," Northfleet commented blandly. " And pretty quick, too. You forgot that it doesn't work quite according to plan if there are islands in the maze."

" Islands ? "

" Bits of the maze completely detached from the rest," Northfleet explained. " We've been circumnavigating one of them for the last few minutes. Naturally, if you walk round an island, you're bound to come to where you started."

" Um ! " said Colin, in a rather crestfallen tone. " Method doesn't pan out so well, after all ? Then what next ? "

" Cross to the other side of the corridor, keep your left hand on the wall there, and start off in the same direction as before. But wait a jiffy till I get this thread untied and reeled in. No use in wasting any of it. "

When the thread had been recovered and re-anchored, they set out once more. Two right-angled turns brought them to the mouth of the new corridor which they had already seen ; and with his left hand on the wall, Colin entered it. A few paces farther on the passage turned to the left, led straight on for some twenty yards, and then bent again to the left.

" All right angles, so far," Colin pointed out unnecessarily. " Now to the right again. Plain sailing this : only one road and no side-galleries.

Now to the left. Hello! Blank wall ahead. Must be a transverse corridor at the—— Good Lord! This is a bit thick!"

His downward-deflected light had revealed a yawning chasm blocking the end of the tunnel and taking the place of his supposed transverse corridor. He advanced gingerly to the verge and threw his beam into the pit.

"I say, you know, this is a bit steep," he ejaculated rather incoherently in his first surprise.

Northfleet gazed down into the pit.

"A sheer drop, as you say," he agreed, with wilful misunderstanding. "Very neat."

"This is a bit more than I bargained for," Colin complained. "Just suppose we had blundered down here in the dark, what?"

"I expect the designer had just that very notion in his mind," Northfleet surmised in a cheerful tone, which Colin rather resented. "I wonder did they come down now and again to dig their prisoners out of the mousetrap, or did they just leave them till they passed in their checks? Not much chance of unauthorised visitors getting into the old castle by this route; and if they happened to come in force, this would be the very place to hold them up. Callers with visas on their passports would get helped with ropes, I suppose. It must be twenty feet deep at least; so even if one man stood on another man's shoulders, he couldn't get out. Besides, a simple stranger would probably fall flop into it and be so damaged that he couldn't climb at all. So far as we're concerned, it's a case of getting a ladder down here before we can go on. A rope's no good—no projections to tie it on to in these passages. Nuisance, isn't it ? "

" Do you want to go on ? " Colin inquired, rather tepidly.

It was all very well to start out to explore a secret passage, he felt ; but when the exploration revealed things like this pit—with perhaps worse traps in store—and when further progress meant hauling a ladder through the windings of the labyrinth, the affair lost its attractions. Still, as he recognised, it would be rather feeble to abandon the business at the first check.

" There won't be any man-traps or spring-guns," said Northfleet reassuringly, as though he had read Colin's thoughts. " Craigmore's workmen would have found them when they came down to wall up the other end, and the Dinnets would have told you about them."

" I suppose so," Colin agreed in a half-hearted tone.

He put the best face that he could on the matter, however ; and after some trouble they procured a ladder and succeeded in getting it down to the pit. By its help they descended into the chasm, after Northfleet had tested the air with burning paper.

Once down, Northfleet transferred the ladder to the farther side of the pit, propping it against the blank wall, and ascended until he got his head above the floor-level. Then with his flash-lamp he examined the walls.

" The tunnel we came down by is the middle one of three, all ending at the pit's edge," he reported. " Which of the other two should we try first ? "

" We want to get away from the centre, don't we ? Try the outside one," Colin suggested.

" The westerly one ? Right ! " Northfleet descended, and shifted the ladder into a fresh position. In a minute or two they were in the new tunnel.

" Stick to the left-hand wall again ? " Colin asked. " Then, here goes ! "

Twenty feet down the new corridor came a right-angled turn ; and on rounding this they found themselves in a cul-de-sac. Retracing their steps, they climbed down into the pit and ascended into the third tunnel. Once more Colin took the lead, his left hand on the wall, while Northfleet payed out the guiding thread and halted at each fresh turn to make careful notes. The ladder hampered them badly, as they had enough to occupy their hands ; but it could not be left behind, lest there were other pits ahead.

Colin's initial zest had worn off. The lowness of the roof overhead, the straitness of the corridors, the continual turnings and windings of the rectangular system, the trouble of easing the ladder round awkward corners : all began to have their adverse influence upon him. He soon lost all count of direction ; and the apparently aimless meanderings of the passages irritated him almost as much as the waste of energy involved in wandering into culs-de-sac and emerging again where he had gone in. Gradually there came a feeling that he was cut off from the daylight, buried under tons and tons of rock and earth. In his normal life Colin was something of a "fresh-air fiend"; and he became resentfully conscious that he was not cut out for this mole-like type of exploration.

Northfleet's methodical procedure added to his vexation. At intervals, Colin was left in charge of the ladder and the thread, while Northfleet, taking the lamp with him, explored some side-gallery. These spells of enforced inactivity in pitchy darkness seemed to last longer and longer each time they occurred.

They came upon a second pit, and the passage through it offered a slight change from the monotonous corridor-pacing. But then the succession of rectangular turns began again. The track wound on hither and thither through the bowels of the earth, confusing Colin's brain by its intricacy. The actual distance he had traversed was less than half a mile; but the snail's pace at which they covered it made it seem like leagues.

A third pit opened before them; and beyond it the maze recommenced. At last, as Colin turned a corner, his flash-lamp showed a long, straight tunnel vanishing into darkness at the far end. It proved, on exploration, to be only a cul-de-sac; but as they returned along the second wall, their system led them into a fresh alley which the lamp failed to pierce. Northfleet halted, and took a bearing at the mouth of it.

"This may be the end of the labyrinth," he observed as he replaced his note-book in his pocket. "I hope so, anyhow, for the stock of thread's nearly run out."

" Better be turning back, then," Colin suggested, hopefully.

He had no stomach for exploration beyond the thread clue's range. Completely confused in the network of the labyrinth, he had come to look on the thread as his only means of extricating him from this man-made molehill. His intellect assured him that the one-hand-on-the-wall method was perfectly sound ; but something more powerful than reason was working to persuade him that these theoretical notions didn't always work out correctly. Already he had seen that the vaunted method did fail in certain cases. That initial circumnavigation of the island site had been a very plain example.

Then another uncomfortable hypothesis flitted across his mind. Suppose the flash-lamp battery gave out ? Or the lamp might fall and get smashed. Nice state of affairs that would be. Even with the thread to guide them, still they had these pits gaping in their path. It would mean crawling through the darkness on hands and knees, feeling for sure ground at every inch of advance. Not for Colin, he decided firmly.

Colin's courage was of the sort which demands daylight for its display, or, if not daylight, at least elbow-room. After his experience underground, he was suffering unconsciously from a slight attack of claustrophobia. He wanted to get up to the surface again and feel the fresh air about him. And yet, he shrank from betraying his feelings to Northfleet, who evidently suffered no such pangs.

" Damn it ! " Colin concluded irritably, " I

can't suggest turning back if he means to go on. Feeble, that. Make me look like a funky kid. If this passage is straight, I'll go down it till the twists begin again. Then I'll really strike."

Not far down the new passage Northfleet called a halt.

"This is the end of the thread supply," he announced casually. "Wait till I tie the end to a piece of paper, so that we can find it easily as we come back."

He did so ; and then, taking Colin's consent for granted, he started forward once more. Colin, acutely uncomfortable at the thought that they had left their Ariadne's clue behind them, kept his hand firmly on the left-hand wall of the passage and held himself on the alert for cross-corridors. The first sign of anything of that sort, he had determined, would mark the end of his explorations, no matter what Northfleet thought of him.

The tunnel continued unbroken in a straight line for some distance ; and then, without branching, it turned sharp to the right. After pacing along this new stretch for a time, they came upon a doorway on their left which opened into a moderately spacious chamber.

"Where the old Chief lived, perhaps, when he was hiding down here after the '45," Colin surmised for Northfleet's benefit.

The room offered nothing of interest to them, and they returned to the passage. Fortunately for Colin's self-respect, it continued straight on, with no side-alleys. Evidently they were now outside the labyrinthine tract. One or two changes in direction occurred, which necessitated fresh readings with the prismatic compass.

Then, at last, Colin gained some relief. They came upon a newly-erected wall of brick and mortar which blocked the passage completely.

"So that's that!" Colin ejaculated. "None too soon, either, for my taste. I'm beginning to feel a bit stuffy down here. Glad to get some fresh air into my lungs again."

Northfleet, busy with his final notes, made no reply; but when he slipped his note-book back into his pocket, he invited Colin with a gesture to retrace his steps. Beyond the door of the old Chief's chamber, Northfleet picked up the thread clue once more; and Colin felt easier in his mind. But when they reached the exit from the labyrinth, Northfleet disturbed him by a fresh suggestion.

"What about going back through the other half of the maze for a change? Stick to the left-hand wall as before, instead of going home the way we came?"

And leave the thread behind! Colin didn't even weigh the matter. His mind was made up.

"I'm all for getting up above ground again," he admitted frankly. "The air of this place is a bit too stuffy for my taste."

Northfleet gave in without ado.

"Very good. I hate to leave a job half-done, though," he confessed in a regretful tone. "I've mapped about half of this place, I believe, and I'd like to finish it. Any objection to my coming down again on my own, some time?"

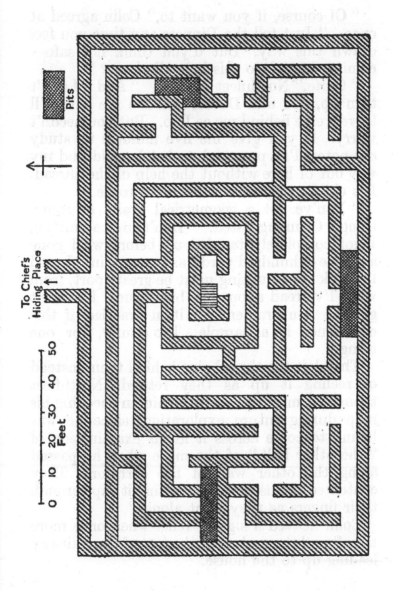

" Of course, if you want to," Colin agreed at once. " Just tell the Dinnets any time you feel drawn this way. But d'you think it's safe—coming down into this hole all alone ? "

" Quite," Northfleet decided. " And if I don't turn up, you and Dinnet can fish me out. I'll leave a clue behind me as I go. But you needn't worry. If you give me five minutes to study my notes, I'm prepared to bet I could find my way out of here without the help of the thread. It's child's play to reverse one's route."

" You've got a geometrical brain, or something," Colin suggested. "Don't mind admitting I got completely tangled up before we'd gone a couple of hundred yards, as we came in. I used to think cave-hunting must be great sport, from what I've read about it ; but I guess I haven't got the temperament for it in practice, if this experience is a sample. Too stuffy, for one thing."

They left the thread clue behind them instead of reeling it up as they retired. Northfleet thought it might be useful to him in checking his map during future exploration, since he was bound to come across it in his examination of " the other half " of the maze when he passed along the other wall of the corridors. They contented themselves with letting it slip through their fingers as they went along.

Colin heaved a sigh of relief when once more they found themselves at the foot of the stairway leading up to the house.

CHAPTER VIII

COLIN rebaited the two hooks on Jean's line and dropped the sprowl over the side of the motor-boat.

"Another mackerel," he remarked disparagingly, with reference to her latest catch. "Must be a shoal of them about. Better chuck it now, dear. I'm not going to insult my palate by offering it mackerel—too coarse for Colin—and you can't possibly eat all this lot yourself."

It was Jean's first experience of hand-line fishing and she was loath to stop.

"The Dinnets can have them," she suggested. "And if they don't want them, they can give them to the gardeners."

"Something in that, maybe," Colin acquiesced. "Bit hard on the gardeners, perhaps, from my point of view. But they can always drop 'em overboard on the way home, if they don't like 'em. There's aye a way, as they say."

"Just one more," Jean pleaded.

"All right. One more," Colin agreed. "And then we'll have to push for the shore. It's getting dark. Don't much care about sitting here with the engine off when all these rocks are about."

Jean glanced up at the cloudy horizon and found to her surprise that the dusk had deepened almost into night as she fished. The outline of Ruffa hung above her, sharp against the dull sky ; but it was only a silhouette on the surface of which shone the lights from the windows of

Wester Voe and Heather Lodge. Suddenly fresh beacons appeared on the headland across the bay from Wester Voe.

" Look, Colin ! What's that over there ? " Jean exclaimed, pointing to them. " See the two lights, like electric torches, over yonder ? What can they be ? "

Colin turned round and examined them.

" Electric torches, right enough, by the look of them. Not moving about, though. Seem as if they were fixed to point somewhere in this direction. It's all heather up there. Rum, that. Must be some of the Heather Lodge people playing about, unless it's Northfleet amusing himself by waking up his bird friends."

He stared at the lights, trying to distinguish something in the surrounding darkness ; but there was nothing detectable. Jean soon lost interest in the phenomenon.

" Colin, do you think it's quite safe for Mr. Northfleet to go down alone into these passages under Wester Voe ? From what you said about them, it seemes a bit risky for him, doesn't it ? Suppose he had an accident, or lost his way ? "

" He's finished down there," Colin explained, reassuringly. " He told me this afternoon that he's got the whole affair mapped now, so he won't be going down again. By the way, he's worked out the run of the passage, and it seems it goes up to Heather Lodge. The bricked-up bit must be somewhere under the Heather Lodge cellars, if they have any. He took the corresponding bearings aboveground, and that's where they led him, apparently."

"Well, I'm glad it's bricked up, then. You know, Colin, I don't like these people at Heather Lodge—except Hazel, of course."

"They don't bother us, anyhow," Colin pointed out.

"That's true," Jean admitted. "Still . . . I rather wish they weren't there, Colin. There's something funny about Heather Lodge. I don't know what it is, but I've got a sort of feeling that there's something queer."

Colin was not a little vexed to find that all his precautions for Jean's peace of mind seemed to have come to nothing.

"Hazel been saying anything to make you feel like that ? " he demanded suspiciously.

"Oh, no," Jean declared emphatically. "It's just that I'm a nervous little beast, Colin ; and I don't quite like the notion of armed men, and big dogs, and so on, over there at Heather Lodge. Hazel's explanation sounds a bit thin, when I think over it. She believes it herself. She's got a sort of contempt for that uncle of hers. But—well, somehow, it doesn't sound good enough, does it, Colin ? "

"She knows old Arrow, and you don't," Colin pointed out. "If it satisfies her, it ought to be good enough for you, shouldn't it ? "

Much to his relief, Jean's attention was diverted before she could press the matter further.

"What's that, Colin ? " she exclaimed. "H'sh ! Listen ! "

Out of the depths of the dusk came a slow throbbing ; then a dim grey shape loomed up and drew nearer over the smooth waters. Soon

119

it passed them at a distance : a small yacht under bare poles, feeling its way cautiously down the channel into the bay. Dimly they could see the man at the wheel, and a second figure which seemed to be kneeling on the deck, busy with some task or other.

" Visitors ? " said Colin, in some surprise. "Looks about a fifteen tonner. Auxiliary motor, evidently. And they mean to stay the night, it seems," he added, as the splash of the anchor and the rattle of the chain came to them across the water.

Struck by an idea, he glanced up at the two lights on the headland. Almost at the roar of the anchor-chain they were extinguished, having evidently served their purpose. Whoever the strangers were, they had friends at Heather Lodge ; for the lights must have been placed as sailing-marks and had been dowsed as soon as they had filled their purpose. That meant a pre-arranged visit, Colin reflected without carrying his inferences further.

" I wonder who——" Jean began, inquisitively. Then a twitch on her line diverted her mind. " I've got another, Colin ! "

She began to pull in her line. Colin detached the fish, peered closely as it in the semi-darkness, and then, without more ado, pitched it overboard again.

" What was it, Colin ? "

" A dog-fish," Colin announced in a disgusted tone. " That's one thing I won't eat, even to please you. Time to chuck it, now, dear."

" I suppose it is," Jean admitted, reluctantly.

"Well, I haven't done badly for a beginner. We'll come out again to-morrow night, Colin."

"H'm!" Colin protested. "Am I supposed to be taking up a fish diet, or what? And next time it'll most likely be lythe."

"What are lythe?"

"Pollack's another name for 'em. A bit like cod. You can have my share of all you catch. If fish is what you want, what about a lobster salad? Or you might go crab-hunting among the rocks and pick up a partan or two. Tastier than mackerel. More exciting to catch 'em, too, with the chance of a good nip thrown in."

"You can have the nips for your share," Jean rejoined. "If you're so keen on crabs, catch them yourself. I hate the look of them when they're alive."

She changed the subject in her next words:

"I wonder who these people are in the yacht. Hazel didn't know they were coming to-night. She didn't say anything about them to me, at any rate; and if she'd known they were coming I'm sure she'd have told me."

Colin made no comment on this, but busied himself with starting the motor.

"That yacht's anchored almost bang in the fairway," he pointed out, after a long scrutiny in the dim light. "Makes it awkward to get in to the pier, confound 'em! We'll have to go in gently so as not to scrape our paint against 'em."

He took the tiller, let the clutch in, and throttled down until the little motor-boat was moving as slowly as possible. He had a good knowledge of the channel from daylight trips, but this was his first attempt at a night-passage and he meant to take no chances. As he drew nearer, he found the position more difficult than he had guessed from a distance. The yachtsmen, either ignorant or inconsiderate, had anchored their vessel in the end of the channel, where the fairway was at its narrowest; and in the deepened dusk this made the passage too tricky for Colin's comfort, since he was still a raw hand with the motor-boat.

"If they're going to stay on Ruffa, we'll need to get them to shift out of that," he grumbled to Jean in an undertone. "Twenty yards farther on they'd have just as good holding-ground and they'd be in nobody's way. I'll give 'em a hint as we pass."

He took out the clutch and let the boat run forward under its own way. As he passed the yacht's counter, he saw above him two dim figures on her deck. One of them, kneeling, seemed to be throwing some powder into the water, handful by handful. Colin got the impression that he was emptying a sack piece-meal. Other small sacks, like ballast-bags, lay beside him on the deck. The second man, put on the alert by the noise of the exhaust, stared intently at the motor-boat as it forged alongside.

Colin stooped forward to throttle down the engine still further, so as to quiet the exhaust while he was speaking. As he did so, a flash-light shone over him; Jean gave a faint cry; and he looked up to face a heavy pistol which covered him from hardly a couple of yards range.

"*Au large!*" said the man behind the pistol, keeping his flash-lamp fixed blindingly on Colin's face. Then, realising that Colin was bewildered, he repeated the order in English. " Sheer off, you ! And quicker than that ! "

The second man rose to his feet in a leisurely fashion and produced an equally ugly pistol from his coat-pocket. As he did so, he seemed to catch sight of Jean, who had been hidden from him before. He whispered something to his companion, who nodded rather doubtfully.

" Is that Mademoiselle Arrow ? " the first man demanded.

Colin's indignation had now swamped his stupefaction.

" What d'you mean by this ? " he exclaimed. " What——"

His interrogator seemed to grow suddenly more menacing.

" 'Ands up ! " he ordered tersely.

Colin guessed from the tone that these people meant to stand no nonsense ; so, shaking with suppressed anger, he obeyed perforce. Nice figure he was cutting before Jean, he reflected furiously. And who were these fellows ? Foreigners, from the accent, like the Heather Lodge guards.

The spokesman on the deck turned to Jean.

" You are not Miss Arrow ? No ? "

Jean had some difficulty in finding her voice.

" No," she confirmed at last, rather huskily. "Our name's Trent. We're living at Wester Voe—that house up yonder. Miss Arrow's a friend of mine. She lives at Heather Lodge, over there."

The two men on deck consulted together in whispers. Colin, who was no linguist, could not follow their rapid interchange ; but the result, at least, was satisfactory. The weapons were lowered, though not pocketed, and the spokesman turned again to Jean. His voice took on a certain underbred oiliness which Colin liked as little as the earlier truculence.

"We make you most 'umble apologies, madame. We 'ave evidently made a very foolish mistake, for w'ich we ask your pardon. You will overlook it, *hein* ? Your sudden appearance out of the dark—very startling ; and we did not see that a lady was in the boat. But that is all right now, *hein* ? You overlook it." He paused for a moment as though to collect his thoughts. "My nerves are . . . out of order a little. I 'ave been ill, recently, you understand ? I am all on edge. And your intrusion gave me a surprise. Yes, that is it. It gave me a start. You would pity me, I know, if you could understand. But that is all right now, *hein* ? You will not be angry with a sick man."

Colin had dropped his hands at the first words of apology.

"Damned liar," was his internal comment on the explanation. "He's no more neurasthenic than I am. Can't have a row before Jean, though. Least said, soonest mended."

He put his hand on the yacht's hull and pushed off gently.

"If you're staying here, may I point out that your yacht's almost blocking the fairway here ? " he said in a tone which betrayed his suppressed anger clearly enough. "If you shift her twenty yards on, you'll be in nobody's way."

"Oh, certainly, certainly," the spokesman

acquiesced eagerly. "We are extremely sorry to give trouble. We shall move, as soon as there is light to see. I hope that will do ? And we are sorry, we are very sorry indeed, that this unfortunate little mistake has occurred. You will overlook it, as between gentlemen, *hein*? An awkward contretemps w'ich we much regret, I assure you."

"Oh, let it go at that," Colin interrupted impatiently.

He let in his clutch, and the little motor-boat purred on past the yacht. Colin leaned over and touched Jean's arm, to find her trembling.

"What a start they gave me," she said with a poor attempt at a laugh. "And what extraordinary people, Colin ! I really thought at first that they meant to shoot, and I was in a perfect panic about you. That's really why I'm trembling like this. I'm all right now. It's just the after-effects. But who can these people be, Colin ? They know about the Arrows. But they don't know the channel well, so they haven't been here often; and they don't know much about Ruffa or they'd have guessed who we were. That we were from Wester Voe, at any rate. That's plain. I'm not sure I like it, Colin. I don't like it one bit. Can you make head or tail of it ? "

A dark object loomed up suddenly ahead and Colin twitched the helm to avoid it. They swept past a small rowing-boat—the Heather Lodge pleasure-craft, Colin guessed—with one man rowing and a second figure in the stern. Evidently it was making for the yacht. Jean gave a violent start as they just escaped disaster, and Colin pressed her arm reassuringly.

"Narrow shave, that" he grunted crossly. "Another time old Arrow goes visiting his friends I hope he'll show a light. I'm getting a bit fed-up with that lot, I'll admit."

Shutting the throttle, he allowed the motor-boat to run gently in towards the steps. As they came into the lee a man's figure on the top of the jetty showed up in clear outline against the paleness of the sky. Colin's nerves had not been shaken by his late experiences, but his temper had been badly frayed.

"Who's there?" he demanded aggressively.

The figure stooped over the edge and peered at the motor-boat.

"Sh!" it said in a vehement whisper. Then in a low voice it added. "That you, Trent? I'm Northfleet. It's all right, only I'd rather you didn't shout my name just now. Is Mrs. Trent there? I hope I didn't startle you."

"Not half so much as these swine on the yacht, there," Colin explained, disjointedly. "Stuck a pop-gun about a foot long in my face just now. Gave Jean the start of her life. Bit thick, what? Of all the nerve . . . Pretty doings, what? Some of the old Arrow's pals, I gather. I'm going to interview that bird before many hours are over. Won't stand this kind of going-on, not from the Grand Mogul."

Northfleet ran down the steps and helped Jean to land. Colin followed them up the stair after making the boat fast; and the three stood at the end of the jetty looking out towards where the yacht lay in the darkness.

"Not even a riding-light showing," Colin growled. "Gang of tinkers afloat."

Northfleet seemed to have gathered something from Colin's jerky explanation, but now he asked for a fuller account. When he had listened to it without comment, he turned to Jean.

"It must have given you a bad jar, Mrs. Trent. I expect you're feeling a bit nervy— most people would, after that sort of experience. There's one thing I ought to say, and you can take it as being just the plain truth. All this affair "—he waved his hand towards the yacht— "has nothing to do with you and Mr. Trent. You can take my word for it that you needn't expect anything more of the sort. These fellows mistook you for somebody else. That I can guess. You mustn't let it worry you in the slightest, please. So far as you're concerned the whole business was a pure accident which won't occur again. And another thing: Miss Arrow isn't in any way mixed up in the affair. I think I ought to make that clear."

"That's all very well," Colin declared bluntly, "but it leaves us much where we were. What's all this monkeying that's going on? What's at the back of it all, exactly?"

"I wish I knew," Northfleet replied, with a touch of irritation which somehow gave the effect of sincerity.

Colin considered for a moment or two. This mystery-mongering—as he regarded it—exasperated him after his recent experiences. Northfleet evidently knew something, and Colin wanted to know it too. On the other hand, he flinched from an attempt to force Northfleet's confidence while Jean was there. Whatever lay behind these mysterious manœuvres, it seemed advisable that he himself should get the full story from Northfleet and then supply Jean with a suitably expurgated version, something which would hold water and yet not alarm her further. After the shock she had she might very well insist on leaving Ruffa at a moment's notice ; and, for many reasons, Colin had no wish for that. The first essential was to discover if possible how the land actually lay, and Northfleet was the only possible source of information.

" Care to come up to Wester Voe with us now ? " Colin inquired.

If he could keep Northfleet there until Jean went to bed, then he might be able to extract something.

" I'm afraid I can't come at this moment," Northfleet said, after a brief pause for consideration. " I've something I must do. But if I may drop in on you, later on in the evening——"

" Right ! " Colin agreed. " Come as soon as you can, will you ? We'll go up there now. Come along, Jean."

They left Northfleet on the pier, staring out into the night in the direction of the yacht.

Colin expected an awkward interview with Jean when they reached Wester Voe ; but, rather to his surprise, she seemed much less disturbed than he had anticipated.

" Do you understand all this business, Colin ? " she began. " I can't make head or tail of it. Why should these men threaten us with pistols just because we came alongside ? It's like an American gangster film, it is, really, Colin. Of course, Mr. Northfleet's quite right ; they mistook us for somebody else. You saw how polite they turned when they found out their mistake."

" Positively greasy," Colin agreed heartily. " For two pins that fellow would have wept on my shoulder, by the sound of him."

" Well, anyhow, it was plain enough that they meant no harm to us, wasn't it ? And Mr. Northfleet said the same."

" Oh, so he's the last word in oracles, is he ? " Colin inquired, as though none too well pleased by this.

A little opposition at this stage, he thought, would confirm Jean in her attitude, which was the very one he wanted her to adopt.

" Jealous, Colin ? " she asked, teasingly.

" No, it's just that he somehow gives me a feeling that one can depend on him and that he wouldn't let one down."

" Strong, silent man, and all that ? I know. Heard 'em often on the talkies."

" Really, Colin, one would think you'd some sort of down on him, by the way you talk. You haven't, have you? Because I like him, and I hope you won't drop him when we get back to town."

" Good Lord, no ! I've got nothing against him," Colin protested, fearing that he had overdone his effect. " And what are we going to do now. Wireless ? Or just sit here ? "

Jean considered for a moment.

" I've got a lot of letters that I ought to write," she said doubtfully. " I hate wasting any of the daylight on that. Would you mind, Colin, if I wrote some of them now ? You could amuse yourself with the wireless, couldn't you ? And you'll let me know when Mr. Northfleet comes in ?"

" Answers to inquiries," said Colin, " No. 1, ' No.' To No. 2, ' Yes.' To No. 3, ditto. You write 'em in here and I'll let the wireless loose in the lounge."

Then, as he was leaving the room, a fresh thought struck him and he turned back.

" Bit stuffy, this evening. I'm going into the garden to smoke a pipe. If you want me, just call through the window. I won't go far away."

Jean made no objection to this, and Colin wandered out of doors, congratulating himself on a neat stroke of diplomacy which would enable him to intercept and question Northfleet before they interrupted Jean in her correspondence.

His visitor kept him waiting rather longer than he had expected ; but when he appeared Colin was able to attract his attention quietly and lead him off down one of the paths just out of earshot of the drawing-room windows.

" Seen anything more ? " Colin demanded. " What's it all about, anyway ? "

Northfleet took out his case and lit a cigarette before answering.

" The easiest thing is to tell you what I've seen and leave you to draw what conclusions you can," he decided. " You may be able to see further into it than I do."

" All right ; fire ahead," Colin agreed, over-looking some of the latent possibilities in Northfleet's suggestion.

"Very well, then," Northfleet began, with apparent frankness. "I happened to be on the moor when I noticed two men fixing up electric torches on the headland yonder."

"Sailing-marks for the yacht," Colin interjected.

"So it seems," Northfleet concurred. "After that, out of curiosity, I went down to the beach. It was deep dusk by that time. By and by old Arrow and another man came down the path from Heather Lodge, carrying what I took to be petrol tins."

An idea struck Colin, and he interrupted with a question.

"What's old Arrow like—in appearance, I mean?"

Northfleet considered for a moment.

"Arrow? Oh, tall, rather thin, if anything, big beak of a nose, cutaway chin, grey-haired, clean-shaven, walks rather like the hind legs of an elephant. That's how I recognised him in the dusk. His gait's unmistakable."

He paused, as though to give Colin a chance to say something, then continued:

"They had quite a pile of these petrol tins on the beach and they began loading some of them into the rowing-boat."

Colin was not the man to shrink from voicing an inference merely because it was self-evident.

"Re-fuelling the yacht, most likely," he suggested. "She's got an auxiliary motor."

Northfleet accepted this contribution politely, but without comment.

"Shortly after that," he continued, "the

second man left the beach and climbed up on the headland. Then I saw the mast and rigging of the yacht against the sky and heard her let go her anchor."

"Ah, I expect the second bloke went up to dowse the lights," Colin said, with another step forward in the obvious.

"Very likely," Northfleet agreed. "The next thing I heard was the sound of your exhaust as you came in. The second man turned up again, and he and Arrow pushed off the rowing-boat and went off into the dark."

"You didn't speak to them?"

"Not I. I've never spoken to old Arrow in my life, and it didn't seem a propitious moment to make his acquaintance when he had a job on his hands. I strolled over to the pier, and the next thing was your descent on me."

"And what happened after we left you?"

"Nothing more exciting than what went before. You and Mrs. Trent seem to have had a corner in all the melodrama business. Arrow and his man must have been aboard the yacht for a while. They came ashore later on, minus the petrol tins; and apparently they brought some stuff back with them. At least, although it was dark, I had an idea they unloaded something and went up, carrying it, whatever it was, to Heather Lodge. They pulled the boat before they left. That's the whole story."

"Stores, perhaps," Colin surmised. "Dinnet said the Heather Lodge people got most of their stuff from a motor-boat that called now and again."

"Stores, most likely, as you say," Northfleet

answered, though with a faint touch of irony in his tone.

" Yes, it is pretty obvious, I admit," Colin confessed. " After all, they've got to have some supplies in a place like this. But if it's merely supplies, where does the gent with the gun come in ? " he added doubtfully. " Can't see why he should be so ready with his gun in defence of a jar of marmalade or a tin of chicken-ham-and-tongue paste."

Northfleet evaded the direct issue.

" It wasn't you and Mrs. Trent they were afraid of," he pointed out. " That's as plain as a pikestaff."

" What's their game, then ? "

" I don't know," Northfleet answered, rather irritably. " Can you think of anything yourself ? "

Colin had another revelation of the obvious.

" Smuggling, eh ? " he suggested. " That might fit. But what's really worth smuggling in these days ? "

" Dope, for one thing. And the duty on saccharin runs up to over six thousand pounds per ton. It's easy enough to find something worth smuggling, if you look round."

" 'S that so ? " Colin was surprised by the figure. " Why, then, look here. Easy to land stuff on Ruffa ; no Customs people within miles. Easy to ferry it over, bit by bit, and land it on the coast hereabouts. Not at Stornadale, where you might be noticed. Land it on the shore somewhere at night. No risk at all. Take it away in a car. Dead easy."

" Why not land it on the shore direct, then,

instead of dumping it here ? And why doesn't Arrow keep a motor-boat ? Rowing to the mainland's a bit of a job at the best ; and quite impossible if the sea gets up at all."

Colin still clung to the smuggling theory.

"Was that stuff they landed heavy ?" he asked.

" How can I tell ? " Northfleet retorted, with another touch of irritation. " I can't see in the dark. All I know is that they did land something. And it can't have been a load heavier than two men could carry easily, or they'd have come back again for a second trip up to Heather Lodge."

Colin, slightly irritated in his turn, resolved to make a frontal attack.

" Look here," he said abruptly. " Just where do you come in, Northfleet ? This bird-watching stunt's all my eye. I could do it better myself. You've some other game on. What is it ? If it's a straight one, I might lend a hand."

For a full minute he got no reply. The tip of Northfleet's cigarette glowed periodically in the darkness ; but the rhythm remained unaltered ; and if Colin had expected Northfleet to betray agitation by quick smoking he was disappointed.

" I'm in a difficult position—a damnably difficult position," he said at last, with a certain irascibility which Colin knew was not directed to his own address. " If I go the length of saying that I'm up here on a confidential bit of work, it's as far as I can go. I expect you'd guess that anyway, so I'm not giving much away. But who my employers are is their own affair and mine."

" Quite so," Colin agreed.

" I don't live on air, and my fees are pretty stiff. It's been worth these people's while to make me drop my practice and come up here for weeks. Therefore they must think the business important. I'm not telling you anything you couldn't infer for yourself."

" I guessed something of the sort," Colin admitted.

" So far as I'm concerned," Northfleet went on, emphasising his words with a movement of his cigarette, " the business is absolutely straight. I wouldn't touch it if it weren't."

" Take your word for that," Colin volunteered at once. " It's old Arrow you're after. And Hazel Arrow——"

He paused, annoyed that he had let that slip out unawares.

" Miss Arrow's one of my difficulties," Northfleet said quite frankly. " But so far as she's concerned—— She has nothing to do with the matter I'm employed on. Is that absolutely clear ? "

" Quite," said Colin, not anxious to pursue this branch of the problem for reasons which seemed obvious to him.

Northfleet smoked for a time in silence.

" Well, there it is," he said at last. " I've broken no confidence in telling you that. I can't tell you any more. You could queer my pitch for me by going to old Arrow, I expect ; but I don't think you'll do that."

" Hardly," Colin protested indignantly.

" Or you can stand neutral," Northfleet continued, without taking notice of the interjection. " Or else you can lend me a hand, if you like.

Unless you choose, that needn't involve you in any risks."

" Meaning the pirate with the pistol ? "

A movement of Northfleet's glowing cigarette-tip showed that he nodded in confirmation.

" I've a notion," he said, after a moment or two, " that a copy of that gibberish which came over the wireless the other night might be useful. You noted it down, you told me. Care to risk the wrath of the Postmaster-General and ' make known its contents ' as they say on the licence ? "

" What makes you think it'd be any use to you ? " Colin asked. " It was short-wave stuff. The sender may be anywhere."

" You got it perfectly clearly on a night when general conditions in the ether were bad," Northfleet pointed out. " That looks to me like a ground-wave ; and the range of ground-wave reception for a weak amateur transmitter is nothing much. *Ergo*, the transmitting station isn't far off. What about the call-sign ? "

" A fake one," Colin declared promptly. " It ought to be Siamese. But if you're right about the transmitter being a local one, then the message never came from Siam, obviously. Couldn't find the call-sign in the directory myself. No such station mentioned."

" If he starts transmitting again you might rig up a frame aerial and try to get the bearing of the transmitter," Northfleet suggested. " In the meantime, if you want to help, let me have your copy of the message. That doesn't involve you to any extent."

Colin considered for a few moments before replying. Northfleet had put some of his cards on the table ; and clearly enough he had gone as far as he could go at the moment, if he was to keep faith with the people who employed him. And Colin had still one bargaining counter left, even if he parted with the code message : he had the gold brick up his sleeve.

"All right," he decided aloud. "I'll give you the copy. What's more, I'll give you a copy of another message I took down this evening. I happened to turn on the set after dinner, and he was shouting away, same as before. Began just like last time : " Hello ! Hello, London ! Attention ! I am calling and testing . . . testing and calling.' You remember how the thing went. And he ended up with the same gramophone record. The message was a lot shorter to-night— the Morse part, I mean—and quite different from the last lot. Just as much gibberish, though. Could make neither head nor tail of it myself."

"Thanks," Northfleet said briefly. "It's good of you to let me have it."

"I'll give you the pair of them when we go inside. Now there's one thing more. Do you know any hare-lipped man mixed up in this affair, whatever it is ?"

"No, I don't," Northfleet answered, with a touch of surprise which vouched for his frankness. "Didn't Mrs. Trent ask me something of the same sort ?"

"She knows nothing about it," Colin hastened to assure him. "Don't go stirring that up. She was just repeating something I'd said. I don't want her worried by this business. Understand ? "

" I shan't mention it."

" Final question," Colin added, as he rose from the seat : " Is this a big business ? Important, I mean. Thing that there's big money at stake in ? "

" Can't tell you that," Northfleet responded curtly.

Colin calculated his effect with care, allowing a long enough pause to make his next words tell effectively.

" Matter of gold, eh ? "

Even in the dark, it was plain enough that Northfleet was startled.

" How the hell did you guess that ? " he demanded, losing his usual politeness in his astonishment.

" So it *is*," Colin rejoined triumphantly. " I rather thought it was. Now come inside and I'll give you the copies."

When he handed over the papers he watched Northfleet's face as he read over the second cypher message :

Ffeou	*natnm*	*etiri*	*hatos*	*iorun*	*itcoa*
fasoc	*cnial*	*srytb*	*ghowb*	*tptat*	*adosy*
hygoo	*hamlu*	*dprca*	*ucuts*	*iteao*	*osgra*
assfs	*canes*	*soaim*	*rohat*	*nkeot*	*olgat*
cprtm	*lftsd*	*bbero*	*mlido*	*lwcfa*	*iascu*
eenep	*irnyp*.				

" Make anything of it ? "

" Not by inspection," Northfleet admitted.

" But cryptograms always interested me. I'll see what I can make out of it."

" You'll let me see the translation, if you solve it ? "

" Of course," Northfleet agreed, stowing the papers away in his pocket as he spoke. " And now, Trent, how did you guess that about the gold ? "

But before Colin needed to answer Jean came into the room.

" I heard you talking," she said. " Colin ! the yacht's gone. " I've just been watching her go out, with the night glasses. I heard them starting up her motor, so I went to the window and looked. The lamps on the headland were lit again, to show her the line of the channel. It was rather a relief to see her go, Mr. Northfleet. These men gave me a regular shock to-night, and I'm much more comfortable now that I've seen them sail way."

" I shan't miss 'em," said Colin lightly.

" Nor I," Jean concurred. " You know, in spite of what you said, Mr. Northfleet, I was still a bit nervous about them, and it's a relief to know they've gone."

" Probably they were just as startled as you were, when the motor-boat slid alongside," Northfleet assured her. " They've gone, any-how, so that worry's off your mind, I hope."

" If they come again, I'll take good care not to startle them a second time," said Jean decidedly.

YOU'VE really got some sense out of that stuff ? " Colin demanded, with a note of suspicion in his tone. " Not pulling my leg, I mean, and planting a fake decipherment on a simple soul ? "

" Your middle name's Thomas, evidently," Northfleet retorted good-humouredly. " No, there's no fake about it. I'll show you just how I solved the thing, if you're so sceptical. Will that satisfy you ? "

Colin paused in lighting his pipe and nodded in reply.

" Been worrying over the thing for a whole day myself and got no further. Be a relief to my mind to see how it's done."

They were sitting at the door of the shieling. Northfleet rose, went into the hut and brought out a camp-table and some papers. He planted the table before Colin and drew up his own chair alongside.

" There wasn't much to work on," he pointed out. " A preliminary call *en clair*, a Morse message of 336 letters, a final call : that was the first message. Then you gave me another cipher of 160 letters which also came over in Morse. With so little material, it's plain enough that we've got to wring the last drop of information out of it. We can't afford to overlook small points."

" That's horse-sense," said Colin approvingly.

" Bother is, they were so small that I didn't see
'em at all."

"Well, take it bit by bit," Northfleet suggested. "The call *en clair* began : ' Hello !
Hello, London ! ' That's not the usual amateur's
way of ringing up a friend, is it ? "

" No, I don't think so," Colin admitted
doubtfully. "You hear that in transatlantic
official stuff."

"So it wouldn't attract attention, eh ? And
it gives no clue to the sender or receiving
station ? But the fellow receiving would be
listening on the right wave-length and when he
heard that call—prearranged, of course—he'd
know who was talking."

" That's so," Colin agreed.

" The next bit was : ' Attention ! I am calling
and testing . . . testing and calling.' Is that
usual—the inversion, I mean ? "

" No," Colin adjudged. " ' I am calling and
testing ' would be enough for practical purposes.
They do say that."

"Then it looks—doesn't it ?—as if that formula
was simply to make it difficult for an outsider to
fake a message : mislead the receiving station,
I mean. It sounds natural enough, and yet it
helps to assure the sender that it's a message
from the right source. That's a guess, merely."

" Let it go at that," Colin agreed, eager to get
to something more definite.

"The next bit's interesting. 'I shall repeat
this message at ten, eleven, and twelve o'clock.'
What do you make of that, Trent ? "

Colin considered for a moment.

"By Jove! Of course! I was a fool not to spot that," he admitted handsomely. "You mean that the receiving station had no transmitter? If it had, it could have asked to get a doubtful bit of the message repeated. Since it hadn't, the sender repeated the message at fixed times, so that the receiver could fill in any gaps due to atmospherics and so forth in the first transmission. Is that it?"

"That's how I read it," Northfleet confirmed. "So it amounts to this: we're dealing with a transmitting station close at hand—as I pointed out to you the other night—and it's communicating with somebody who has no transmitter and can't reply. Well, that's always something learned."

"Guessed seems nearer the mark," Colin commented sceptically.

"Guessed, then, if you like," Northfleet conceded without ado. "Now we come to the Morse cipher. Here's a copy of it.'"

He spread the paper out on the table as he spoke, and Colin stared again at the jumble of letters which had puzzled him completely.

Teiil	lfilh	tcetu	fdhso	oenpr	yyugo	hngof
lovtu	gchan	noatn	aehat	isuwe	etfst	gscad
ofrgh	pelpe	hasle	gasth	hgsmr	lhlar	arnif
thrdl	nitfo	sswsg	nyile	efalt	odect	iesol
ntsnt	cooue	aodnt	iutsi	tioom	leanr	iigot
ahnom	finhe	ylmfd	attts	manhh	ofeii	etodd
otpca	motie	fmong	imcla	ttchb	yimnn	etrox
emcou	vsfhe	elmpn	nctaw	etrwo	oahee	iycna
oirbt	rtxet	peizn	rscsa	tikoh	nitht	emfne
nnruo	gotgp	enetp	syans	z		

" Well, barring odds and ends like ' hat ' and ' cad ' and ' lean ' there's nothing in it that suggests any language under the sun to me," Colin declared as he ran his eye up and down the page. " Why, you don't know what language the original was in, even."

" It isn't Spanish, anyhow," Northfleet affirmed.

" Why not ? "

" Because Q is fairly common in Spanish, and there isn't a Q in the whole cipher. There's no K in Spanish, but there's one in the message. It might be in a proper name, of course."

" Pass that," Colin conceded.

" The message *en clair* was in English," Northfleet pointed out. " So the chances were that the cipher was an English message also. It might have been enciphered in various ways. There's simple substitution, where you agree to use, say, M instead of A, S instead of B, and so forth. You can complicate it by a double substitution if you like—it's called the ' Beaufort cipher,' then."

" I've heard rumours of the sort," said Colin sardonically. " We used that at school."

"There's an entirely different brand of cipher," Northfleet went, on quite unperturbed. " It's called the ' transposition cipher '. In it the letters remain unchanged, but during the enciphering their order in the message is altered."

" I follow you, Watson," Colin acknowledged.

" Then follow on," Northfleet continued. " The letter T occurs about once in every ten letters in an English message. That is, about

10 per cent. of the letters in the message are T's. Suppose you find only one or two T's in a longish message in cipher, then either the original message was not in English, or else it's a substitution cipher and the T in it stands for some other letter like J or K, which doesn't occur frequently in ordinary English."

"Faint, but still pursuing," Colin assured him. "You've got to prove the message was in English originally, though. How about that ?"

"That wasn't so difficult, though it was troublesome," Northfleet explained. "There are 336 letters in the long cipher message. I counted the number of times each letter occurred in it—so many A's, so many B's, and so on. Then I took the first passage in English that came into my mind. It happened to be the bit in the Bible starting with : 'Now there arose up a new king over Egypt which knew not Joseph,' and so forth. I counted off 336 letters and tabulated their frequencies as before. Then I put the two sets of results side by side. The stars represent the number of times a letter occurs in the passage from Exodus ; the dots represent the number of times the letter occurs in the cipher message."

He put down another sheet of paper before Colin. (See opposite page.)

"It's not a question of getting exact agreement, naturally," Northfleet went on, pointing with his pipe-stem as he proceeded. "But even so, you can see that in nearly half the alphabet the frequencies run side by side almost exactly.

```
A  ************************
   ...................
B  *
   ..
C  *****
   .
D  ***********
   ........
E  ********************************************************
   .............
F  *******
   ...........
G  ******
H  ************************
   ..................
I  *****************
   ..................
J  **
   .
K  ***
   .
L  ****************
   ...............
M  *********
   ..........
N  *********************
   ....................
O  ************************
   .....................
P  *********
   .........
Q
   .............
R  ***************
   ................
S  *****************
   ..................
T  **********************************
   ..............................
U  *********
   .........
V  **
W  *********
   ....
X  ..
Y  *******
   ........
Z  ..
```

The general run of the likeness is all that really matters; and you can see at a glance that the similarity's far closer than chance could make it. That's enough to satisfy me that the message is an English one and that the letters haven't been altered. In other words, these are the letters of the original message in English, but they've been jumbled up in accordance with some prearranged scheme."

"That sounds all right," Colin admitted.

"If the original message had been in German it would have had more Z's in it," Northfleet said, to reinforce his argument. "Same if it had been French. Spanish would have had more Q's."

Colin nodded.

"Admitted," he said. "You've proved it's English, all jumbled up. Now what about un-jumbling it? That looks as much of a job as getting the eggs back out of an omelette, to me."

"Well, obviously there must have been some plan in the jumbling : a definite system of trans-position applied, letter after letter. If you can hit on the plan, the thing's solved."

"Maybe," Colin conceded ; "but I'm not the lad for the work. I admit that straight off. I don't so much as see how you'd begin."

"Look at it this way," Northfleet suggested. "In English there are a lot of digraphs—I mean a pair of letters expressing one sound, like TH, CH, CK, and SH. Some of these must have occurred in the original message. Since TH occurs fairly often in English—in words like THE, THEM, THEIR, THIS, THAT which turn up again and again in the simplest sen-tences—I started on that pair of letters. Some of the T's in the cipher had no H's as com-panions : they may have occurred in words like TEST or TEN or PUT. But some T's must have had H's as neighbours in the original message. If we can identify these T's and their mates among the H's, we'll have a clue to how the transposition was done."

Colin rubbed his ear with a whimsical air to suggest that he was getting out of his depth at this stage.

" Going's a bit rocky, now," he confessed.

" You'll see it clearly enough soon," Northfleet assured him. " Struggle on, for a moment or two. What I did to start with was this. I wrote out the message and numbered each letter in succession, like this :

$$\text{T e i i l l f i l h} \ldots$$
$$1 \ 2 \ 3 \ 4 \ 5 \ 6 \ 7 \ 8 \ 9 \ 10 \ldots$$

so that the last Z was No. 336, since there are 336 letters in the message."

" I see *that* all right."

" When I'd done that, I found that the H's were numbered 10, 18, 31, 43, 53, 75, 81, and so forth, while the T's were numbered 1, 11, 14, 39, 49, 55, 65, and so on. The next thing I did was this : I wrote down in a horizontal line all the numbers of the H's, and in a vertical line all the numbers of the T's. Then by subtracting each T number from the H numbers in turn, I got a series of differences. When the H number is smaller than the T number, I added 336—the total number of letters in the message—to the H number before doing the subtraction. Here's part of the table—enough to illustrate the results."

Northfleet spread another sheet of paper on

the table, and Colin stared at it rather un-comprehendingly.

H numbers + 336	346	354	367	379						
H numbers	10	18	31	43	53	75	81	91	97	107
T numbers 1	9	17	30	42	52	74	80	90	96	106
11	335	7	20	32	42	64	70	80	86	96
14	332	4	17	29	39	61	67	77	83	93
39	307	315	328	4	14	36	42	52	58	68
49	297	305	318	330	4	26	32	42	48	58
55	291	299	312	324	334	20	26	36	42	52
65	281	289	302	314	324	10	16	26	32	42

" You don't see it ? " said Northfleet, after a glance at Colin's puzzled face. " Well, isn't it clear enough that there's a repetition of 42 as a difference in six lines out of the seven, and that no other number turns up so often ? I've under-lined the 42's so that they'll catch your eye."

" Plain enough, that," Colin admitted. " But I don't see what it means."

" Think again. Take the first letter in the cipher. It was T. If an H was next to it as part of TH, then that H would have been No. 2. But during the enciphering this H No. 2 has got shifted along until it is now No. 43, so that between it and its original companion there's an interval of 42. Similarly, the T numbered 11 was followed by an H in the original. That H has got shifted forty-two places farther on ; so that instead of being No. 12 it is now No. 53. On the other hand, the T numbered 14 doesn't yield the common difference 42 with any of the H's. Evidently it wasn't part of a TH digraph

at all, but belonged to some word like 'true'
or 'two' or 'turn' where no H follows the T.
Do you follow me, Watson ? "

"I get a glimmering," Colin asserted. "But
I'd like it put in words of one syllable, just to
make sure I do understand it."

"Very well," Northfleet agreed. "Take a
simple example. Suppose I want to encipher
the words : 'This is my message.' I write them
down in groups of three letters, like this :

```
T  H  I
S  I  S
M  Y  M
E  S  S
A  G  E
```

Then I rewrite the letters as they occur in
downward order, column after column, and I
get

```
T S M E A H I Y S G I S M S E
1 2 3 4 5 6 7 8 9 10 11 12 13 14 15
```

Now your H, which was the second letter in
the original, has got shifted to place No. 6 ; and
the I which was the third letter in the original
has dropped into the eleventh place. Subtract
1 from 6 and you get the difference 5. Subtract
6 from 11 and again you get 5 as the difference.
Now do you see what the 5 corresponds to ? "

Colin studied the paper for a moment or two.

"It's the number of letters in each vertical
column, isn't it ? " he said as he looked up
again.

"Yes. And in the Morse cipher we got a
common difference of 42, didn't we ? "

" Jove, yes ! I see now," Colin exclaimed excitedly. " The original message must have been arranged in vertical columns, like yours, only with forty-two letters per column instead of your five. Is that it ? "

" And since the message contained 336 letters, there must have been eight columns," Northfleet suggested. " Unfortunately, it's not quite so simple as that. There's a second regular series of differences in addition to the 42 set. When I went over the whole of the H's and T's, I found that the H's numbered 18, 31, 177, 184, and 199 were linked up with the T's numbered 142, 155, 301, 308, and 323, with a common difference of 212, instead of the 42. Here you have the thing without any extraneous figures to confuse your eye."

He laid another sheet of paper before Colin.

H numbers + 336		354	367	513	520	535
H numbers		18	31	177	184	199
T numbers	142	212				
	155		212			
	310			212		
	308				212	
	323					212

Colin gazed at the figures disconsolately.

" Frank and honest's my motto," he declared at length. " I do not follow you this time. In fact, if you gave me a month of Sundays in the next blue moon I doubt if I'd get much further forward on my own wheels. I give it up. How d'you set about it ? "

"We'll leave it aside for a moment," North-fleet said. "Go back to your own suggestion and arrange the letters in vertical columns with forty-two letters in each column. Here's how it works out when you do that."

He produced yet another sheet of paper and confronted Colin with the following arrange-ment:

1.	T H e f n o f n	22. e s t o d t e n
2.	e a g a r T H r	23. n T H u s c e n
3.	i n a l i p a s	24. p g r e T H i r
4.	i n s t i c e c	25. r s d a t b y u
5.	l o t o g a l s	26. y c l o t y c o
6.	l a n d o m m a	27. y a n d s i n g
7.	f T H e t o p t	28. u d i n m m a o
8.	i n g c a t n i	29. g o t t a n o t
9.	l a s t h i n k	30. o f f i n n i g
10.	h e m i n e c o	31. h r o u h e r p
11.	T H r e o f T H	32. n g s t h t b e
12.	c a l s m m a n	33. g h s a o r t n
13.	e T H o r o w i	34. o p w i f o r e
14.	t i l l i n e t	35. f e s t e x t t
15.	u s a n n g T H	36. l l g i i e x p
16.	f u r t h i r t	37. o p n o i m e s
17.	d w a s e m w e	38. v e y o e c t y
18.	h e r n y c o m	39. t h i n t o p a
19.	s e n t l l o f	40. u a l l o u e n
20.	o t i c m a a n	41. g s e e d v i s
21.	o f f o f T H e	42. c l e a d s z z

"I've underlined the TH digraphs which have been brought together again by this arrange-ment," Northfleet pointed out. "You can see from that alone that this puts us on the right track. No mere chance would bring them all into positions, side by side, like this."

" Yes, but the damned thing doesn't make sense," Colin broke out in exasperation. " It's just as much of a jumble as it was at the start. You haven't solved it—or got anywhere near solving it."

" Think so ? " said Northfleet, imperturbably. " Well, we'll take no short cuts, then, although one's staring you in the face there. We'll proceed logically, step by step. You see the letters I have put in italics ? These are the T's and H's which fit into the 212-interval series I showed you a minute ago. The T in line 7 is the partner of the H in line 9 ; the T in line 14 is the mate of the H in line 16 ; the T in line 16 ought to be associated with the H in line 18 ; and the two T's in line 29 are the companions of the H's in line 31. Does that suggest anything to you ? "

" Not a damned thing," Colin admitted despairingly. " This cipher business seems to need a special brand of head, like mathematics."

" Well, look again," Northfleet advised. " Each T is associated with an H ; and that H is not in the line immediately below, but in the second lower line. There's the T in line 9. Its mate is not in line 10 but in line 11. You skip a line before you come to the mate. See that ? "

" Yes, I see that, now it's pointed out. It holds for the lot."

" Then look at it again, and you'll see also that the T and its mate are either in the first group of four letters of their respective lines or in the last group of four letters. In other words, the components of the digraph always lie in the right-hand half of the column or in the left-hand half. You don't find one in the left-hand half and the other in the right-hand half."

" That's so," Colin admitted.

" That suggests that the two halves of the column are really independent, doesn't it ? And that the line intervening between the two components is out of its place proper owing to a second transposition introduced during the encipherment. Well, then. Try lines 7 and 9 together, splitting them into two groups of four letters each, and omitting line 8. You get this :

7. f <u>T H</u> e   t o p *t*
9. l a s t   *h* i n k

Read each section as you would read a book, and you can see the left-hand bit is '. . . f the last . . .' while the right-hand bit is '. . . top think . . .' That looks a bit more like English, doesn't it ? "

" I get you, Steve ! " Colin ejaculated in relief. " This it ? Split the big column into two columns-of-fours. Miss out all the even-numbered lines ; and read the odd-numbered lines like a book, the left-hand page being the left column-of-fours and the right-hand page being the right column-of-fours But what about the even-numbered lines ? Where do they come in ? Or are they just duds ? "

" No, they fit in all right. Here's how it goes :

(1a.) T h e f (1b.) n o f n (2a.) e a g a (2b.) r t h r
(3a.) i n a l (3b.) i p a s (4a.) i n s t (4b.) i c e c

```
5a.l o t o    5b.g a l s    6a.l a n d    6b.o m m a
7a.o f t h    7b.t o p t    8a.i n g c    8b.a t n i
9a.l a s t    9b.h i n k    10a.h e mi    10b.n e c o
```

And so on. You see how they enciphered it? They wrote their message in columns-of-four. That gave eighty-four lines each of four letters. Then they split the single long column into four short columns and put them side by side, which gave the arrangement I've just shown you. Then they wrote 1a and 1b as a single line, and made the next line 2a and 2b, this way:

```
        T h e f n o f n
        e a g a r t h r
```

And, finally, they re-wrote the thing in the order of the letters down the columns, t e, and so on. To decipher it, all the receiver had to do was to write the message in vertical lines of 84 letters, then arrange the columns as I did just now, and so read the thing straight off."

"And how does it read?" Colin demanded impatiently.

Now, surely, he would come a step or two nearer to the key to the mysteries of Ruffa.

"Here's the transcription. You'd have had it sooner if you hadn't been so suspicious about its genuineness."

He laid a final sheet of paper on the table, and Colin read the result of all this labour:

"The final lot of the last three thousand was sent off on Thursday and got through safe stop Nothing seen of Nipasgal stop Think of throwing them well off the scent by using another port next time stop Advise against landing chemicals till further notice stop Grey cloud in offing stop Will give you all clear thrice comma at nine comma, nine thirty comma and ten thirty comma on night before I expect you Ends Z.Z."

" And this is the transcription of the second message," said Northfleet, pointing with his pipe-stem lower down the page.

" Fishery gunboat has now left district and coast is clear comma so far as can be seen stop All ready for you to-night comma but approach cautiously stop Wait for lights at dusk before coming in stop."

" Well," said Northfleet, a trifle sardonically, " there's your guaranteed decipherment. And what do you make of it ? "

CHAPTER X

COLIN seemed in no haste to show his hand. He re-read the two messages with care before opening his mouth.

"Second one's fairly straight," he declared at last. "Taken with what we know already, it's just directions to those artists on the yacht about coming in here. Only rum thing about it is the obvious relief they show at the Fishery gunboat clearing out. Quite evident they didn't want her poking her nose into their affairs, eh ? "

"Quite," Northfleet agreed tersely.

From his tone it was clear that Colin's inference was not new to him.

"Put that alongside the bit about the ' grey cloud in the offing ' in the other message," Colin proceeded. "That Fishery gunboat was grey painted. Think there's anything in that ? "

"I expect that was their pet name for her," Northfleet agreed indifferently.

"' Advise against landing chemicals till further notice.' " Colin read out. "They did land something, you said. But why all this fuss and secrecy about landing a few chemicals ? That rather beats me. But perhaps they landed something else along with the chemicals. How'd that fit ? "

"What else ? " Northfleet demanded.

"Search me, and you'll find nothing," Colin admitted. "It was just a brain-flash."

" Flash a little brighter next time," Northfleet suggested. " It wants a good illumination to light up this business, let me tell you."

Colin returned to the manuscript.

" ' Nothing seen of Nipasgal. Think of throwing them well off the scent by using another port next time.' H'm ! Nipasgal ? Sounds like a patent medicine. Sure you haven't slipped a cog in the deciphering there ? No ? Well, then, I suppose it must be a pet-name for some acquaintances of theirs. It's plural, evidently, since it has ' them ' as a relative. And I gather Nipasgal aren't pals of this lot, since there's talk of throwing them off the scent."

He looked inquiringly at Northfleet.

"*You* don't know who they are, by any chance ? "

Northfleet shook his head.

" Can't identify them. But it doesn't take a Sherlock Holmes to connect them with the need for these two guards at Heather Lodge."

" As fierce as all that, you think ? " Colin commented in a reflective tone. " Secret society, what ? Or something in that line ? Sounds a bit far-fetched. And yet, one can't deny that old Arrow has these two sudden-death merchants on his premises. Unless he's got a persecution-mania, there must be something behind it all. But what ? "

He paused, evidently conning over possibilities in his mind.

" Here's what I make of it. Something there's big money in. Something that isn't just too straight. Something that somebody else has

tumbled to and begun to threaten unpleasant-
ness."

If he hoped to draw Northfleet by this, he failed.

" What do you make of the reference to a
fresh port ? " the chemist asked, instead of
following Colin's line of thought.

" Nothing much," Colin admitted ruefully.
" Only one bay in Ruffa, so it doesn't refer to
this end. Must mean he wants to change the
port that yacht comes from or goes to, eh ? "

" And Nipasgal are trying to intercept something *en route*, evidently," was Northfleet's
comment.

" Yes. Reads that way, certainly."

" What do you make of the first sentence :
' The final lot of the last three thousand was
sent off on Thursday and got through safe ' ?
Does that suggest anything to you, Trent ? "

" It isn't three thousand articles. They're not
running a factory at Heather Lodge," Colin
asserted. " Ever seen them send off a big cargo
of any sort—a cartload of stuff, I mean ? "

Northfleet shook his head.

" Then it isn't three thousand pounds," Colin
inferred, " for that would be over a ton weight."

" There are pounds and pounds," Northfleet
pointed out with a satirical smile.

Colin sat up suddenly.

" Now *that's* a notion I'd never struck.
Forgery, what ? Packets of bank-notes ? "

" You can put that out of your head. It isn't
that."

" Well, it must mean three thousand pounds
of some sort. A tidy sum to handle in one

transaction. And," he added reflectively, "that fits in with the fact that both you and I know there's gold at the back of this business, somewhere. Ruffa must be another name for Tom Tiddler's Ground:

> "*Here I stand on Tom Tiddler's Ground,*
> *Picking up gold and silver.*"

He broke off abruptly, struck by the accuracy of the parallel. He himself had stood on Tom Tiddler's Ground picking up gold not so long ago—and it was no mere metaphor. There was the gold brick.

Northfleet also seemed to recognise an aptness in the nickname.

"Tom Tiddler's Ground?" he echoed. "That's not bad, Trent. I can tell you this much. The Heather Lodge lot are making money on Ruffa—big money. It's Tom Tiddler's Ground for them, at anyrate."

An earlier speculation of his own flashed back into Colin's mind.

"Placer mining!" he ejaculated.

Northfleet shook his head decidedly.

"That notion won't wash," he said bluntly. "In the first place, there isn't a stream longer than half a mile in Ruffa. You'd never find placer deposits in them. Secondly, I've been over every inch of the island, bar the Heather Lodge grounds, and there's no sign of any workings— no digging, no cradles, nothing. Thirdly, these fellows keep to Heather Lodge, except when they take the dog for a walk. I'd have seen them if they'd been working a deposit. No, you can dismiss that notion."

Colin was downcast for a moment, but a fresh idea came to his aid.

" Hold on, though ! Suppose an alluvial deposit got buried by a cave-in of the banks of an old river. The gold would be underground, then. What about that subterranean tunnel ? Might be some stuff down there. I mean, we don't know anything about it beyond the bricked-up part. The Heather Lodge lot may have found a deposit near their end and dug an adit into it from the tunnel. Then they could dig away as they pleased, underground, and you'd be no wiser."

" The streams here are too short."

Northfleet reiterated his objection in a slightly impatient tone. But Colin had an answer ready.

" Yes, if Ruffa had been an island from the Creation onwards. But it was part of the mainland once, I guess. The gold may have been laid down then, when there was plenty of room for a river. After that, the land round about may have submerged and left Ruffa sticking up."

" I see you're set on that explanation. Don't let me disturb your mind," Northfleet begged ironically. " Divert your attention for a moment and I'll show you something. See that big white motor-launch in the offing yonder ? She's the Heather Lodge supply-boat. See ! She's coming up in our direction hand over fist."

Colin followed Northfleet's gesture and saw the white hull of the visitor cutting through the waves in the distance. For a moment the sun gleamed dazzlingly on the windows of the cabin as the vessel changed her course by a point or two.

" I've never seen her before," Colin said, as he watched the swift approach of the vessel. " Fairish size, she is. Could stand up to weather not badly. Not a bad turn of speed, either. Does she call here often, in the usual run ? "

" Irregularly. She was here last week."

"Last week ? I never saw her," Colin objected.

" No. You were out all day with Mrs. Trent, down the coast in your motor-boat. The launch was away again before you turned up in the evening. Do you remember what day that was ? "

Something in Northfleet's tone as he uttered the last sentence made Colin look up sharply.

" What day it was ? One forgets the days of the week in this place. Lemme see . . . Last Thursday, was it ? I mean Thursday in last week."

" That's correct. Does it suggest anything ? "

Thursday ? Colin knew he had seen the word somewhere. Of course ! It was in the cipher message. He pulled the paper towards him and re-read the sentence : " The final lot of the last three thousand was sent off on Thursday and got through safe."

" You mean that motor-launch took away the stuff, whatever it is ? "

" Very curious coincidence, if it didn't," Northfleet commented. " At least, it took 'part' of it away."

" And the rest went in the yacht, eh ? "

" If it did, it went disguised as petrol."

" Petrol tins might hold anything, and you didn't see inside them," said Colin weightily. " What did the launch bring in, did you see ? "

"A lot of boxes and parcels," Northfleet answered, making no concealment of the fact that he had watched the whole affair. "They might have been simply groceries and so forth. In fact, one box at least was that. It had no lid and I could see tins and jam-jars in it as they carried it up from the jetty. I was up on the hill with a good pair of glasses—the ones I use for bird-watching," he explained with a faint grin.

"Ha! Thrilling, no doubt," said Colin, acknowledging the thrust. "But what's more to the point : what did the launch take away with her when she went ? "

"Two wooden boxes, like ammunition boxes, rather. They were iron-clamped, I could see. And they seemed pretty heavy, to judge by the way they carried them—two men to the box."

"Ah ! " said Colin, in what he hoped was an indifferent tone.

How many of these gold bricks could one pack into an ammunition box, he wondered. If the box was full, it would make a heavyish load to carry over rough ground, certainly. Then a fresh thought prompted him to ask a question.

"What crew has she, did you see ? "

"Two men. That was all I saw."

"Like these foreign scoundrels on the yacht ?" Colin inquired.

Northfleet shook his head.

"I didn't go near them, so I didn't hear them speak. But I had a good look at them through my glasses. English, I'd say. Gentlemen, possibly—or, at any rate, they'd been gentlemen at one time. Miss Arrow mentioned them to me once, and that's the impression I got from the way she spoke. It fits in with some other information I have from another source."

Colin was busy with his new line of thought.

"Four men at Heather Lodge; two fellows at least on the yacht; and these two on the motor-launch. That's eight men to divide the profits, whatever they are. If all that gang are making a good thing out of it, the receipts must run into big figures."

"They do," Northfleet confirmed succinctly.

As well they might, Colin thought, if those boxes were packed with gold bricks. Ruffa must be Tom Tiddler's Ground and no mistake.

"Another thing the launch brought was a load of petrol tins," Northfleet went on, supplementing his earlier list. "Some of them may be for re-fuelling the yacht and the rest must be benzene for the Heather Lodge gas plant."

He paused for a moment, then and added:

"Do these points suggest anything to you, Trent?"

Colin pondered for a while without hitting upon anything.

"No, I don't see much in it," he confessed.

Northfleet put forward his interpretation with obvious diffidence.

"Perhaps this is straining the thing a bit, but here's an explanation, for what it's worth," he said. "If the yacht needs re-fuelling, she must have come a longish distance without touching a port. On her looks, she had a far bigger effective radius than the motor-launch, and yet it's the launch that brings the petrol tins, and the yacht that takes them away."

"If it *was* petrol that they held," Colin objected. "It might have been poteen. Perhaps Arrow's running an illicit still. He may be, for all we know."

"Pigs might fly," said Northfleet contemptuously. "Stick to the facts. That short-radius motor-launch brings the tins. Therefore its trips are well within its ordinary radius of action. The yacht's engine's only an auxiliary, and yet she has been eating up her supply, apparently. Obviously she's had a far longer trip than the motor-launch. Besides, the launch drops in here fairly regularly, whilst I've only seen the yacht once or twice since I came to Ruffa. That points the same way, on the probabilities of the case. I don't say the thing's proved, naturally. Still it suggests things."

But Colin was in no mood for idle discussions about the effective radius of yachts or motor-launch. A new and brilliant idea had crossed his mind, and he blurted it out on the spur of the moment.

"I say, you know. Remember the Traprain Law business over on the East Coast. Archæology stunt. They dug up a place there and found a sea-rover's hoard. Gold vessels all bashed up and squashed for easy carriage. Heaps of them. Some old Norse pirate had looted an abbey on the Normandy coast, or somewhere thereabouts. Going up the North Sea he'd got into trouble, somehow. Came ashore at Traprain Law, cached his plunder, and probably got scuppered on the way home. Never came back for the stuff anyhow."

" Well ? " Northfleet prompted, with more interest than he had hitherto shown in Colin's speculations.

" Well, don't you see ? " Colin pursued in high excitement. " That tunnel's the very place for a cache—under the floor or behind some of the stones in the walls. Suppose somebody had played the old Norseman's game. And suppose Arrow happened to come upon the stuff by chance. That would cover every inch of the ground."

" Why all this secrecy business, then ? " Northfleet inquired sceptically.

" Law of Treasure Trove, of course ! If any gold plate or such-like stuff's found and there's no traceable owner to it the Crown steps in and grabs it. You may get something for finding it, but it's Crown property. I don't know whether you get a percentage for your pains or not. You certainly don't scoop the lot. So if you bleat about it publicly—snap ! in come the law officers and take it off your hands. But if you keep your mouth shut—who's going to know anything about it, except yourself and your pals ? There's your solution, down to a dot."

Northfleet made no reply for a full minute.

" You may have come near it," he admitted frankly, at last. " I don't know whether you're right or wrong, Trent ; but it would be a devil of a relief, I can tell you, if that proved to be the true solution. In more ways than one," he added, as though musing aloud.

CHAPTER XI

COLIN would have liked to demand some elucidation of Northfleet's meaning, but his tact suggested that he should refrain. The chemist's final phrase pointed straight to Hazel Arrow, though her name had not been mentioned; and Colin felt that a direct question might freeze up the stream of information which had just begun to trickle. For some moments he sat silent, his eyes on the stretch of sea across which the white motor-launch was chipping through the waves on its way toward the western cape of Ruffa. His restraint was at length rewarded; but when Northfleet spoke again he seemed to choose a fresh topic.

"You seem to gather up out-of-the-way information, Trent. Did you ever read anything about the Philosopher's Stone?"

Colin shook his head rather doubtfully. His store of knowledge in that field was no greater than the average man's.

"Not much," he admitted. "Stunt of the alchemists, wasn't it? Something that changed lead into gold? Fake, mostly, if not entirely, so to speak. Pot of molten lead; a few powders to give a flash; a metal rod to stir up the ingredients: that was the outfit, wasn't it? Only, the rod was really hollow, plugged with wax at both ends, and with some pellets of gold in the cavity. When they stirred the lead with that, the wax melted and the gold slipped down into the crucible. Then they could show their patrons that the lead contained gold and get a subsidy to carry on the good work. That sort of thing."

"That sort of thing, as you say," Northfleet confirmed. "It was a stock joke with generations of lecturers on chemistry Nobody believed in the possibility of changing one element into another. Anyone who said a word in its favour got laughed at. Then came radio-activity, and it turned out that every specimen of uranium was a bit of the Philosopher's Stone. Know anything about recent work on the transmutation of the elements, by any chance ?"

"Just what I read in the newspapers," Colin confessed modestly. "All this stuff about split-ting the atom, and so forth."

"And what do you think of it ? You're a plain, unscientific person."

"It doesn't mean much in my young life, and that's a fact," Colin admitted. "Thrilling to you chemists, no doubt. But beyond that, it's just a toy affair. Nothing on a big scale can come out of it, 's far 's I can see."

Northfleet smiled rather wryly.

"I expect some honest citizens of Alexandria said the same when they heard about Hero's aeolipile. And yet it was one of the first steam engines."

"Something in that, perhaps." Colin s tone showed no enthusiasm. "But, so far, this atom-splitting's uneconomic. Uses some frightfully expensive stuffs or machinery and doesn't yield enough gold to make a flea wink if you put the lot into its eye."

" Like the fellow in Lamb's essay who burned down his house every time he wanted roast pig ? Yes. But according to Lamb they weren't so very long before they found a cheaper way of doing the job, once they got the right notion into their heads. And it might be the same with gold-making. Some bright lad might strike the right method."

Colin shook his head decidedly.

" That's rot," he affirmed bluntly.

" Think so ? " said Northfleet. " I'm not so sure."

" But it would have made a stir, if it had been done," Colin objected. " It'd upset things a bit. Newspapers would be on to it like terriers after a rat."

Northfleet made no attempt to conceal his amusement.

" Yes. And the wiseacre in the street, like you, would turn up his nose and say : ' Fake ! ' immediately. And then he'd forget it, eh ? But here's an actual case. I'm not inventing it. I read about it in an old volume of *Pearson's Magazine* that was kicking about the house when I was a kid at school."

Colin snorted contemptuously.

" Is that where you get your chemical information ? " he inquired ironically. " Wish I'd taken up chemistry myself. It must be light reading."

" All I'm trying to do is to convince you I'm not inventing," Northfleet assured him. " You'll find the business mentioned in Fournier d'Albe's life of Sir William Crookes. There's a fairly full account of it in Commander Gould's *Enigmas*, too. That's surely enough to satisfy you that I'm not trying to pull your leg."

" All right," said Colin ; " give us the yarn, whatever it is."

" Towards the end of last century," Northfleet began, unperturbed, " there was an American chemist by the name of Emmens. He invented an explosive called ' Emmensite,' which I believe was taken up by the U.S.A. Government. In 1897 Emmens gave out that he had discovered how to convert silver into gold. He started with Mexican silver dollars, and by using some machinery or other—he called it a Force Engine—he claimed that he had turned the silver into a stuff called ' Argentaurum,' which was half-way between silver and gold. From this argentaurum he could go on a further stage if he liked and change it into gold by continuing his treatment."

" Fake ! " was Colin's comment, accompanied by a shrug of his shoulders. " You don't swallow that, do you ? "

" Not as it stands, I admit. Modern ideas don't allow for any such half-way materials as argentaurum was supposed to be. But let that go, for the moment. The point is that Emmens took his argentaurum gold to the United States Mint. They tested it, found it was gold right enough, and bought it from him over the counter. Between April and December, 1897, they purchased between six and seven hundred ounces of his gold—close on eight thousand dollars' worth of gold at the price then current. And that's no newspaper yarn."

" Not pulling my leg, really ? " Colin demanded suspiciously.

" Not in the slightest."

" But why didn't someone else repeat the experiments and—— "

" Suppose you yourself made a discovery of that sort," Northfleet interrupted, " what would you do ? If you were a pure dyed-in-the-wool scientific man with no interests beyond the search for truth and the advancement of knowledge, you'd publish your method and throw the thing open to the world. But science is a dashed poorly-paid industry, let me tell you. Wouldn't you be just a trifle tempted to stick to your discovery and make money out of it, instead of giving the show away ? I don't mind admitting that I'd suffer a qualm or two if I had to come to a decision myself about that. And, besides, it might be made well worth your while to keep your jaw shut. The gold industry has a lot of ramifications, and some people might prefer to pay you for secrecy—pay high, too."

" Hadn't seen that side of it," Colin admitted handsomely.

" Emmens made no bones about it," Northfleet went on. " He went into the thing purely as a case of Mammon-seeking. He said so himself : ' No disciples desired and no believers asked for ' ; that was his attitude when Crookes tackled him about his process. Now if you'd been in Emmens's shoes, what line would you have taken ? "

"Keep it dark, I suppose, and go on selling the gold."

"And suppose the newspapers got hold of it and made a mild stunt of your alchemy, what then?"

"Keep on saying nothing, and let them tire of it."

"Or else publish a wholly misleading account of your process to keep the really dangerous people—your fellow-chemists—clean off the track. Keep them guessing as long as you could. And, if they bothered you, tell them that science could go and cook itself, for all you cared. In fact, behave in a wholly unscientific manner, with a dose of rudeness thrown in."

"And was this stunt really run at a profit?" Colin asked in a less sceptical tone.

"His figures show that he made a profit of one pound six shillings on every ounce of silver transmuted, after all costs had been deducted. Nowadays, with gold up in price, the profits would be far bigger."

"H'm!" Colin ejaculated thoughtfully.

"I only spoke of Emmens to knock some of that cocksureness out of you, Trent," Northfleet explained. "You can forget about him now. He hasn't the remotest connection with the present affair. I just want you to realise that gold-making is quite on the cards, and that economical gold-making isn't an impossibility. You can't rule it out entirely; we've got a bit more careful about saying 'Impossible!' nowadays in chemistry. Now, does the name of Leven suggest anything to you. F. A. Leven, with a lot of the alphabet after it."

"Lemme see." Colin pondered. "D'you mean the scientific fellow?"

"He was Professor of Chemistry at the Western Adelphi College in Bayswater, in our day."

"Oh, yes!" Colin had a sudden recollection. "I remember. Didn't he get into a row with the police over some pretty ladies in the street and get hauled off to the lock-up, once?"

"Here's Fame!" said Northfleet sardonically. "Be a distinguished scientific man for years, and the man in the street never hears of you. Get into some squalid row at a street-corner and you print yourself on the public memory. That's what happened in Leven's case, anyhow. He was one of the smartest men in his own line; but his line wasn't the sort that the man in the street could make head or tail of; so Leven's name meant nothing to the public until he was had up at Bow Street."

"Well, what about it, anyway?" Colin inquired. "That scandal's ten years old now. I read about it when I was in my first year at U.C.L."

"Don't be in a hurry, Trent. That incident's important. Straws show the way the wind blows."

Colin caught the hint.

"Bad lad, eh? Bit of a rip, and all that sort of thing, you mean?"

"Draw your own conclusions," Northfleet grunted. "I've stuck to the facts, pure and simple. I prefer that course, for certain reasons. But I'll say this. Leven had very expensive tastes and he drew a salary of seven hundred

pounds a year. I dare say he had a private
practice to help him. Still, if there was any
truth in rumours, he must have found it a stiff
business. He got in amongst a lot of very
queer fish, too. I don't need to say any more.
You can read between the lines yourself."

His shrug was very expressive.

"All right. Skip that, and get on," Colin
suggested.

"Very well. The next stage of the thing
is pretty vague. It was mostly a matter of
hints dropped here and there to different
people. He'd got on to a big thing, had Leven.
He didn't push it on the world, as if he wanted
the world to know all about it. No, he seemed
to let it out in spite of himself. At a dinner he'd
do himself extremely well off the wine-list, and
then he'd grow a bit talkative. Something
would be blurted out on the spur of the moment ;
then he'd wake up to the fact that he'd let his
tongue run away with him, and he'd shut up as
tight as an oyster."

"Rummy, that, certainly," Colin commented.
"And no particulars ? "

"No particulars whatever. The result was
that the chemical world got the notion that he
had something up his sleeve—something big ;
but exactly what it was they couldn't define.
If they'd gone into committee and pooled all
they'd heard individually I doubt if they'd have
made much out of it. The nearest thing was
when he was put up to speak at a Chem. Soc.
dinner. He'd mixed his drinks a bit, and in
proposing a toast he turned aside to make a

lot of sneering remarks about the 'fiddling methods' and 'paltry results' of the transmutationists. Without putting it into plain words, he made it sound as if he were an expert patting a lot of beginners on the back for their little efforts. I heard that speech myself. It was in damnably bad taste, but that made it all the more convincing, in a way."

"What sort of man is he?" Colin interjected.

"I've never spoken to him in my life," Northfleet explained. "But I've watched him often at meetings of the Chemical. He's an egotist of the extreme sort. Number One is all that counts with him. That sticks out all over him. He built up no school at the Adelphi College, because he took care that no student working with him ever got a spark of the credit. ' We ' simply wasn't in his dictionary. It was 'I' all the time. ' I was the first worker in this line ': ' I foresaw this difficulty and I devised means to get over it '; ' I brought out the important fact that——— '; ' I said the last word on this subject in my paper of such-and-such a date '; and so on and so forth. He quarrelled with all his old students, too; and with most of his colleagues as well, I've heard. Naturally he wasn't liked. But a clever man can do without people's liking—up to a point at any rate."

"Don't flatter him, do you?" was Colin's comment.

There was a personal note in Northfleet's description, in spite of his carefully-assumed indifference; and Colin now had little difficulty in guessing the origin of it. With an effort he refrained from making the obvious identification aloud. It would come better when he had listened to the whole story, he felt.

"Well," Northfleet continued, without noticing the interruption, "things went on like this for a while. Then, in 1924, he walked up Tower Hill, dropped in at the Royal Mint, dumped some gold on the counter, and demanded payment. In those days you could insist on having gold of a certain purity converted into sovereigns. Naturally, they didn't take his word for it. The stuff was assayed, and it turned out to be what he said it was—fairly pure gold. They had to pay him for it. I've been told that he went back several times, always with sound stuff, and in fair quantities too."

Colin had no need to feign interest. With the gold brick in his pocket and the mysteries of Ruffa in his mind, he wanted to hurry Northfleet's narrative, for he could see whither it was trending.

"In 1925," Northfleet resumed, "that little game came to an end. Free coinage of bullion at the Royal Mint was abolished. I don't suppose he had much difficulty in finding an alternative market. The fact that he had sold his stuff to the Mint was pretty convincing. And any jeweller who bought from him would take good care to have the stuff assayed by an independent expert. It wasn't spot-pure gold, but it was quite worth refining. It varied from sample to sample. There was always a fair amount of silver in it, some copper, and a little platinum. These, in case you don't know, are impurities found in specimens of natural gold, at times. Here are the results of the analysis of a sample of Leven's gold. The figures are percentages."

He handed over a paper and Colin read :

Gold	.	.	.	.	61·63
Silver	.	.	.	.	28·71
Copper	.	.	.	.	8·62
Iron	.	.	.	.	0·75
Platinum	.	.	.	.	0·25
Zinc	.	.	.	.	0·04
					100·00

" Seems to be a lot of silver in the stuff," Colin commented.

" Not more than you find in some specimens of native gold," Northfleet assured him. " I've seen analyses of some Transylvanian gold where the silver content went as high as thirty-eight per cent. Gold and silver always seem to be associated in Nature."

" This percentage business conveys nothing definite to me," Colin admitted, tapping the paper as he spoke. " What's the fineness of this stuff ? How many carats ? "

" Round about fifteen. Pure gold's reckoned as twenty-four carat."

" How do you know these figures are O.K. ? " Colin demanded in a slightly sceptical tone.

" Because I did the analysis myself. You needn't ask me who gave me the stuff. I shan't tell you that," said Northfleet bluntly.

Colin thought he could read between the lines.

Some jeweller had employed Northfleet to make the assay. Naturally, he could not give his employer away. It was stretching things quite far enough to show the analytical results.

"So much for that," Northfleet went on. "I've no notion how much gold Leven managed to get off his hands through the jewellers and bullion dealers. His sales varied in amount and were at irregular intervals; but judging by his standard of living he must have driven a pretty brisk trade. And then, apparently, somebody split. The thing leaked out, anyhow. A couple of cheap sensational papers came out one day with a portrait of Leven and headlines : ' Alchemists' Dreams Come True ' ; ' British Scientist Makes Gold ' ; ' Interview With The Inventor ', and all the rest of it.

"That interview was a bit curious. Leven took the stand that he was a purely scientific person ; the process was still in its early stages ; he didn't care to say much about it just yet ; in due course his results would be communicated to the chemical journals, etc., etc. That choked off the journalists—too dull for them. So they dropped the thing instanter. As for the man in the street, he'd never heard of Leven before. Leven might be a distinguished scientist, as the papers said. But making gold ? The man in the street wasn't going to be such a ruddy fool as to swallow *that*. So he just muttered ' Fake ! ' and turned over to the sporting news. In another couple of days the public had forgotten about the whole affair. In chemical circles there was a certain amount of *Schadenfreude*, some rather cheerful rubbing of the hands, and nods and winks among the people who hated Leven most. In their view he'd come down badly—been fairly caught out in a bluff. They thought it was an attempt at self-advertisement on Leven's part, and they rather rejoiced at it having gone wrong. Most of them simply disbelieved the whole tale and thought the reporters had invented the story about the Mint.

" Perhaps it was another of Leven's calculated indiscretions. Or possibly his hand was forced in some way. I don't know. Anyway, the thing had a very brief publicity, of a kind—and then there was dead silence on the subject. But Leven went on selling his gold. It was as good as the next man's, whether Nature made it or Leven, and he easily found a market.

" But that newspaper stunt made one change in the situation. Leven got frightened, I judge. After all, if you get a reputation of being a gold-maker, you may be worth burgling. That must have been the real factor behind the story Miss Arrow told you the other night. He got into a funk and he hired a guard—that creature Zelensky. Doesn't that suggest that gold-making's a paying business for Leven ? "

" Suppose it does," Colin agreed. " But who is this Zelensky cove ? "

Northfleet pondered a few moments before answering.

" Well, you've more or less promised your help," he decided at last, " so I don't see why I shouldn't tell you what I know in the matter. Zelensky's biography's been looked up. One extract will be enough. You remember the Separatist stunt in the Rhineland ? Zelensky commanded one of the squads that played a part in that show. By and by the Separatist business fizzled out, and Zelensky's paymasters were left with his gang of ruffians on their hands. They didn't want them any longer. What was to be done ? They put it to Zelensky, and he got them out of the difficulty—easy enough, too. He got his pack of armed scoundrels together ; filled them up with drink ; proposed a raid on some villages up in the hill-district near by ; loaded his crew on to a motor-lorry and started them off in great glee at the treat before them— loot and all the rest of it. Zelensky himself contrived to get left behind. He walked straight off and phoned up the road, warning the villagers of the coming of the looters. The country people had no use for Separatists ; they'd heard all about them. So they just ambushed the lorry on a steep gradient—— "

"And ? " Colin interjected as Northfleet paused.

" Oh, they got 'em at a disadvantage, of course. Killed the lot with scythes, pruning-knives, or anything else that came handy. No one asked any questions. Why should they ? "

" You mean the beggar betrayed his own men ? " Colin ejaculated, aghast at such cold-blooded treachery.

" I don't suppose that worried him much," was Northfleet's comment. " His paymasters wanted a job done. They paid him to do it. He did it. That's how he'd look at it, I expect."

Colin looked sharply at Northfleet. The

chemist's matter-of-fact tone almost suggested that he felt no particular disapproval of the episode. In fact, the neatness and efficiency of Zelensky seemed to have extracted a faint tribute of respect. Northfleet met his eye with a sardonic expression.

"Not going into mourning for them, are you?" he asked. "My own view is that the fewer scoundrels there are the better world it'll be. So I don't weep when a few ruffians get their deserts. One ought to look at these affairs dispassionately."

Colin abruptly changed the subject.

"Leven—that's old Arrow, I suppose, under a false name?"

Northfleet nodded.

"Yes. He took Miss Arrow's name to hide under. Probably she would have refused to masquerade under a false name herself; so he chose hers to save bother when he brought her up here."

Colin plunged into reflection for a few moments before he spoke again.

"Leven must be putting a fair strain on a scoundrel like this Zelensky—having him around with all this gold-making going on."

"I doubt if Zelensky has even a glimmering that there's gold at all," Northfleet answered thoughtfully. "Leven wouldn't need to tell him. Zelensky's hired as a bodyguard. No need for him to be taken into Leven's confidence. Nor Natorp either. He's a Lett of some sort, I believe, with a Russian record no better than his colleague's."

"Take it as read, then," Colin suggested.

"Makes one sick to hear about that sort of thing. Go on with the story."

"Very well. It looks as though Leven evidently didn't feel safe in London, even under the guard of these two beauties. Or there may have been another reason. I'm merely guessing there. To stick to facts, he resigned from the Adelphi College—which in itself shows he was doing pretty well out of his gold-making—and he disappeared from London. He covered his tracks, came north, and settled down in Ruffa here, to carry on his work. He brought his niece along with him, probably so as to leave no one behind who could let out where he was. She's entirely dependent on him, so she had to do as she was told, I gather."

"How much of all this does Miss Arrow know?" Colin asked with some reluctance.

"Next to nothing," said Northfleet curtly. "She was at school when the newspaper stunt happened, and I've learned that it was one of these weird boarding-schools where the girls aren't allowed to see a newspaper of any sort. So she heard nothing about the gold-making business, I expect. I've never questioned her— I prefer to play the game in this case—but she speaks quite freely about some chemical work that her uncle carries on in his laboratory here. She's not the sort of girl who could lie easily. *Ergo*, she doesn't know what's going on, or she'd have been told to keep her mouth shut. She knows nothing, so she can tell nothing. That's old Leven's point of view, I believe."

"No use asking where *you* come in, is there?"

" None whatever. Guess for yourself as much as you like. Who'd be affected if Leven took to making gold on a huge scale ? No, you needn't bother suggesting possibilities, because I'm not going to contradict you and give you a chance of worrying it out by elimination."

Colin was satisfied that Northfleet had treated him fairly, within his self-imposed limits. Something seemed called for in return. He put his hand in his pocket and fished out the gold brick, which he had brought with him to use in case it seemed fair to do so.

" What d'you make of that ? " he asked with a faint tinge of triumph in his tone as he laid it on the table.

If he had hoped to surprise Northfleet, he was successful.

" Where the devil did you lay your hands on this ? " demanded the chemist, with more excitement than Colin had yet seen him betray.

Colin, having made up his mind to be frank, gave him the whole story without reservation.

" What do you make of it ? " he asked, when he had told his tale.

" H'm ! " Northfleet said thoughtfully. " He wasn't so far out after all when he hired a bodyguard. I'd no idea there was as much in it as this. Your hare-lipped pal must have been a cute beggar to get past Natorp & Co. and burgle the gold store."

" Fits in, doesn't it, with those hints about Nipasgal's activities in the cipher message ? "

Northfleet nodded.

" What puzzles me is how Master Hare-lip

got away from them all, including the wolf hound," he said in a doubtful tone. " Seems a bit strange."

Colin had another of his bright ideas.

" S'pose old Arrow—Leven, I mean—called them off, eh ? If he'd let Natorp & Co. get hold of Hare-lip they'd have searched him for arms, and the gold brick might have turned up. That would have made Natorp and his pal open their eyes a bit. Gold in quantity's a big temptation. And most likely old Arrow—Leven, I mean—hasn't got a childlike trust in the honesty of his guards. He'd want to keep 'em in the dark at almost any cost."

" Something in that, possibly," Northfleet admitted frankly. " I wonder how your hare-lipped friend got away finally—if he did get away at all," he added meaningly.

" A pal with a boat, I suppose," Colin suggested, ignoring the darker alternative. " There must have been a boat there, or he couldn't have landed on Ruffa at all."

" Yes. And I suppose a boat can be sunk in deep water all right," Northfleet added, obviously pursuing his second line of thought. Then with a change of tone he went on, " By the way, Trent, would you mind letting me have that ingot ? It would be a useful bit of evidence for me to show to my employers. You'll get paid full value for it, of course."

" Not my property," Colin pointed out. " May be Leven's, though I've no proof of that. Fact is, I'd just as soon get it off my hands, since I've no claim on it. Suits us both, that ? "

" Put in that way, certainly."

He picked up the ingot from the table and slipped it into his pocket.

" That's all right," said Colin. " But look here. Another idea. Is this Leven's first visit to Ruffa, or has he been here before ? "

For a moment Northfleet seemed puzzled by the question, then his face cleared.

" Oh, I see, now. You're still harping on that treasure-trove notion, are you ? I can't help you there. Dinnet might be able to give you the information if you asked him."

" Which I'll do immediately I get back to Wester Voe. Another idea. Why is Leven worried about the Fisheries gunboat ? "

" Can't say," Northfleet answered frankly. Then, after a pause, he added, " Leven deals with a number of chemical firms, buying reagents for his private practice. Since the newspaper stunt he's bought nothing from these people but the commonest kind of chemicals—just the usual analytical stuff. I happen to know that. But if he's the man I take him for, he's done that of set purpose. If any out-of-the-way stuffs are needed in this business of his he's managed to camouflage his purchases. Probably he does his buying through agents of his own, so that his name never appears on an invoice."

" I see ! " Colin interrupted. " The yacht brings these stuffs direct from the Continent, perhaps. That would fit in with what you said about petrol supply and effective radius and so on. If the yacht brings 'em, they don't go through the Customs. There's no trail left for

Nipasgal to pick up by any mishap. There's no clue to Leven's processes in his gold-making. But of course that means he's smuggling, if the stuff's dutiable ; and so he's not keen on landing chemicals while the Fisheries boat's in the offing. She might spot his game and pass the word to the nearest Customs people."

"That might be it," Northfleet admitted, rather grudgingly.

"Don't see *one* thing, yet," Colin confessed. "S'pose old Arrow—Leven, I mean—*is* making gold and selling it at a profit, as you say, well, what's the odds ? Gives him a nice little income, I'd imagine. But is anybody a penny the worse for that ? People who buy his stuff aren't swindled. Get full value for their money, don't they ? Couldn't have him up for false pretences, even if they tried, I take it. Then why all this fuss ? Why not let him push along with his gold-making in peace, instead of poking a nose into his private affairs ? Seems to me a bit uncalled-for, don't you know. He's not doing anybody any harm, 's far 's I can see. And he's got troubles enough on his hands without you butting in, surely ? I'm not criticising you, you understand ? It's your own show and none of my business. But what I mean to say is : aren't you and your pals—whoever they are—making a mountain out of a molehill ? "

Northfleet looked at him keenly.

"You're not trying to draw me. I quite see that. And I'm not going to be drawn, in any case. My employer is Lord Knows Who—a recent creation, not in the Peerages yet. Now

I'll put the thing in general terms, just to correct your perspective a bit. Suppose—as you say—that Leven's process requires an expensive plant. Say, for instance, that it needs a radioactive material at some stage or other. Leven's not a rich man, as I've told you. His spare cash wouldn't go far in buying any of the really strongly radioactive stuffs. Assume, then, that he has managed to scrape up a small quantity—enough for transmutation on a very moderate scale. In passing, I'm quite sure that he's not doing it in that way; I'm merely giving you a concrete illustration."

"Right," Colin agreed. "I see your point. Go on."

"Under such conditions, Leven could turn out a very modest supply of his gold. As you say: what's the harm in that? None whatever, so long as things remain at this stage. But if Leven can turn out a small supply with his present plant, he could obviously turn out a bigger supply with a bigger plant. Or if somebody with big resources got hold of Leven's secret, the same thing would happen. If you can make a pound of gold economically, it's not likely that you'd be unable to turn out a ton of it at a profit if you extend your plant sufficiently. Suppose Leven or anyone else were put in a position to turn out gold by the ton instead of by the ounce, what results would follow? Just think that over."

"Slump in the Kaffir market," said Colin sapiently. "Drop in all gold-mining shares. Grass growing in the streets of Johannesburg and all that sort of thing. Um! Yes, I suppose it would be disturbing."

"Because the price of gold would drop, once the secret leaked out? And what about all the gold deposits that the nations are holding in their Treasuries?"

Colin began to open his eyes as these aspects of the matter dawned upon him.

"Zooks! This begins to look serious. It does, really. I hadn't seen it on quite that scale. International problem, eh? And half the governments in the world wondering where they stand? Y'know, Northfleet, this is a bit disturbing, when you come to look at it."

"Waking up, are you?" Northfleet said cynically. "Better wire your stockbroker to sell your Rand shares, if it's as bad as all that. I'll give you a tip for your next investment. If gold went out, what metal would take its place?"

"Silver?"

"And what about the countries on a silver basis? How would they be affected?"

"Meaning that silver would appreciate when gold dropped out, and so countries with a silver coinage would stand to gain?"

"I'm no economist," Northfleet pointed out. "I'm just suggesting problems. I don't profess to solve them for you. But if silver were to appreciate in value, who'd stand to gain by it? The Americas between them produce two-thirds of the world output of silver. Mexico alone represents a third of the silver output of the globe. What sort of country's Mexico, Trent?"

"A bit unsettled, according to my newspaper."

"Hardly good for the world if one-third of its total supply of the most precious currency-metal came from an unstable country. Somebody would have to put that right, wouldn't they? A little war on somebody's hands, perhaps? See, the horizons opening up a bit?"

Colin turned in his seat and looked up at the rock- and heather-strewn slopes of the island. Then he swung round again and gazed at the shore, where the fulmar petrels were going about their little affairs or sitting placidly, two by two, on the shelves of rock. It seemed an incongruous setting for a chemical process which, if Northfleet were right, might shake the world and give a new tilt to human affairs.

"Funny to think that an acre or two of an islet like Ruffa should hold all that," he reflected aloud in a faintly awed tone.

"Oh, I don't say it's likely to come to that," Northfleet pointed out. "I merely drew a pretty picture for you, to show you some of the possibilities behind gold-making. Lots of things might happen before it got to that stage. For instance, some people might feel justified in calling a halt by pretty drastic methods applied to Leven & Co. Say a treatment with lead pills—the nickel-coated brand, or something of that sort. Or, again, Leven might join up with somebody who could provide him with the sinews of war, so that his gold-making plant could be extended immensely and his output vastly increased."

"I say, you know," Colin protested, "this is a bit of a nightmare. You don't really think all this is likely to happen?"

Northfleet shrugged his shoulders in a non-committal fashion.

"I started by saying : ' Suppose . . .'" An economist would give you worse goose-flesh on the subject, I dare say."

"I'm just trying to think out who would be mainly affected by somebody flooding the market with gold," Colin said tentatively. "The South African mines, obviously ; the bullion dealers ; the banks, of course ; the big financiers, too ; and any governments that have stuck to the gold standard. Jove ! That's a pretty formidable lot."

"And the governments that are off the gold standard as well," Northfleet pointed out. "The whole international finance situation would be shaken up."

"And I suppose your Lord Knows Who amongst them ?" said Colin ironically. He glanced at his watch and added : "Well, time's getting on. I'd better be pushing along now."

Northfleet made no attempt to detain him.

As Colin climbed the ridge which separated the shieling from Wester Voe he felt like a man who has just come to the end of a very vivid short story. There had been a dispassionateness about Northfleet's exposition which lent to it a remarkable convincingness ; and the occasional lapse from that attitude had made the thing even more real to Colin. But as he trudged up the heathery slope, the standards of everyday feelings came back to him slowly, just as they do to a reader when he lays down the book which has been holding his attention. The impression of a world out of joint began quickly to fade from his mind, among the bell-heather and the rocks of Ruffa, with the little streamlet tinkling into pool after pool as he walked beside it. Natural things appeal to simple minds, and Colin was of the simple cast. Without knowing it, he was being soothed by his surroundings and relieved from his nightmare.

When he reached the watershed, he stopped for a time and scanned the landscape. Down below him, alongside the jetty, lay the white motor-launch, spick and span in the sunshine, with a man in a yachting-cap lounging aboard her. Nearer in, on the path leading across to Heather Lodge, were two laden figures. One of them, from his clothes, evidently belonged to the launch; the other Colin assumed to be Beeston, the assistant, whom he had not seen before. They were carrying up stores from the launch, apparently.

Colin's eyes passed on to Heather Lodge itself, a stiff-architectured house, built to withstand the winter storms of Ruffa, but unimpressive in the extreme. Was it credible that an ordinary-looking place like that could be the danger-spot of the world's finance ? Nonsense ! Colin assured himself. Northfleet had been doing a bit of leg-pulling, seeing how far he could go without raising Colin's suspicions. There was nothing in all that stuff.

And then, like a cloud on a summer sun, came the recollection of the armed guards. One couldn't call *them* ordinary or wave them aside out of the affair. Whether Northfleet had told a straight tale or not, Messrs. Natorp and Zelensky were something that Colin had seen with his own eyes and didn't need to take on trust. There *was* something rum about the crew at Heather Lodge. And there was the gold brick also to fit into the scheme. There was no hearsay about it either.

But then, as Colin assured himself, the whole gold-making business might well be—as he phrased it to himself—"All my eye and Betty Martin." The gold brick and the gold sales had to be explained, certainly. But gold-making! Colin's robust common sense assured him that people didn't make gold. Not in quantity at any rate. The gold could be accounted for in far more plausible ways. A Norse pirate's hoard, for instance, or . . . And as Colin's eye travelled beyond the bay to the black fangs of the skerry a fresh idea crossed his mind. There was the Armada treasure-ship in the bay. That stuff, too, would be treasure-trove, with all the inducements to secrecy if its store were tapped. One could go on selling gold in quantity for long enough, if one had an Armada galleon to draw from.

His glance passed on to Wester Voe ; and the figures of Jean and Hazel on the tennis-court drew his thoughts in another direction. Was it good business to let himself get entangled in Northfleet's schemes. Colin stood to gain nothing from them, and there was Jean to consider. After all, he knew nothing about Northfleet, except that they had been through University College at the same time. For all one could tell, Northfleet might have turned out a rank wrong 'un since then. Colin would never have heard about that. Perhaps he had been over-hasty in parting with that gold brick, he reflected.

But it is difficult to be a pessimist when one stands on a ridge above the sea, with a faint breeze rippling the heather at one's feet and a summer sun making diamonds on the waves below. Colin reacted to his environment and brushed aside his forebodings. After all, he wasn't really involved. He could draw out whenever it suited him. And so far, except in the matter of the gold brick, he had done prac-tically nothing in the affair. In short, why worry?

It was a much more cheerful Colin who arrived at Wester Voe and rang the bell for Dinnet.

" Oh, Dinnet, do you remember Mr. Arrow visiting Ruffa before this ? "

The factotum pondered for a while, then he shook his head.

" No, sir. Before Mr. Arrow took it, Heather Lodge was let to a gentleman retired from the Navy. He took the house year after year, I remember. He was here in 1926, sir, when I first came to Ruffa ; and he'd had the house for a year or two before that. He's dead now, sir. I've heard, somewhere, that before him there was a Mr. Leven, who took the house one summer. But that was before my time, sir.'

" Ah ! Thanks, Dinnet. That's all I wanted to know. Idle curiosity, and all that."

Dinnet retired, evidently surprised at this digging up of ancient history ; and Colin was left to put two and two together and to make what he could from them.

"THE 'fac-to-tum's' late to-night, Colin," Jean complained as they stood outside Wester Voe and gazed in vain towards the little cape round which the motor-boat would appear on its return from the trip to Stornadale with the gardeners.

"Running it a bit fine, certainly," Colin agreed, glancing at his watch. "Wonder what's kept him."

"Isn't it funny, Colin, how Ruffa changes things?" Jean went on. "At home, with four posts a day, I never bothered about letters. They just came or they didn't come. But here, when we get them only once a day, I seem to spend my time longing for the post; and when Dinnet brings nothing, it always feels like ages until the next evening. It's not that I particularly want letters : it's just because one doesn't get them as usual, I suppose."

"Like salt in soup—you never think of it until it's missing," Colin suggested. "Doesn't worry me, though. Never was much of a hand at putting bright thoughts on paper. Can't see, myself, what you find to say in all these letters you write. Hardly decent to be so free with the ink-gusher on a wedding-trip, take my word for it. Gives friends the impression you're bored stiff, I should fear."

He glanced at her, slightly perturbed by his own suggestion.

"I say, darling, you *aren't* bored, are you? Honest?"

Jean shook her head to reassure him.

"Not a bit of it. Really and really, Colin. And now I must fly and change. Don't keep me waiting for dinner. I'm simply famishing."

She hurried into the house. Colin, after another glance at his watch, decided that he had still time to smoke the best part of a cigarette. He had just opened his case when the motor-boat rounded the point, and Colin was surprised to find that it carried someone in addition to Dinnet.

"Wonder who this can be?" he reflected, and walked back into the house for a pair of glasses.

When he emerged again, the motor-boat was coming on towards the skerry. Colin put up his binoculars and took a long look at the tiny craft. Dinnet's companion was a stranger: a middle-sized, heavily-built man. As the boat drew nearer, Colin could see him clearly: clean-shaven, square-faced, with something in his appearance that suggested imperturbable self-reliance. Colin had an inclination to go down to the jetty and meet the boat; but a final glance at his watch assured him that he had no time to spare for conversation just then; and he could hardly escape at a moment's notice if he once became involved in talk. He slipped the binoculars back into their case, returned to the house, and went upstairs. After all, Dinnet would give him any information about the man, later on. There was no particular hurry. Still, the arrival of a fresh inhabitant of

Ruffa seemed peculiar, considering the restricted housing on the island. And quite obviously this man had come to stay. He could hardly expect Dinnet to take him to the mainland again that night.

During dinner, Colin's curiosity led him to broach the subject to Dinnet's slight though obvious confusion.

" Brought a passenger with you, I saw, Dinnet ? "

" Yes, sir. He was waiting at Stornadale, sir."

" Friend of yours, I suppose," Colin said indifferently, " or does he belong to Heather Lodge ? "

" No, sir. He has Mr. Craigmore's permission to stay on Ruffa for a while, sir."

" Oh, indeed ! " Colin was faintly resentful. It seemed hardly handsome of Craigmore to dump a visitor on himself and Jean, especially without so much as " By-your-leave." " He's staying here, I suppose ? He'd hardly get a room at the hotel here on the spur of the moment."

Dinnet smiled in polite recognition of the jest.

" As you say, sir, he would find some little difficulty. But it iss all right, sir. He will not be troubling you and Mrs. Trent at all. He has come up for an open-air holiday, and he means to camp out for a week or so while he iss here. He has got a little tent and some stores with him."

" Oh, that's all right, then," Colin conceded, with a certain relief which he failed to conceal.

" Of course he could not have stayed here," Dinnet explained, as though stating a fact so obvious as to make its formulation supererogatory. " Mr. Craigmore had lent Wester Voe to you, sir, and he would not think of sending anyone here."

" Quite so," Colin agreed, feeling a certain reproof behind this defence of Dinnet's employer.

" Mr. Craigmore telegraphed to me, sir, about the matter. I found the wire at the post office when I went there for the letters. I will show you it after dinner, sir."

" Oh, don't bother," said Colin, half-ashamed of himself at having betrayed his feelings. " No business of mine, Dinnet."

" I wonder who he is," Jean mused when Dinnet left the room. " Another recruit to the inner circle of Ruffa society. Does he look much catch, Colin ? "

" I only got a glimpse of him in the boat. Dressed for the part, all right—heather-mixture plus-fours and trimmings to match. Got one of these heavy, square-jawed physogs you see on the American captains of industry. Or he might be a middle-weight boxer on his vacation. Unplaceable sort of type. Might be anybody, in fact. Anybody who's quite able to look after himself, at any rate."

He paused, evidently rather pleased with his effort at description. Jean's ironical laugh disabused him.

" You'd make a fortune as a descriptive writer, Colin. Wonderful ! "

" Well, he *is* like that."

The re-entry of Dinnet set them talking on other subjects until dinner ended. Colin rose and opened the door for Jean; but as he was about to follow, Dinnet detained him with a gesture.

"This iss the telegram, sir."

Something in the factotum's manner showed Colin that he had been separated from Jean for some purpose which had nothing to do with the message itself. He could not help admiring Dinnet's resource in the matter.

"Let's see it, then, Dinnet," he said, pushing the door to and turning back into the room.

Dinnet held out the familiar form and Colin read:

Dinnet Wester Voe
Pick up Mr. Wenlock at Stornadale and take him to Ruffa he will explain matters himself Craigmore.

"Handed in at some London office," Colin noted. "Mr. Craigmore isn't in London just now, Dinnet?"

"No, sir, that iss quite true. Still, sir, I think the message iss quite in order."

"No business of mine, anyhow, Dinnet. Not's far's I can see."

"Mr. Wenlock, sir, would be glad if you could spare him a few minutes just now. Alone, sir. That was why I took the liberty of stopping you at the door, sir."

"Ah, indeed. Quite right, Dinnet. What does this man want with me? I never heard of him till this minute."

197

" I think he would rather explain, himself, sir. If you will wait for a moment I will send him to you."

" Very good, Dinnet. Send him along."

Dinnet vanished discreetly through the service-door. Colin, his half-smoked cigarette between his fingers, stared round the familiar dining-room mechanically. Who could this unexpected visitor be ? And why should he apply at the earliest possible moment to Colin, of all people, who had never even heard his name before. Another of these mysteries which seemed to hang over Ruffa like mist over a marsh. Well, this one could be cleared up without much waiting ; that was one good point.

The door opened. Dinnet's voice announced : " Mr. Wenlock, sir." Mr. Wenlock stepped into the room with an air of reserved assurance. The door closed behind him. Colin was face to face with the latest arrival.

" Good evening, Mr. Trent," said the new-comer briskly as he advanced into the room. " You're surprised to see me, I expect. I apologise for interrupting you ; but it was essential that I should see you at once."

He paused, evidently intending that Colin should speak next.

" Yes ? "

Colin did not propose to give himself away in the slightest until he knew more about his visitor.

" I'll put my cards on the table at once, Mr. Trent. I've come to ask you some questions, and, if possible, to prevent you asking awkward questions about me. You've seen that telegram? I asked Dinnet to show it to you to establish my bona fides and save trouble."

Colin looked at the face before him, with its humorous creases about the corners of the mouth. A good mixer, this fellow, he inferred. A rather likeable cove, in fact. If faces were fortunes, the bloke would be quite well-to-do, so long as beauty wasn't demanded as a *sine qua non*. But Colin didn't see why he should be cross-questioned merely because his would-be examiner could show a good set of teeth when he smiled. Come to think of it, this gent seemed to be a bit of a rusher in the way he took consent for granted. Colin wasn't going to be taken in by that sort of bluff.

" I've seen a telegram, certainly. But, if you don't mind my pointing it out, anybody can send a wire in someone else's name. Not necessarily evidence, if you see what I mean."

Mr. Wenlock's smile broadened.

" You're cautious, Mr. Trent. Quite right, in the circumstances. In fact, I'm glad of it."

He felt in his pocket, produced an official card, and handed it across to Colin.

" Detective-Inspector Wenlock," Colin read aloud, in a tone which betrayed a mingling of surprise and relief.

So Scotland Yard was taking a hand in the affairs of Ruffa! Northfleet's hints about Governments came back to his mind. Evidently there must be something pretty big behind the business, after all. Anyhow, Colin reflected with satisfaction, one knew exactly how one stood with the police. If they wanted assistance, they were entitled to get it.

" Wasn't over-keen to be cross-examined by total and unauthorised strangers," he explained ; " but this is a different pair of shoes, naturally. If you're from Scotland Yard, it's all right."

Detective-Inspector Wenlock made an expressive grimace to indicate that the situation was not yet straightened out entirely.

" You're frank, Mr. Trent. So am I, so I'll say this. I've no official footing up here. This place is north of the Border and outside English jurisdiction, you see. Of course I got in touch with the local constabulary before coming here. They know all about me. But, for all that, I'm practically a private person like yourself, so far as authority goes. If I ask questions, I've got to rely on your courtesy for my answers."

Detective-Inspector Wenlock had not attained his grade without acquiring a very sound judgment of human character. By throwing himself on Colin's generosity he did a very good stroke of business for himself.

" But why come to me at all ? " Colin demanded. " I'm only a visitor here."

" To prevent you asking awkward questions, just as I said. That was one reason. You see, Mr. Trent, except for yourself and your man Dinnet I'm here incognito. Or at least I hope so. If I hadn't come straight to you, what would have happened ? This place is about the size of a pocket-handkerchief and a new arrival can't escape notice. There's not much to talk about on an islet like this, I imagine. You and your friends would have begun to talk about me. I don't want any more of that than can be helped. You can stop it to some extent if you like. Once people think they know all about a man, they take no notice of him. If you say you've met me and that I'm a geologist, you'll be telling no lies. I am a bit of a geologist. It's my hobby. And if people hear that, they'll ask no more. Especially if you show you're bored by the subject. Whereas, if they don't know anything they'll get inquisitive. Will you do that for me?"

"No harm in that, 's far's I can see," Colin admitted. "But this island's getting a bit overcrowded with nature-students. There's an amateur bird-watcher on the premises already."

Wenlock gave a deliberate nod.

"Yes, Mr. Northfleet. Dinnet told me about him. We know something about Mr. Northfleet."

Was Colin mistaken, or was there just the faintest sub-tinge of hostility in Wenlock's tone in his reference to Northfleet? Colin could not be sure. Still, there was enough in it to give him a qualm. After all, what did he really know about Northfleet? Only what the man himself had told him, so far as recent times went. Was it possible that he, Colin Trent, had got hold of the wrong end of the stick in the affairs of Ruffa? Suppose that, under cover of all that wild yarn he had told, Northfleet was really playing a game of his own, what then? "But what game?" Colin asked himself. And then, in a flash, he had another of his scintillant ideas. Suppose Northfleet was out to get the gold-maker's secret—for himself. And then another name joined to Northfleet's in his mind: Nipasgal! Northfleet himself might be one of that gang, whoever the rest of them were. Suddenly Colin felt himself in rather deep waters. That gold brick loomed up in his mind. Should he have handed it over to Northfleet quite so readily? This detective might ask awkward questions about that affair, even although Colin had been innocent enough in his methods.

" What strikes you as curious about Ruffa? " said Wenlock, unexpectedly breaking in on Colin's rather chaotic musings.

" Curious? " Colin repeated, defensively.

" Oh, come now, Mr. Trent," Wenlock protested in an injured and disappointed tone. " This is hardly fair with me. You've been more days on this island than I've spent hours, myself; and yet I've picked up quite a number of points that I'd call curious. There's a house where some hush-hush chemical process is going on; there's an armed guard over it; there's a wolf-hound, too, to help the guard; craft of one sort and another drop in from time to time, and they land stuff or embark it; and finally there's a bird-watcher "—he smiled with a shade of contempt—" who doesn't know a heron from a cormorant by sight. Your experience must have been strange and varied if you don't call such goings-on ' curious '."

Colin realised that Dinnet must have been talking freely to the detective, much more freely than he had done to Colin himself. His respect for Scotland Yard went up. " Why," he reflected, "this man's a promoted policeman, and he talks better English than I do." Which was true, though rather humbling to Colin. He failed to realise that frequent service in the witness-box gives an unequalled training in the precise meaning and use of words. One thing was quite clear; if Dinnet had been talking, then he, Colin, had better make a clean breast of things now; otherwise he might involve himself in an awkward tangle. The only matter in which his hands were tied to any extent was his conversation with Northfleet. That, to Colin's mind, had been a confidential affair; and he could hardly bring himself to divulge its tenor.

"Well," he said at last, "I'll add an item or two to your list, if you like. Haven't been altogether blind, you know."

And with that he plunged into a detailed recital of what he had seen on the island since his arrival : the wounded man, the gold brick, the wireless cipher messages, the coming of the yacht and its sudden departure. Wenlock interjected a question occasionally ; but for the most part he was content to let Colin tell his story in his own way. The detective's face betrayed nothing of his thoughts, and Colin could not make out whether the fresh facts pleased Wenlock or not. He admitted that he had shown Northfleet the cipher and that Northfleet had unravelled it ; but he said nothing about Northfleet's tale of modern alchemy.

"A somewhat exciting time you seem to have had," was the detective's comment when Colin had finished his story. "Just one point, Mr.

Trent. You say you think these men on the yacht were foreigners. Could you be sure of that ? "

Colin considered for a moment or two, seeking definite evidence.

" Tell you one thing," he said, suddenly. " When we barged into them unexpectedly, one of the fellows bawled out : ' *Au large !* ' on the spur of the moment. Taken aback, I expect, and used his native language—second nature, in a flurry. Then he corrected himself and said : ' Sheer off ! ' That's a bit of evidence apart from the mere matter of accent."

Wenlock nodded.

" You mean he was a Frenchman, Mr. Trent ? "

" Looks like it," said Colin, cautiously. " Look here, Inspector, if there's anything crooked going on, is it an international affair ? "

" *If* there's anything crooked going on," the detective answered with equal caution, " then it *is* an international business. But I don't want to give you a false impression, Mr. Trent. I don't know whether there's anything crooked or not. That's the plain truth. Curious things have been happening, and naturally it's our business to make what we can of the matter. We can make inquiries. That's justifiable enough ; and that's why I'm here now. But I'm frank when I say that I've nothing definite against anyone on this island. I'm merely a seeker after knowledge in a small way."

" Does Scotland Yard usually detach an Inspector and send him to the Back o' Beyond to look into things ' in a small way ' ? " Colin asked shrewdly.

"A match isn't much in itself, but it might lead to trouble in a powder-magazine," Wenlock analogised.

The illustration reminded Colin unpleasantly of Northfleet's gloomy forecasts.

"Now about this gold ingot," the detective went on briskly. "You handed it over to this Mr. Northfleet, you say. In a way, that's a pity. I should like to see it."

"I could get it back from him," Colin pointed out.

Wenlock shook his head decidedly.

"That would simply set him thinking, and then he'd begin to ask questions. The fewer questions the better, Mr. Trent, if you don't mind. My arrival here is suspicious enough in itself without firing off a cannon to draw attention to it. What makes you think the thing was gold ? "

"Well, it was as heavy as lead, and when I cut into it with my knife it was uniform all through, so far as I could see. It wasn't a lead block gilded over, anyhow. It looked like gold; and there's no other soft yellow metal anything like so heavy, bulk for bulk, is there ? "

"No, I suppose you're right there," the detective conceded. "Now let's get this fairy-tale straight, Mr. Trent. This is the way it runs. I've come to you with an introduction from Mr. Craigmore. Beyond that you know nothing about me. That saves all bother about inventing a history of me. I've told you I'm

an amateur geologist with a theory about the
north-west coast-line that I'm trying to prove
by an examination of the rocks on Ruffa. You
don't understand my theory, which saves you
explanations. I'm not just of the social class
you usually mix with. That accounts for your
not asking me to the house here. I'm a fresh-
air fiend, and prefer to camp out. Further, I'm
such an enthusiast on my hobby that I bored
you stiff. That will discourage people from
taking too much personal interest in me. I can
make my own opportunities for interviewing the
inhabitants of this island when I want to. Now,
could you remember all that ? "

" Easy enough," Colin admitted.

" Then I mustn't detain you any longer, Mr.
Trent, or Mrs. Trent may begin to wonder what
you're doing. By the way, how are you going
to account for all the time spent in this palaver ? "

" Listening to a monologue on your theory of
the west coast," Colin said with a smile. " Could
hardly tear myself away from your eloquence,
and all that."

" Excellent ! " Wenlock agreed. " And now
I'd like a few more words with Dinnet, if I can
get him alone."

Colin took the hint and rejoined Jean in the
drawing-room. To his relief he was not called
upon to tell her even the smallest white lie.
Mrs. Dinnet was with her, but withdrew hurriedly
and apologetically when Colin appeared.

" Colin," said Jean, as the door closed, " poor
Mrs. Dinnet's lost her mother."

" Oh," Colin interjected sympathetically.

"She died very suddenly, it seems. Of course, she was over eighty, so it had to come some time. But still, Mrs. Dinnet's very cut up about it. Dinnet got word when he went over to Stornadale to-night. It's been a bad shock to both of them. It seems Dinnet was very fond of the old lady too."

Colin made a sympathetic noise. He had a kind heart, but his powers of expression in these cases were very limited.

"You know, Colin," Jean went on, "these Dinnets are awfully decent people. What do you think was worrying her ? She and Dinnet want to go over and look after things ; there's only an unmarried sister on the spot. But Mrs. Dinnet was in a state about leaving us here to look after ourselves for a day or two. 'Of course, ma'am, we ought to go, but if you'd rather we didn't, then I can stay and look after you while Dinnet goes by himself. I'm really terribly put out, ma'am, to think of giving you trouble.' And so on. She was quite genuinely worried, poor old thing. Of course I told her she must go. But she would hardly be per-suaded until I threatened to get cross with her. As if I couldn't manage to cook well enough to feed you for a couple of days ! The very idea ! "

"Poor old thing," said Colin. "Jolly decent of her, as you say, dear ; but as if we'd think of such a thing. Pity these old family retainers are dying out. They don't make 'em nowadays. We'll manage quite O.K. You do the cooking and I'll do the washing-up. Make a bit of a picnic of it, what ? And Dinnet can let me see how to run the electric light plant, if it needs looking after. Poor old Mrs. Dinnet. Must be feeling very sad. So unexpected and all that."

He glanced out of the window and his eye was caught by lines of white horses on the sea.

" Hope they'll get off all right. Looks as if it might be blowing up a bit before long. When are they going ? "

" First thing after breakfast to-morrow morning. Mrs. Dinnet would not hear of going to-night, when I suggested it. ' Oh, no, ma'am, we couldn't think of it—leaving you here at a moment's notice, like that ! ' And when I tried to insist she told some story about not being able to get a conveyance of any sort at Stornadale to-night, anyhow. So that clinched it and she got her own way, of course."

" She's a decent old soul. We'll manage all right. By the way, they'll be taking the motor-boat. You'll have no chance of getting off your beloved island until they come back, my young Crusoe. If you want to get to the mainland, you'll have to borrow the Heather Lodge skiff and row yourself across. Can't count on me for *that* job, I give fair and clear warning. Too much like work, for Colin."

" I shan't worry," Jean assured him.

" By the way, I suppose the Dinnets will be away for a couple of days ? There's the funeral and all that."

" I said they weren't to hurry, Colin. But I expect they'll hurry home again as fast as they can, for all that. Mrs. Dinnet really seems to think we're not fit to look after ourselves. Quite worried about it."

Colin shrugged his shoulders. If the Dinnets chose to look at things in that way, argument would do no good.

"By the way, Colin," Jean went on, "who was the man in the boat with Dinnet this evening? I happened to look out of the winddow and caught a glimpse of him as they landed. Did Dinnet tell you any more about him? Ruffa seems to be filling up. We'll be overcrowded, if people come rushing over at this rate."

"I saw the fellow himself a minute or two ago," Colin acknowledged. "He told me he was a bit of a geologist. Trying to prove some theory or other, he said. He's going to camp out. Won't disturb us at all."

"Nice?" Jean questioned.

"Not our style," Colin assured her hastily. "Likely to be a bit of a bore, if let loose."

He congratulated himself inwardly on having kept strictly within the bounds of veracity. But it seemed advisable to change the subject.

"By the way, dear, *can* you cook? I engaged you without a character, you know."

"I'm not a bit worried about my cooking capacity," Jean averred. "The real question is whether I can get you to eat what I've cooked, Colin. If you don't like it, then you can just massacre a tin. Mrs. Dinnet says there's heaps of tinned stuff in stock, and it won't do you any harm to live on it for a couple of days. I asked what there is. Five minutes with a tin-opener will give you a dinner fit to make your mouth water. Soup: Clear Mock Turtle or Thick Mulligatawny; Fish: Prawns in Aspic or Sardines in Oil; Joint: Corned Beef or Ox Tongue; Game: Wild Duck in Glass; Sweets: a Pudding Paste—whatever that means—or Pineapple Chunks. That leaves me with only the coffee to brew. Why, Colin, you'll live like a lord, my dear, and give no trouble at all. If you want potatoes, you'll have to dig and peel them yourself."

"Oh, I don't mind," said Colin placably. "In fact, it's a good notion. We can stand it for a couple of days."

"Whether we stand it or not," Jean said, getting up from her chair, "I've got to get the hang of the range or stove or whatever it is they keep in the kitchen premises. I'll go and ask Mrs. Dinnet to show it to me now and give me tips. We'll need hot water, no matter what we live on. And you'd better see Dinnet and ask about the electric light plant."

"I've a notion it's a motor-dynamo charging batteries," Colin answered. "In which case it might run for a day or so without any meddling. However, best to be on the safe side. I'll see Dinnet about it."

CHAPTER XIII

"MUST you fidget so, Colin ? "

Jean's voice betrayed a touch of irritation quite foreign to her usual temper. Gales made her nervous ; and all through the afternoon she had been listening to the bluster of squalls about Wester Voe, the swishing of the trees around the house, the intermittent rattle of the rain upon the streaming window-panes, and the periodic crash of the waves against the rocks of the shore. As she glanced up, she saw through the broad window a dull, leaden sky, across which clouds scurried in tumbled masses before the wind. With a slight shiver of mental unease she snuggled into the depths of her big arm-chair, before the fire which they had kindled for the sake of cheerfulness. At her movement, Hazel's dog Peter, stretched out on the hearth-rug, opened a sleepy eye, gazed up at his mistress, and then dozed off again, with his muzzle between his paws.

Leaving the window with its dreary seascape, Colin turned back towards the two girls by the hearth. Hazel, leaning forward with her chin propped on her hands, seemed to have dropped into day-dreams as she sat. From her expression, Colin could guess that her reverie was a pleasant one.

She had come over just after lunch, before the gale got up, and Jean had insisted on detaining her, since there was nothing to amuse her at Heather Lodge. Northfleet, uninvited by chance, had not put in an appearance ; and the trio had been forced to fill in time as best they could. It was one of those days which bring with them a feeling of petulant boredom ; but they had done the best that they could to ward it off. Jean had resolutely refused to set foot outside the house in such weather. They had played cut-throat bridge without enthusiasm, and then turned to snooker in the billiard-room, until this palled in its turn. The girls had shared the work of preparing tea and dinner, and had thus made a break in the monotony ; but Colin, left to his own devices, had found time hang heavier and heavier on his hands as the day dragged on. As host, he felt it his duty to try to " make things go," even under these unpromising conditions.

" Feeling a bit under the weather ? " he asked, sitting down on the arm of Jean's chair. " Spot of bridge ? . . . No ? Care to have a shake or two at poker dice, Hazel ? There's a set on the premises, I noticed."

Hazel lifted her head and declined with a nod which was tempered by a smile.

" No ? " Colin persisted, undeterred. " Amuse you with a little sleight of hand—a few card-tricks by Signor Colino Trento ? "

" No ! ! " said Jean vehemently.

"Something in that," Colin admitted. " You've seen 'em all before. Novelty's lacking in your case. Ah, well ! Might dress up as Father Christmas, or a ghost, or something, and give you a treat ? . . . No ? Well, I'm not proud or highbrowish. If Old Maid's your fancy, I'm game. Or Consequences. Or Heads, Bodies, and Legs. . . . No ? A bit discouraging, this reception. I tell you what's wrong with us all. No fresh air. A bit of a stroll to blow the cobwebs off ? Those in favour will say ' Aye ' in a loud clear voice."

" I'll join you, if you like," Hazel agreed, though with no marked enthusiasm. " You can drop me at Heather Lodge."

" Nonsense," Jean protested. " You've nothing to do at Heather Lodge and the evening's young yet. Let Colin go out and get wet if he wants to, Hazel. He'll come back refreshed and buck us up with all the gossip of the neighbourhood. Don't you go."

Hazel leaned back in her chair.

" To be honest, I'm not keen about going to Heather Lodge just yet," she admitted. " If you'll put up with me, Jean, I'll stay on for a while. I'm enjoying myself, no matter how I look, really."

" Then that's that, Colin. You're not going to lure Hazel out into that storm until she has to go. By the way, why not stay the night here ? It's beastly weather and you're not needed over there."

" No, that's a bit too much," Hazel decided. " It's awfully good of you, but it's no distance to go, and it would be silly to put you to trouble, since the Dinnets are away."

Jean turned to Colin.

" That's settled, then. Off you go, Colin. Don't take too long about it, though. Go up to the Heather Lodge headland and bring back the weather report. And, Colin, just switch on these lights as you go out, please. This kind of half-light gives me the creeps, with that storm on the windows."

Colin rose from the arm of the chair, drew the curtains, and went to the door. As he switched on the lights, the contrast struck him between this safe and comfortable room and the wild weather which raged outside the walls. He glanced from Jean, curled up like a kitten in the huge arm-chair, to Hazel, back again in her day-dreams. Complex world, and all that, he reflected; but here was a corner out of reach of wind and tide. The thought gave him an extra zest for his plunge into the gale. Nice to come back again out of the buffeting of squalls and the lash of the rain into this warm tranquillity.

He put on his shooting-boots, pulled a cap well down, and belted a trench-coat about him. Then, on the offchance that he might see something, he picked up his binoculars and slung them round his neck. The front door nearly wrenched itself out of his hand as he opened it; and the rain, driving before a gust, made him blink as he emerged from the loggia.

"Dirty weather, sure enough," was his mental comment. "Just as well these girls didn't come out. No fun for them, this."

At the gate he halted and looked about him in the stormy twilight. The gale had played havoc with the lupin field; swathes of the plants had been blown down, making broad gaps in the blue. Down below him great waves were bursting among the skerry rocks, spouting huge spray-fountains as they broke. The roar of wind and rain, deadened within the house, resounded now like distant artillery. Colin enjoyed a good storm : the feel of the wind beating about him like a live thing, the thrill of the rain driving into his face, and the tumult of wind and water in his ears.

He had meant to go down to the jetty, and from that point of vantage watch the lashing of wind and tide upon the coast ; but, as he gazed, a burst of spray rose from a breaking wave and fell heavily, drenching the pier-top with tons of water. Evidently that was not the post for him. His sensations there might cost more than they were worth.

He turned his back to the wind and followed the path through the field of lupins in the direction of Heather Lodge. Up on the headland he would get the best view that could be had. The Heather Lodge skiff, he noted, had been carried up the beach far out of danger.

Among the heather beyond the lupin field he had to pick his steps. The wind was unsteady and intermittent : fierce squalls were followed by sudden calms. Like the wind, the rain came in gusts, sometimes stinging his ears and driving past him in clouds across the slope, at others falling almost gently on the heather.

" Don't envy Northfleet," Colin reflected as he trudged along. " All right to be here in the thick of it. O.K. to be behind a good stout house-wall. But in that shieling he gets the worst of it, both ways : all the draughts and none of the comfort."

Then it occurred to him that someone must be even worse off than Northfleet in this weather : the detective, camping out on the moor. Colin had an impulse to seek out Wenlock and invite him to take shelter at Wester Voe. No tent could ever stand up to this gale. Further consideration led him to put this charitable notion aside. If Wenlock wanted shelter he knew where to find it. Colin could hardly be expected to wander over the hill-sides on the offchance of running across him.

He climbed the headland, where the wind blew even more fiercely, and sat down on an outcropping rock to take in the panorama. A blink of angry light fell on the sea from a rift in the cloud-banks, and Colin could see the white horses, rank behind rank, in endless advance from out of the mists which hid the horizon. Here and there a squall raised a cloud of spindrift, an acre or two in extent, and drove it swiftly over the furrowed sea like some fast-moving wraith. Down below the waves surged and thundered upon the skerry, churning up sheets of foam, which drifted into the bay and whitened its waters. Suddenly the wind fell and grew steadier. The rain ceased, and Colin could see more clearly, now that its veil was withdrawn.

All at once his eye caught a dark speck out on the waste of tossing water : something hidden at times by spray which broke over it, but reappearing as the waves passed by. He lifted his binoculars and stared intently, unconsciously rising to his feet to get a better view. In the field of his glasses he saw a black motor-boat, larger than the Wester Voe craft but smaller than the Heather Lodge supply-vessel. It was making heavy weather; the waves seemed to be dashing over it, and at times Colin's heart came to his throat as it vanished in a cloud of spume. It seemed to carry a crew of six; and from the vague glimpses which he caught, most of them appeared to be baling hard.

"Fairly catching it, out there," was Colin's comment. "Shouldn't care to be aboard that boat just now. Silly owls! Why don't they get down into the lee of Ruffa, instead of barging out yonder into the thick of it? Lucky for them the wind seems to be dropping."

The tail of his eye caught a movement beside him, and he turned to find the muffled-up figure of the detective approaching.

"See that boat out there?" Colin asked, pointing as he spoke. "Here! Take the glasses."

He unslung his binoculars and passed them to Wenlock.

"Over yonder, see?"

The detective put up the glasses, fiddled for a moment with the focusing, and then swept the grey waste below him.

"I see them now, quite plain," he reported. "The wind seems to be going down, out yonder, but they're baling hard. Now they're coming round. I shouldn't care to risk that, myself, with a following sea. They might be swamped

at any minute. Now they've got her head round
and they're coming this way."

He passed the glasses to Colin, who gazed in
his turn.

"Making for the bay," he commented, peering
out into the failing light. "Must be mad, surely.
Never get through that skerry channel in
weather like this, unless they know the coast
well. Even then it's taking a bigger chance than
I'd care about myself. . . . By Jove ! . . . No,
they're all right still, but a few more waves like
that might kill the engine and leave 'em scuppered. . . . Damn fools, they must be. Why
don't they run for shelter ? "

As the minutes passed the wind dropped more
and more. The black hull of the motor-boat
crept doggedly shoreward in safety, though
Colin marvelled at the courage or ignorance of
the men aboard her. Time and again it seemed
nothing short of a miracle that she escaped
swamping. At last the wind fell till there was
a comparative calm, and the motor-boat's crew
evidently decided to take the risk of running the
channel. On she came, riding up on the
advancing waves as they passed her, or falling
almost out of sight into the trough as the crest
went by. Colin's excitement grew as he watched.
There was no need of the glasses now ; the boat
was close in. They could see the balers at work
and the helmsman braced at the wheel.

"By Jove ! They've done it ! " Colin ejaculated with a gasp of relief.

For a few moments the boat had been almost
hidden from the watchers by the clouds of

spray which dashed about it from the rocks, but now it rode clear out of the jaws of the channel and into the bay. It neared the jetty.

"Look!" Wenlock exclaimed involuntarily.

A sudden squall caught the vessel, drove her off her course, and dashed her against the end of the pier just as she was about to round it into safety.

"Stove in! She's done for!"

With a shudder of sympathy, Colin saw the little human figures in frenzied movement: struggling, scrambling, leaping to the stone-work of the jetty in a desperate effort to gain a safe foothold before the next wave came upon them. Five of them were successful. Colin caught his breath as the sixth, too late in his jump, fell short and vanished in the boiling waters as the wreck of the motor-boat drifted clear of the pier-end and went down. Then, as he watched in impotent compassion, a wave lashed across the jetty and hid the survivors in its foam. When the smother cleared, Colin counted only four figures. It was almost incredible to him that two men had been swept out of existence in a time which he could count in heart-beats. Suddenly he was galvanised into action.

"Come on!" he cried to the detective. "Run!"

He had no very clear idea in his mind except that help was needed and that it was shameful to stand there, an idle spectator. But Wenlock, who had been watching intently through the binoculars, checked him with a gesture.

"Not much use," he said coolly. "That wave washed one of them against a stanchion before it swept him over. I saw his head hit it. There's no hope for a stunned man in that kind of water, Mr. Trent. The other fellow—the one who missed his jump—never turned up on the surface again, so far as I saw. I guess the boat crushed him. They may drift ashore on the sands, down there——"

He broke off in surprise, then continued:

"Well, their mates don't seem to bother much about them. Look!"

The four survivors had made a dash to the landward end of the jetty; but they did not stop there, as Colin expected they would when they reached shelter. Instead, all four raced up the rude stairway which led to Wester Voe.

"Gone for ropes?" he suggested.

"It doesn't take four men to borrow a rope," the detective said sceptically. "Why don't some of them stand-by, in case their mates turn up and need help? Blind funk, if you ask me, Mr. Trent. It takes some men like that, at times."

Colin was still quivering with the excitement of the disaster, and to him the detective's cool psychological reflections seemed wholly ill-timed.

"Come on!" he repeated. "May need help of some sort, these fellows. Broken bone or what not. And there are only two girls in the house. You know something about first aid, I s'pose? Come on!"

Wenlock unslung the binoculars and handed them back to Colin.

" Better run for it," he agreed, briefly.

The wind had died down again to a steady breeze, which made progress easier than the earlier squalls, and the rain had almost stopped. For a minute or two Colin ran with his attention fixed on Wester Voe; but as they skirted the descent to the bay a fresh idea crossed his mind.

" Look here ! " he said. " It's just on the cards one of these poor devils may be washed up on the sands and need help. You go on to the house. I'm no good there. Couldn't put a broken arm in splints if I tried. Tell my wife I sent you. I'll go down to the beach and see if there's anything I can do. If not, I'll follow on. Right ? "

" Very good," said the detective, without slackening his pace.

Colin diverged to the left, halted on the edge of the descent, and peered out over the water in the hope of seeing some sign of a human form. A sullen dusk had fallen, and he found his range of vision narrowed down in comparison with that which he had a few minutes before. He could see nothing that looked like a body in the waves ; but to make sure he climbed down the declivity to the sands and ran hither and thither along the strand where the foam-drift lay thick at the edge of the water. It did not take him long to realise his mistake in tactics. From sea-level he could see no distance over the tumbling waves. He left the beach and climbed back to the path above once more. But even from this vantage-point he could detect nothing. The skerry thundered and threw up ghostlike pillars of spray in the half-light; intermittent waves broke on the jetty. But in the bay there was no sign of any survivor. Wenlock had been right in his reading of the situation.

Against his will, Colin at last recognised the hopelessness of waiting where he was. At Wester Voe he might be of some use; here he was serving no purpose. Reluctantly he turned away and ran along the path towards the house. As he did so, from ahead of him there came down the wind a sound which made him pull up in his tracks and strain his ears. Then, almost immediately, a second followed: an unmistakable pistol-crack. And, close upon it, clear in a lull of the wind, the scream of a girl in sheer terror.

Colin in a subterranean passage was one person; Colin above ground and in an emergency was a very different creature. He dashed off again in the direction of the cry, forcing his passage through the wind-blown heather, his mind filled with only one idea: to reach Wester Voe and protect Jean from whatever might be threatening her. That shrill, inarticulate cry had carried no personality with it, only horror and dismay; but he knew it for Jean's voice, and at its message his throat thickened with anger and apprehension. Whoever had drawn that cry from her would have to pay for it to the full, if Colin could manage it.

He broke out of the heather-path and was crossing the narrow belt of grass between it and the lupin field when an urgent voice made him pause in his stride.

" Pull up, you fool ! " it said. " They've got me. You can't do anything. Wait ! "

Colin halted in his tracks. Now that memory had time to work, he recognised Wenlock's intonation, though the voice was changed by pain.

" Lie down ! Quick ! Don't let them see you."

Colin obeyed involuntarily, and crept on hands and knees in the direction of the detective.

" What is it ? " he demanded. " I can't wait. I must get to the house. My wife's there. I heard her crying out."

" Get under cover," Wenlock ordered. " Have you got a gun in your pocket ? . . . No ? Then you can't do anything. They shot me on sight and they'd pick you off too, if you let them know you're here."

" Who ? "

" Your split-lipped friend. He's back again, with a gang like himself. I blundered right into them on my errand of mercy "—even through the pain Colin recognised the irony of the tone— " and your acquaintance pulled his gun on me instanter. It got me in the shoulder. We'll have to get out of this. They'll be hunting for us in two ticks, I guess, though I tried to pretend they'd done for me with the second shot.

" Sorry," said Colin, wholly ignoring Wenlock's advice. " You'll have to look after yourself just now. I've got my wife to look after. And there's another girl there, too."

" Have some sense," the detective pleaded, in an exasperated whisper. " They'll shoot you as soon as they see you. What better will your wife be for that ? Reinforcements are what we need, and you must beat them up. I can't, in this state. It's the only chance, I tell you. The people at Heather Lodge have pistols. Get help from there."

The cold common sense of this overcame Colin's resistance, but only after a struggle. The thought of Jean at the mercy of these scoundrels —whoever they were—dominated his mind and impelled him to choose direct methods ; but reason, in the end, forced him to see that Wenlock's plan was the only one possible. Without fire-arms, he was helpless ; and except for the Heather Lodge armoury Ruffa held no weapons outside the Wester Voe gun-room.

The detective sat up with a groan of pain.

" We'll need to get out of here at once. You crawl ahead and I'll try to follow. If I drop out, then go ahead yourself. Don't bother about me."

For a time they crept from cover to cover until at last they reached a safe distance among the heather.

" Who are these fellows ? " the detective demanded. " Can you make it out ? "

" Nipasgal," said Colin curtly, after a moment's thought.

" Nipasgal ? " Wenlock repeated uncomprehendingly. Then apparently he recalled Colin's narrative of events. " Oh, you mean the people who were mentioned in that cipher wireless ? The gang Leven was on the look-out for ? Likely enough. All the more chance of recruiting the Heather Lodge lot to help you, then. You'd better hurry off there now, Mr. Trent. There isn't any time to waste. I'll follow as best I can. I seem to have lost a lot of blood and can't keep up with you. Go now."

Colin needed no further orders. He was burning to do something active. He wanted to feel that he was really moving to Jean's help, instead of standing by inactive and impotent. That terror-stricken cry lingered in his ears and filled him with the gravest fears. With a last reluctant glance at Wester Voe, he turned his back and set off through the rain and dusk, making for Heather Lodge. Even if the people there denied him their assistance, they could hardly refuse him a pistol. That would give him at least a sporting chance when he returned to Wester Voe ; for return he must—and soon—if Jean was to be rescued from the hands of these scoundrels.

Then, as he sped along, a fresh thought occurred to him. Northfleet's position in the scheme of things was still obscure. If he were hand in glove with the Nipasgal lot—as Colin had once suspected—then the soundest plan would be to enlist his help at once. He could hardly refuse it, and his influence might do the trick. If, on the other hand, he had no connection with these gunmen, Hazel was in their hands as well as Jean, and Northfleet would have the best of all reasons for coming to Colin's aid. Either way, Northfleet would be useful and a surer ally than the Heather Lodge people. And once Northfleet was enlisted they could both go to Heather Lodge and get weapons. Old Leven, no matter what kind of person he was, would be bound to help them for the sake of his niece.

At the thought of these reinforcements Colin felt a slight encouragement. He quickened his pace as he turned in the direction of the shieling. Soon he was panting and scrambling among the heather of the watershed. But at the back of his mind there was the dreadful thought that perhaps already he was too late. The callousness with which the survivors of the landing-party had abandoned their friends to their fate without an effort to help or even a sign of interest, had thrown a flood-light on the character of the Nipasgal company. Only sub-human beasts could have behaved like that. And Jean was in their hands now.

As he topped the rise Colin saw a light burning in the shieling. At least his detour had not been in vain. Northfleet must be there. He gathered himself together and raced down the farther slope, heedless of risks on the broken ground. Once, losing his foothold, he fell headlong and rose with blood oozing from his cheek. Now he was on the grassy strip between heather and sea, with clear going before him. He gathered himself together for the last lap.

A few seconds later, panting, dishevelled, blood-stained, and with fear for Jean's safety tearing at his heart, he beat frantically on the locked door of the shieling.

CHAPTER XIV

A CHAIR was roughly pushed back within the shieling, the key grated in the lock, and Northfleet appeared, propping the half-open door against the wind with his foot.

"What's up ? " he demanded curtly, as he caught sight of Colin's face.

Colin was in no condition to give a coherent account of his experiences.

"Gang of gunmen landed on Ruffa," he gasped disjointedly. "Up at Wester Voe now. Shot the detective. Got Jean and Hazel in their hands ; they were alone in the house. Jean screamed ; I heard her. Lord knows what's happening up there. Wenlock wouldn't let me risk going. We need guns for the job. It's the Nipasgal lot, I think : the gang in the cipher message."

At the sight of Northfleet's amazed expression, one of Colin's shreds of hope vanished. It was plain as print that Northfleet knew nothing about the raid. He had no connection with Nipasgal.

"Have you a pistol ? " Colin demanded, turning to the other alternative in his mind.

Northfleet motioned him to enter ; slipped on a coat ; went to a drawer and pulled out an automatic pistol which he dropped into one pocket ; loaded the other with several boxes of cartridges, and some loose ammunition.

"We must go up to Heather Lodge and get them to help," Colin continued breathlessly.

" Right ! " said Northfleet, speaking for the second time. "Come on. And tell me the details as we go, if you've enough breath left. We can't stand here chattering."

He ushered Colin out with another gesture, and they set off at their best pace up the slope towards Heather Lodge. Colin was hard put to it to find breath to amplify his tale ; but bit by bit he managed to convey to Northfleet all that he himself knew of the episode. As he told it, he had the feeling that ages had elapsed since the events occurred. Time seemed to have become distorted under the emotional strains through which he had passed. Northfleet made few interruptions : a sharp question from time to time, to clear up some incident. When Colin had been pumped dry, Northfleet dismissed the past without comment and turned to the immediate future.

" Four of them survived. Against that we may rake up ourselves—two—and the Heather Lodge guards—that makes four—and perhaps Leven's assistant—five in all. Leven's not likely to be much good ; and you say this detective's knocked out and useless. H'm ! Are you any sort of a shot with a pistol, Trent ? "

" I know how to fire either a revolver or an automatic. Can reload it, I mean. But I'm no crack shot."

" Close thing, then, at the best. These fellows seem to be the real gunman brand, if they shoot on sight. Four of them. Against that, I'm a fair shot myself ; Natorp and Zelensky are first-class, from all I've heard ; you're not much good ; and we can neglect Leven and the other fellow. The odds aren't in our favour, and that's a fact."

This cool reckoning up of chances came as a cold douche to Colin. Thinking only in numbers, he had put the odds as six to four against the gunmen and had counted on a speedy and certain victory. Now, however, it looked as though the actual superiority lay with the invaders. His heart sank at the thought. The fate of the two girls hung on the chance of a swift turning of the tables ; but the facts warranted no optimism in that respect.

He wasted no breath in talking, once his tale was told ; and Northfleet, on his side, remained grimly silent. They topped the ridge and were able to look down over the southern shore of Ruffa. To their right, Wester Voe was dark, save for one window on the upper floor.

" What room's that ? " Northfleet demanded.

" Jean's bedroom," said Colin, with a gulp. " Can't see the public rooms from here. All on the other side of the house except the dining-room, and it's dark."

" I remember that."

On the other side of the bay people were astir in Heather Lodge, for lights glowed in more than one window. Colin and Northfleet spent no time in further survey, but set off down the slope at their best pace. Colin had got his breath again during the brief pause. Now, driven by his fear on Jean's account, he made rather better time than his companion over the broken ground of the descent. It mattered little to him if he risked his neck in the race against time. North-fleet—equally spurred by the thought of Hazel's peril—went with more caution. A twisted ankle or a broken leg might mean the shattering of any chance of rescue, since already the odds were against them. To his mind, it was better to lose a few seconds in order to make arrival a certainty.

Colin, having gained on the down-slope, was well ahead of Northfleet when he reached level ground. Without waiting for his companion, he dashed off towards the Heather Lodge lights, and in a minute or two he reached the boundary wall. Abruptly, from a little ahead of him broke out the harsh wail of a Klaxon horn, rising far above the noises of wind and rain. Then he felt his ankle catch on something; he tripped, failed to recover, and came down heavily on his face as a brilliant flare illumined the ground about him. As it died away he heard Natorp's voice :

" Hands up ! "

Something in the tone kept Colin from protest. He scrambled to his feet and held his hands above his head. His ear caught the noise of quick steps behind the wall. Evidently the Klaxon had called up reinforcements for the guard at the gate.

" Who are you ? " demanded Natorp sharply. " No funny business now."

" Trent, of Wester Voe. There's another man with me. I must see Mr. Leven or Mr. Arrow, or whatever he calls himself. At once. His niece is in the hands of a lot of scoundrels at Wester Voe. Hurry, man. Don't waste time."

"Come ten steps forward," Natorp ordered impassively. "Keep your hands up."

Colin had the sense to see that protest was useless. He began to advance as directed.

"The other man keep back," Natorp added in a loud voice.

As he came up, Colin could see very dimly the outline of Natorp's figure in the gloom. Then a pistol-barrel was thrust against his head and he was hustled unceremoniously through the gate by a second man. A flash-light dazzled him for a moment as his captor examined him.

"Ziss is all right," a second voice announced.

Colin gathered that he was in the hands of Zelensky.

"Now you—the other man—you come forward with hands up," Natorp directed. "Mind the trip-wire," he added considerately.

In his turn Northfleet was brought inside the garden and examined under cover of the wall. Evidently the guards had no intention of disclosing their position by using the flash-light in the open. Natorp and Zelensky held a brief conversation, in German Colin thought. At the end of it, Zelensky turned to his captives.

"You want to see ze boss? Zen komm zis way."

Shepherding them before him, he led them off the path and by a circuitous route up to the front door. Evidently trip-wires had been planted freely inside the grounds.

"In zere," their guide ordered, pointing to the door of a room with the barrel of his pistol. "And no larks. No fonny business. Or I get cross."

The gross jocosity of Zelensky's tone in no way veiled the reality of the underlying threat.

Colin turned the handle and entered a sitting-room which had all the appearance of being furnished with discards from Wester Voe. Everything in it was good of its kind; but no one had left the mark of a personality upon it. Those who had lived in it had been mere birds of passage, people who had rented it for a summer and given it none of the character which a permanent abode acquires from its owners.

By the hearth sat a small, dark-moustached man, who at Colin's sudden entry started nervously. Colin ignored him and turned to the other occupant, who was lounging against the tall mantelpiece with his hands in his jacket-pockets. A big, loosely-built man, he looked larger than he actually was, owing to the slack cut of the grey lounge suit he wore. Colin recognised him as Leven by the peculiar tilt of his eyebrows, which Dinnet had once described. But in a vague way Leven reminded him of someone else. For an instant he was puzzled; then it flashed across his mind that the chemist bore a not-too-distant resemblance to Tenniel's drawings of the Mad Hatter. The unruly wisps of hair on the temples, the heavy-lidded eyes, the curve of the predatory nose, the two big projecting front teeth, the cut-away chin: all were there. But instead of the mild Hatter of his childhood's reading, Colin saw before him a ruthless egotist. One glance was enough to tell him that Northfleet had exaggerated nothing.

in his description of Leven's character. Here was a man who would move under the springs of self-interest alone.

Leven straightened himself up as Colin entered, and stared at his visitor with pale-blue eyes which betrayed nothing of his thoughts.

"Ziss is Trent. From Vester Foe," Zelensky explained abruptly. "And a friendt of his. Zey have somezing to tell you."

Leven wasted no breath on conventional openings.

"Well, what is it? What is it?" he asked impatiently, like a man interrupted in some important work by a child's intrusion.

Colin was too overwrought to resent the rudeness of this reception. He broke into a concise account of what he had seen since he left Wester Voe. Leven listened, but his first sign of interest came when Colin mentioned the man from Scotland Yard.

"I'd like to know what he's doing here."

"I don't know. He didn't tell me," Colin assured him irritably, and continued his tale.

When he had finished, Leven clicked his tongue once or twice as though in vexation; but otherwise he made no comment. Colin was aghast at this lack of response.

"Don't you understand?" he demanded. "Your niece is in the hands of these scoundrels at this moment. So is my wife. Have to act quick, if we're to be any use."

Leven's heavy lids drooped a little over his fishy eyes.

"I think my niece is very well able to look

after herself, Mr. Trent," he said phlegmatically. " I don't know your wife."

Colin lifted his hands in a gesture of exasperation.

" That's rubbish," he said bluntly. " Two girls are helpless against four men, even if the men weren't armed. We're wasting time. You can't sit here, twiddling your fingers, with this sort of thing going on. Besides, it's you who've brought on this trouble. I'm not responsible for these people coming here. Neither's Northfleet. They must have come on your account. They're out for you. I know a bit more than you think."

Leven stepped back a pace and set his shoulders against the mantelpiece in what was evidently a favourite attitude.

" I don't admit that," he answered. " Still, even if it's as you say, I've nothing to worry about. I've laid my plans. You didn't take us by surprise, you may have noticed. I can meet these people on ground I've chosen—here. Am I to disarrange everything and put myself at a disadvantage because a fool of a girl blunders into a mess ? Girls aren't so important as all that, Mr. Trent."

Colin's anger choked him at this callous estimate. Before he had time to reply Northfleet broke in :

" Look at it reasonably, if you like, Professor Leven. There are four of these fellows ; and there are four of you here. You might win if it comes to shooting ; or again you might not. I'm a fair shot myself ; Trent can hold a pistol.

Isn't it worth your while to buy our support at a price ? If Trent and I act alone we'll get knocked out and you'll have thrown away two useful allies. If we all act in common we've a sporting chance."

From Leven's expression it was plain that he was more impressed by this argument that by Colin's appeals. He lifted his head and glanced across at Zelensky, as though asking his opinion.

" Zat is sound sense," the mercenary agreed. " Neffer difide your forces w'en zey are small."

Leven seemed to consider the question for a moment or two longer.

" I'll buy you then," he said, with a shrug which might have meant contempt or vexation. " I suppose your price is some Don Quixote act—rushing to the aid of beauty in distress," he added, with a sneer. " I don't think the girls will come to any serious harm ; these fellows won't cut their throats. Have it your own way. But I hope you'll turn out to be worth buying. I laid my plans for defence, not offence ; and you're making hay of all my arrangements. I suppose you won't change your minds, though, even now ? "

" No," said Northfleet decisively.

Leven lifted his cold eyes and scrutinised Northfleet for a moment.

" I don't suppose you're doing this out of pure altruism ? " he questioned with an obvious cynicism.

" No," answered Northfleet. " I'm doing it on your niece's account pure and simple."

Colin was surprised to see Zelensky throw a

peculiar glance at Northfleet. What it meant he could not interpret. Northfleet, apparently, did not notice it.

"Ah! Very pretty," Leven commented on Northfleet's admission.

A blast on the Klaxon horn startled Colin. At the sound of it, the black-moustached assistant made a convulsive movement. Zelensky slipped swiftly out of the room, and they could hear him clatter along the parquet of the hall. Leven seemed the least perturbed of them all. He heaved himself forward from the mantelpiece and stood alert on the hearthrug, his hands still in his jacket-pockets, listening intently, though the wind drowned all but the loudest sounds.

"If that's them," said Colin ungrammatically, "you'd better fork out a pistol for me. I haven't got any. You've got a spare one, I s'pose, with all your preparations."

Leven nodded.

"Get him an automatic, Beeston," he said to the dark-moustached man, who rose obediently and left the room. In a few moments he returned with a pistol and some ammunition, which he handed over to Colin. As Colin took it he noticed that Beeston's hand was trembling violently.

"Good Lord!" Colin reflected. "That beggar's in a blue funk. He won't be much good if it comes to the pinch, when he's in this state already."

They heard Zelensky's lumbering tread in the hall, accompanied by a light pattering. The door opened, and Hazel's dog Peter rushed into the room and began to frisk round Leven's legs. Zelensky followed with a paper in his hand.

" Zis vas tiedt to ze dog's collar," he explained as he handed it to Leven.

Leven opened out the paper carefully, since it had been badly wetted by the rain. As he did so, an expression of approval crossed his face.

" I told you she could look after herself," he said in a tone which suggested that he was entitled to credit for this. " She's written it in Morse. I don't suppose these fellows could read it, even if it had fallen into their hands."

He perused it slowly, evidently finding some difficulty in deciphering the code. Then he handed it across to Northfleet. Colin leaned over and read it also. The message began with carefully-inscribed dots and dashes ; but at the end the writer evidently had grown more agitated and the signs were hastily dashed down. Between that and the moisture on part of the sheet Colin had some difficulty in making out the sense :

" *We are shut up in Jean's room. Four armed men are here. Jean saw them shoot Colin. Then they hustled us up here. Jean is nearly out of her mind with shock. We can't escape. Patrol goes round house. Shall lower Peter out of window with this. Send help. They look ugly. I'm afraid of them. Tell Cyril Northfleet at shieling. He'll help. Come soon.*"

Here the script became wild and straggling, betraying only too plainly the consternation of the writer ;

" Someone is trying our door. Locked. Message. Lights. Hazel."

As Colin deciphered the message, a tumult of emotions swept his mind : bewilderment, bitter anxiety, gloomy foreboding of worse to come, vengefulness, and an anger all the more furious because of its impotence. Rage finally swallowed up all the others, a rage so hot that it left him quivering. In his mind he had a picture of Jean, dishevelled, terrified, struggling vainly in the grip of some sinister ruffian, crying for the help which he could not bring her. And the other brutes looking on, gloatingly. . . . He made an involuntary gesture at the thought.

Colin's anger was of the kind which flares up and betrays itself on the surface. Northfleet was of the more dangerous type, which grows cooler as its rage increases. He read the missive without a quiver, stooped to reward the dog with a pat, and then, ignoring Leven and the mercenary, turned to Colin.

" Of course Jean didn't know Wenlock was about. When she saw him shot she must have imagined it was you, coming back from your walk, that they had intercepted. Better relieve her mind at once ? "

" How ? " Colin demanded uncomprehendingly. " If they're patrolling about the house nobody can get near enough to give a message."

Northfleet picked up the paper and pointed to the last incoherent part of it.

" Don't you see what she means ? There's electric light in the room, and the window faces this way. I taught her Morse. She means to send flash-signals, obviously. She's kept her head through it all."

Colin's emotions had prevented him from analysing the message so minutely. A general impression was all that he had drawn from it. But Northfleet's coolness had its reaction upon him, and he even drew some encouragement from it. Northfleet and he were in the same boat : Hazel was in the same danger as Jean. And then, by a curious trick of memory, he heard a mental echo of Jean's own verdict on Northfleet : " He looks so—well, so dependable." It was something, on this damned island, to have somebody on whom one could rely.

Northfleet had turned to Leven.

" There's some room upstairs that looks towards Wester Voe ? Show me it."

Leven evidently disdained to act as guide.

" Take them up, Beeston," he ordered.

" I want a lamp too," Northfleet said.

The assistant brought an incandescent paraffin lamp from another room and then led the way upstairs, followed by Colin and Northfleet.

" This looks out almost directly on Wester Voe," he said, opening the door of a bedroom.

" Then you can clear out," said Northfleet, taking the lamp from him. " No need to have that fellow reading our messages," he added when the door was closed. " Phew ! He *is* in a funk, poor devil ! We can count *him* out, so far as help's concerned."

Colin had walked straight to the window and gazed out towards Wester Voe. The light still shone from Jean's room; but it disappointed Colin, who had hoped to see some kind of signalling. The girls must have known how long it would take the dog to find its way home, and he had expected that they would begin to send a message as soon as possible.

" See nothing ? " asked Northfleet at his elbow.

" Hazel's clever. Lend me these binoculars."

Colin unslung them and Northfleet gazed through them at the yellow-lit window in the distance.

" The curtains aren't drawn," Colin said, as he stared into the night. " See anything in the room ? "

" Clever girl ! " Northfleet ejaculated. " She's thought of that. Take the glasses, Trent. If she'd signalled with the room lights, that damned patrol would have spotted what she was doing. She's kept the main lights on, and under cover of that she's signalling with a reading-lamp at the back of the room. You can pick it up with the glasses."

Colin glued his eyes to the distant lights and read off the repeated dots and dashes of the code:

$$\bullet \; \bullet \; \bullet \; \text{—} \; \text{—} \; \text{—} \; \bullet \; \bullet \; \bullet$$

While he watched, Northfleet had been busy. By placing the lamp on the floor and pulling the mirror of the dressing-table into a certain position, he improvised a crude heliograph which could be worked by swinging the glass up and down on its axis.

" Stand clear of the window," Northfleet ordered when he had finished.

He began signalling slowly and Colin read off the flickers :

— — — · — — — — · —

"She replies ' *M K* '," he reported. "Thank the Lord ! They must be all right or she wouldn't be able to send. Tell her I'm all sound, will you ? Jean, you know—— "

Northfleet signalled again and Colin saw Hazel's reply :

"*So glad. Don't send too much. They might see. No one has come near us since they found door locked. We've barricaded it now. Some time ago heard them moving about. Now all quiet except patrol under window. Cannot escape. Did Peter come ?* "

Northfleet answered briefly, and added a request which made Colin fasten his gaze on the window. The thin curtains were drawn and suddenly between them and the glass appeared two tiny figures, sharply outlined against the translucent background. Colin looked hungrily at the smaller of them ; then, recollecting himself, he passed the glasses to Northfleet so that he might see Hazel. The taller figure waved its hand with a courageous gesture. Then both stepped back from the window.

"Just as well to be sure there was no hanky-panky," growled Northfleet. "With only the signals to go on, we might have been diddled by that gang, if they had the wit to spot what Hazel had done. That's why I asked them to show themselves."

Colin repossessed himself of the binoculars and read off a fresh message :

"*Can you help, Cyril? Jean's feeling the strain.*"

Ere they could frame a reply the raucous shriek of the Klaxon horn broke out in the darkness.

"Enter the gunmen," said Northfleet between his teeth. "Here, Trent. Send '*Will call you again.*' Don't say more. No use alarming them."

He drew his automatic from his pocket and raced down the stairs into the hall. Colin followed him in a few seconds, after having transmitted his signal.

CHAPTER XV

COLIN, his nerves alert for the first sound of the expected attack, was amazed to find no stir in house or garden. The door of the sitting-room was ajar; and when he pushed it open he found Northfleet, Leven, and the assistant there, in attitudes which suggested no preparation for immediate action.

"Come in, Trent," Northfleet invited. "They've sent an embassy. They'll be with us in a moment. I think we'd better scatter ourselves about the room and not stand in a clump. No use trusting them."

At the word "embassy" Colin's heart gave a leap. That implied bargaining of some sort, he assumed; and he would be no party to a bargain which did not include safeguards for the two girls. What there was to bargain about he had no idea, though evidently the gunmen must intend to get something out of Leven. In any case, the coming parley would show where they stood; and an agreement would be better than open hostilities, with the chances evenly poised as they were between the two sides.

"Here are ze zhentlemen from Vester Foe," Zelensky announced in his most genial tones, as he ushered two strangers into the room.

In the leader Colin recognised the man he had found in the lupin field. Behind him, heralded by a violent sneeze, came a much smaller individual grotesquely attired in one of Colin's own suits, which hung baggily about him. Colin was conscious of a shock of red hair, a snub nose over a wide mouth with an array of bad teeth, and a pair of small, sherry-coloured eyes which shifted restlessly as their owner's gaze flickered from point to point. Remembering that Jean had been in the hands of these men, Colin felt an involuntary shudder pass over him. Each was sinister in his own way. The hare-lipped man suggested sluggish brutality; the other had the quick malignancy of an ill-tempered terrier.

"Zere vill be no fonny business," Zelinsky explained, with the air of one bestowing a benediction.

The hare-lipped man nodded and advanced a pace.

"I'm no talker. See?" he began abruptly. "No need for a lotta palaver. Which o' you's Leven?"

Leven made a gesture.

"You, eh? Well, we know about you. See? You've got the trick of making gold. Right. We've come for our share of it. That plain; And we're gonna have it. Thasso, Hawes?"

"Thasso, Leo," echoed the red-haired man.

Leven laughed unpleasantly.

"You're too late, my man. The bird's flown. I've sent away every grain I had. If you don't believe me, you can search this place from top to bottom. I shan't mind, because you'd find nothing, not a trace. It's gone, out of your reach."

The gunman seemed taken aback but not discouraged.

244

" You talk too much. See ? " he retorted seriously. " If you've sent away the stuff, what's the odds ? You can make more. We're not gonna hurry you. Take your time and make plenty. Thasso, Hawes ? "

" Thasso," confirmed the echo.

Leven made an impatient gesture.

" Do you think it's likely ? " he demanded. " Why should I ? Go and make it yourself, if you're as clever as all that. Besides, if I did it for you once, what's to hinder you from coming back and blackmailing me again and again ? "

" Nothing," said the gunman, with a grin. " You've hit it, mister. You've discovered one kind of gold-mine. We've discovered you. You're gonna be *our* gold-mine after this. See ? Thass all there is to it. Thasso, Hawes ? "

A convulsive sneeze took the place of the usual reply.

Leven paused to consider for a moment or two.

" Nothing doing," he said tersely.

The gunman seemed in no way discomposed by the answer.

" Mister," he began, in the tone of one explaining to a child. " if I held weak cards I'd get peevish with you. I would. Seein' we hold a straight flush, I'm gonna keep my rag. I can afford to. See ? Mebbe you don't know we've got two girls over at the big house. We haven't done 'em any harm—yet. ' They're as pure as the daisy in the dell ', like Harry Lauder sings. One o' them's your niece. See ? Well, mister, unless you get a gleam o' reason in the next minute or so, these girls'll suffer for it—and you can take your oath on that. See ? "

Colin made a movement which brought the eye of the gunman round to him. But before he could do anything rash Northfleet spoke out.

" Leave us to talk this over together for a minute or two," he suggested.

The leader consulted his jackal with a glance ; then he turned back to Northfleet.

" I'm gonna give you ten minutes. That do ? Right. Then there's just one thing I'm gonna say to you, mister,"—he swung round to confront Leven—" and that's straight. You see reason, or when we're done with the girls we're gonna come after you ; and we'll handle you in a way to make you wish you was dead, but we'll screw what we want out o' you. And you can kiss the Book on that, mister. Thasso, Hawes ?"

" Thasso," the jackal agreed with an air of indescribable relish. " Put you through it, we will. And proper, too."

Colin saw Zelensky give Leven a look the precise meaning of which he could not fathom. Then the mercenary stood aside to let the gunmen leave the room.

" You komm viz me," he invited them cordially. " Ve haf a little gossip togezzer to pass ze time w'ile zey make up zeir minds. All goot friendts togezzer, and no ill feelings till ze shooting begins, eh ? Zat is ze right spirit, *nicht wahr ?* "

The leader of the gunmen nodded in rather gloomy acquiescence as he passed out. The grotesque acolyte paused in the doorway and threw a mirthless grin to the company.

" Just you think," he said to Leven with an air of sinister suggestion. " If we have to set about you . . . my word ! "

He spat on the floor ; then passed out in his turn. They heard a paroxysm of sneezing followed by a muttered oath. Then the footfalls of the party receded down the hall and a door slammed.

Colin turned to Leven.

" Tried to bluff them, and it didn't come off, you see," he said contemptuously. " Now we'll talk sense for a change. You'll have to climb down and do as they wish."

" No ! " Leven answered with a coolness that was more impressive than bluster. " That's barred, my good man. Find some other way out, if you can."

" Now, look here," Colin pursued with rising temper, " my wife's at Wester Voe—in danger. You heard what they said ? Well, she and Hazel have to be got out of there, at once, no matter what it costs you. Get that clear. This trouble's all of your making. You've got to settle it. And you've got to settle it soon. Grasp that. If anything happens to my wife you'll wish you'd never been born, Mr. Leven. I mean it."

" The girls will come to no harm," Leven declared sullenly.

" That's a lie, and you know it," said Colin furiously.

Northfleet intervened again, before Leven could answer.

"Wait a moment, Trent. There *is* a simple way out."

He turned to Leven with a sardonic smile.

"Trent and I have only one interest in this affair : to get the girls back safe. These gunmen's quarrel is with you, Professor Leven. The girls are the merest pawns in the game. And they're of even less value now, owing to your peculiar attitude with regard to them. As counters in the gunmen's hands, they're worthless. Very well, then. What's to hinder Trent and myself from withdrawing our support from you in exchange for the girls ? That will leave you and your friends very much up against it. I've no moral scruples about it, and I don't suppose Trent has, either."

"Not I," said Colin. "Very smart notion."

"And what's more," Northfleet went on icily, "if that offer isn't good enough for Mr. Hawes and his pal, I'm quite prepared to go further. I'll change sides with pleasure, after what I've seen of you."

"Count me in too," Colin volunteered.

Northfleet made a gesture of acknowledgment.

"Tot that up, Professor Leven. Four gunmen and ourselves—six. Against that you and your two hired ruffians, plus Mr. Beeston here. You'd be scuppered in no time," he ended with a touch of contempt.

Leven made no reply for a long time.

"Very pretty," he admitted frankly. "You seem a practical fellow, with no nonsense about you. But," he added maliciously, "suppose you and your good friends do come out on top, what then ? I'll pay very special attention to you both if there's any shooting, you may count on that. And when you've disposed of us, you'll be left in a minority compared with the gunmen. What about the girls then ? "

" They'll be no worse off than they are now," Northfleet observed. " Better, in fact ; for while we're all busy polishing you off, Professor Leven, they can get arms from the Wester Voe gun-room. A girl with a shot-gun is safer than they are just now. I'm not much worried on that account."

" You think of everything," said Leven in mock admiration.

" That's my alternative plan," Northfleet pointed out, taking no notice of the jeer. " It lands you in Queer Street, you see. Why not be sensible ? Have you really no gold to stop their mouths with ? A little down, and a promise of more, might get us out of all this tangle. You're up against it."

Leven shook his head.

" Not so much as a pennyweight," he declared, in a tone which carried conviction. " All the last lot went off by the motor-launch."

" You've got some chemicals on hand, haven't you ? HCl, nitric, ammonia—the common stuffs ? "

Leven seemed surprised by this question, but he answered it without hesitation.

" Oh, yes, I've got a winchester or two of each in my lab."

Northfleet seemed to consider for a moment before speaking again.

" Can't you—h'm—*procure* some gold in the

course of a day or two ? ' he asked in a peculiar tone.

Leven shook his head definitely.

" No, I haven't got the materials just now. We've run out of them, and I'm waiting for fresh supplies."

Northfleet nodded as though he had expected some such answer.

" That's a pity. Well, then, there's nothing for it but to draw on my private supply."

Colin was amazed by this, and Leven's face showed that he was equally surprised.

" But there's no gold on Ruffa ! " he exclaimed.

" Oh, isn't there ? " said Northfleet ironically. " I think you're mistaken. I'll guarantee to give these fellows all the gold they want. But they'll have to wait a day or two for it."

Before they had time to question him he switched to a fresh subject.

" There's a cellar down below this, isn't there ? Have you ever been down into it ? "

" Beeston has."

" Notice anything about it ? " Northfleet asked, turning to the assistant.

" There's a trap-door in the floor of it that leads down into a sort of store-room or something, down a flight of steps," Beeston explained. " It's quite a small place, but it looks as if it may have been bigger at one time, for one of the walls is fresh. The bricks and mortar are new, I mean, as if part of the original room had been bricked up. At least, that's what I thought had been done."

Northfleet seemed much relieved by this information, though he made no comment aloud. Colin thought that he saw the idea. This sub-cellar was the terminus of the tunnel to Wester Voe. By opening it up they could gain access to the house across the bay and might thus be able to get the two girls out of the hands of the gunmen. In his excitement he almost blurted this out ; but his total distrust of Leven stopped the words at his lips.

"If I pay the piper, I call the tune," Northfleet went on in a sharper tone. "These negotiations will be carried on by me, Professor Leven. That's understood ? You'll endorse what I say, and apparently it will be your gold that we're talking about. If you don't agree—then Trent and I secede at once, and you're in the soup. There's no misunderstanding ? Very well, then. We can have these fellows back now."

"You bring them, Beeston," Leven directed.

He set his shoulders against the mantelpiece with an air of indifference which Colin could see was only a bit of good acting. The assistant left the room and soon returned, accompanied by Zelensky and the gunmen.

"I'm speaking for the three of us," Northfleet said concisely. "Professor Leven has no gold on hand. But in two days' time we can give you all the gold you want. In exchange for that, we must have three things. First of all, you'll hand over these girls, unharmed. And you'll do nothing to frighten them in the mean-while. You'll treat them courteously. Secondly,

I'm not going to carry out delicate chemical operations with an eye on the window to see if some fool's covering me with a pistol. There must be a truce while we're doing our work. And, thirdly, if the Dinnets—the people who keep house for us at Wester Voe—turn up on Ruffa, they're not to be harmed in any way. You can prevent them going off to give the alarm if you choose; that's fair. But ' no fonny business ', as our friend Zelensky puts it. Now, yes or no."

" Thassa mouthful," said the gunman leader admiringly. " You talk straight and sensible, mister. But I'm gonna put my finger on a bit where you've been too smart for my ideas. If we give up the girls, what grip are we gonna have on you, so's you'll have to do what you say ? None, says you ? No, no, mister. We'll have to think again. This is how it goes. We keep the girls till you hand over the gold. We'll not hurt 'em. We'll not frighten 'em. We'll feed 'em well and let 'em have the run of the cellar—and there's some prime stuff there, we've found. You'll get your beauties back *after* the gold's been passed over."

Colin's heart sank at this proviso, though it was obviously an inevitable one.

" Very well," said Northfleet, without arguing the point. " That's agreed."

" But, look here, mister," the gunman went on. " How much gold do we get ? Isn't there a snag there ? "

" You'll get enough to satisfy you," said Northfleet in a convincing tone. " More than

you can spend in the rest of your lives. And if
any of you thinks he hasn't got enough, he's
only to come back and ask for more."

" Straight ? "

" Straight."

" Sounds like a dream," said the gunman
suspiciously. " I'm gonna pinch myself and
wake up."

" You're a fool," said Northfleet contemptuously. " What does gold cost to a man who
can make it ? It's as easy to make a ton as an
ounce, except that it might take longer."

The tone of his voice evidently convinced the
gunman.

" You're not polite, mister," he complained.
" Still, you sound as if you meant it."

" I mean every word of it."

" Kiss the Book on it ? "

" Yes, if you want that. Can't you recognise
truth when you hear it ? "

Colin was staggered by the coolness of Northfleet's lying, for such he took it to be. These
promises could never be fulfilled. And if they
were not implemented, what hope was there of
securing the safety of the captives ? All that
Northfleet could gain was a respite of two days ;
and if the gunmen were at liberty to seize the
Dinnets when they landed, no rescue from outside could be expected within forty-eight hours.
Northfleet's procedure seemed to border on
madness, in Colin's opinion. Then the thought
of the tunnel recurred to him, and he felt
ashamed that he had not seen the point at
once. All this bargaining had only one aim :

to safeguard the girls until they could be extricated from Wester Voe via the underground passage. What a fool he had been, not to tumble to Northfleet's game immediately! He was beginning to sketch out a plan of campaign on these lines when the gunman's voice interrupted his chain of thought.

"Just in case you think of getting up to any games, we'd best straighten things out. Zelensky, you speak your piece."

The stout mercenary fingered his pistol affectionately and glanced alertly from face to face.

"I am a man of few vorts," he began, with faintly comical pomposity. "I haff had a little talk wiz zese gentlemen. Zey haff toldt me von or two facts, and I haff guessed some more. So I resign from ze service of Herr Professor Dr. Leven. Ze pay is too small. Ridiculous, really. And I associate myself viz my goot friendts here." He indicated the two gunmen with a gesture. "Ze prospects are better. Natorp, he does ze same."

He paused for a moment or two, an obviously rhetorical trick.

"Eizher way, zis leafs me on felfet. If ze goldt is O.K., zen I get my share. And if zis little speculation falls down, why—zere will be compensations. I haff long admired Miss Arrow. Very pretty. A goot little girl—— Take your hand avay from your pokket, Mr. Norzhfleet. No fonny business."

He swung his barrel round to cover Northfleet, whose face had gone white and tense.

"Zere is just von more point. I haff smashed

up ze short-wafe sender. You might have used it to get help, you see? Zome people are so treacherous, it vould surprise you to hear it. And now I haff finished. Goot night, Mr. Norzhfleet. If you do not manage to keep your vort to us, I shall not be altogezzer sorry."

He retreated backwards from the room, keeping Northfleet covered as he launched his final jeer. The two gunmen followed him without a word.

"An amusing card," said Northfleet, with white lips. "So now if it comes to 'fonny business' they're six to four. A bit awkward."

He whistled a little tune below his breath for a moment or two, as though deep in consideration. Then he turned round to Beeston.

"You'd better mount guard at the gate. Nobody will come; but it's best to be on the safe side. The Klaxon will bring you help if anything does turn up. Got your pistol? Well, go now."

Beeston showed obvious reluctance for the work, but he left the room without oral protest, and they heard him putting on his coat in the hall. The rain had ceased to lash the windows, but squalls still shook the casements from time to time, though they were less violent than before. Northfleet turned to Leven.

"You can do what you like," he said, "so long as you're ready to support that fellow at the gate, if there happens to be an alarm. He's no good. Trent, you'd better go up and let the girls know what's what. Be as optimistic as you like. We must keep them from thinking about the worst, if we can. Don't be too long over it, for fear your signals are spotted. I've got to go out for a while. Don't let that genius at the gate loose off on me on the way in again. I'll be back in less than half an hour."

" I'll see to it," Colin assured him.

He followed Northfleet into the hall and, leaving him, went upstairs. Evidently Hazel was on the look-out, for his first signal was answered immediately. He gave her a summary of the truce conditions ; and from her reply he gathered how great a relief the girls felt at the news. He sent a further encouraging message and then bade them good night.

As he came downstairs again, it occurred to him that Beeston must be uncomfortable at his isolated post. Good-naturedly, Colin decided to look him up. As he stood on the doorstep, he glanced up at the sky.

" Going to last for a while yet," was his judgment of the gale.

> *First the rain and then the wind,*
> *Halliards, gaffs, and topsails mind . . .*

Seems to be working out all right, this shot."

He walked cautiously down to the gate, picking his steps to avoid stumbling over the trip-wires. When he came near the entrance to the garden, he thought it well to give Beeston a hail. There was no answer. When Colin reached Beeston's post the assistant was gone.

" Another rat left the ship," was Colin's angry comment. " Hope the omen's wrong this shot. Wonder where the beggar's gone."

He called into the dark, but there was no reply.

"Well, he was no great catch at the best," Colin consoled himself.

He established himself in Beeston's stead, merely for the sake of feeling that he was doing something definite. He had no desire for Leven's society at any price. Leven was as repulsive to him as the gunmen themselves. Leading the life he had led—Colin remembered Northfleet's hints on that subject—Leven probably thought less of women's honour than most people. But to throw his niece to the wolves as he had proposed to do—— "A bit thick," was Colin's rather inadequate digest of his own views.

He had not been very long at his post when Northfleet returned, empty-handed, so far as Colin could see. He received the news of Beeston's defection without comment.

"Not much use bothering about the gate, now we're down to three," he decided. "If they come at all, we'll be scuppered anyhow. You'd better come inside now. I'll need some help in this job."

They re-entered Heather Lodge and stripped off their dripping Burberrys in the hall. Leven was still in the sitting-room, hunched in his favourite posture at the hearth.

"I want some tools," said Northfleet curtly. "Files, metal-cutting saws, and a pick, if you have one amongst your garden stuff. Or, if you haven't it, a hammer and a cold chisel will do at a pinch."

Leven had evidently accepted Northfleet's

leadership. He made no protest against being given orders, but went off at once to fetch the requisites. When he had left the room, North-fleet pulled from his pocket the gold ingot which Colin had given to him and which he had gone to fetch from the shieling. He studied it for a moment or two before speaking.

" That man makes my gorge rise," he said bitterly.

" Mine, too," Colin concurred. " But, I say, what are your plans ? Didn't quite catch on, I admit, when you were telling them all these lies—— "

" Lies ? " Northfleet interrupted sharply. " I told no lies. I gave 'em the literal truth. What would be the point in telling lies when the truth will serve ? I promised 'em gold, didn't I ? Well, there it is."

He held out the golden ingot.

" You promised 'em a bit more than that," Colin protested. " By the way you talked, I thought you must have discovered a new Rand on Ruffa."

" I promised them precisely what they'll get," said Northfleet with perfect seriousness. " No, I haven't time to explain it just now. We're in for a busy time, I promise you. Here's that swine coming back."

He re-pocketed the gold brick as Leven entered, carrying the tools.

" Now I want to see your lab., and the way down to your cellar," Northfleet informed his involuntary host. " After that, you'd better go upstairs and get some sleep. Trent and I are standing watch for a while. We'll rouse you when your turn comes."

As soon as Leven had gone upstairs, Northfleet led the way to the laboratory. A brief search unearthed some eighty-ounce stoppered bottles, which the chemist placed on one of the benches. Colin read the labels as they came to hand: HYDROCHLORIC ACID (Concentrated); NITRIC ACID (Concentrated); AMMONIA (Sp. Gr. 0·880). Colin's knowledge of chemistry was elementary, but he had sufficient to tell him that none of these reagents contained any trace of gold. A mixture of nitric and hydrochloric acids formed the *aqua regia* of the alchemists, that king-solvent which attacked even the noble metals. And, of course, ammonia neutralised acids. Colin, staring incuriously at a muffle furnace, did not find these facts very suggestive.

" Zelensky seems to have run true to form, from what you told me about his earlier career," he commented, as Northfleet rummaged in cupboards in search of large porcelain evaporating dishes.

" Yes. I expected something of the sort as soon as the deputation gave away the show about gold-making. Neither Zelensky nor Natorp knew what was really going on; but they were quick enough to pick up the hint when it was put in front of them. And once they saw which side of the bread the butter was on, they ratted without hesitation. It was bound to happen as soon as they had a talk with the gunmen. There was no way of preventing that."

Colin nodded rather absent-mindedly. After all, the thing was done and there was no more to be said. Then he opened a subject nearer to his heart.

" We're going to get the girls away by the tunnel, I suppose ? That's your plan ? "

Northfleet shook his head, much to Colin's surprise.

" We'd never manage it. These gunmen will be keeping an eye on the stairs, to see that the girls don't slip down and escape. That's self-evident, since they're not imbeciles. We could never get two girls downstairs, into the passage, and past those chasms before the whole pack was after us in full cry. There'd be shooting, and the girls might get hurt, even if we did get them away. No, that's no catch, Trent. Now, look here, we haven't time for chattering. There are two jobs on hand, and you can take your choice. One is to saw up this gold brick or file it down. I must have it in small pieces. The other job is to open up that tunnel by breaking through the new brick wall that Craigmore put up. Choose whichever you like. We've got to get busy. Time's the thing we can't spare."

" All right," Colin decided. " Give me the pick and I'll start on the tunnel."

The idea of breaking down the barrier appealed to him. Somehow, the removal of that wall would make him feel nearer to Jean, fanciful though the idea was.

But as he was leaving the laboratory there came a faint shout from outside the house.

"Good Lord!" Colin ejaculated in contrition as he recognised the voice. "It must be that poor devil Wenlock, the detective. I'd forgotten all about him; and he's hurt, too. I am a beast."

He was about to hurry out to help the wounded man when Northfleet stopped him.

"Get on with your job, Trent. I'll patch this fellow up. And as soon as you're finished, come and lend a hand with this filing. I want this gold to dissolve as quickly as possible."

261

THE night passed without alarm. Northfleet worked far into the morning in the laboratory, snatched some sleep, and returned to his task. Colin lay down, but found that sleep was out of the question for him. The detective, in pain with his wound, kept an unnecessary watch. Leven, apparently, slept soundly, for they heard him snoring upstairs at intervals.

During the forenoon, Colin found the enforced inactivity getting on his nerves. He wanted to be up and doing, to feel that some progress was being made towards the rescue of the captives at Wester Voe. Anxious and restless, he wandered into the laboratory with the idea of questioning Northfleet about his plans. The reception he got was sufficient to put this notion out of his head.

" For any sake, Trent, get out of here—and stay out ! " Northfleet exclaimed irritably. " I'm at a tricky stage now, and I can't afford to have my attention distracted. Sorry if I sound rude ; but I really mean it. The least thing might put the whole business in the soup. Do keep away. Take a walk up to the headland and show yourself to the girls. They'll recognise you by your walk, if they can't see your face ; and it'll assure your wife that nothing's happened to you. Wave to them if you like, but no semaphoring, remember. We don't want to set these swine thinking."

Colin was only too glad to take his colleague's advice. It would always be something : to wave to Jean and see her answering signal from the window. And, as Northfleet said, the sight of him would ease her mind about his safety and take one worry off her shoulders.

He set off, but in a quarter of an hour he was back in the laboratory.

"What is it *now* ? " snapped the chemist. "Stand back at the door, there. Don't come fussing about."

Colin resented the tone ; but his good nature reminded him that Northfleet could hardly be expected to be normal just then. He must be half-mad with anxiety about Hazel, just as Colin himself was on tenterhooks about Jean.

"Just dropped in to tell you one thing. The bloke Beeston didn't rat to the other lot. He must have been in a blue funk about them, poor devil. He went down to the beach, and managed to launch the skiff. Evidently meant to risk the sea that was running rather than be mixed up in any shooting. I found his body on the sands down below. The skiff's gone."

He halted for a moment, then added gloomily :

"That's our last boat. No chance of getting the girls away now, even if the wind went down and we could risk the passage to Stornadale."

"There are the rockets at Wester Voe," said Northfleet.

"Get help, you mean ? That's why you wanted the passage re-opened ? Of course, the rocket-case is just alongside the secret door."

"Oh, get out of here," Northfleet adjured him.

" I simply can't have you lounging about while
I'm at this job. That's a fact, Trent. Please
shift yourself."

" All right," said Colin sympathetically. " I
know how you feel. I must do something, though."

" Then scratch up some lunch, if you can.
I don't suppose Leven will condescend to make
himself useful. And there's another thing. See
if you can find some garden-stakes and cut them
to a six-foot length. Half a dozen will be enough
and less might do. But get a couple if possible."

" I'll see to it," Colin assured him, glad to
have something to do which promised to be
useful ; though what part garden-stakes could
play was beyond his imagination.

" Say six foot six inches, just to be on the
safe side," Northfleet revised.

Colin noted this. Then, irrevelantly, he remarked :

" The Dinnets won't come back to-day.
Sea's still too rough for the motor-boat. And,
naturally, they don't know there's anything
amiss here."

" Just as well," Northfleet commented.
" They'd only be a complication for us."

Colin saw signs of impatience in Northfleet's
face, so he hastened to withdraw.

" Well, I'll fix up these stakes and then hunt
up some grub."

" And, by the way, just see if there's any
motor-grease on the premises," Northfleet suggested as an afterthought. " They may have a
tin or two : supplies for the motor-boat or
something."

Colin went off on his errands, feeling less depressed now that he actually was making himself useful.

Their lunch was a scratch one, and the conversation did little to brighten it. Colin had given Wenlock a sketch of events; and the detective shared his distaste for Leven, apparently, since he never addressed a word to him. Northfleet was silent, evidently deep in thought. Colin himself had no great desire to say anything. As time wore on with nothing to show for it he was growing more and more anxious.

Late in the afternoon he blundered into the laboratory again and was swiftly turned out by Northfleet, who seemed to be busied with pouring some olive-green powder into what looked like large test-tubes, and who was even more irritated than before by Colin's intrusion.

" You go and bury Beeston's body, if you've nothing better to do," he suggested. " No use leaving it there for the girls to see, is there ? "

Colin had forgotten that the corpse on the beach might be within sight of the Wester Voe windows.

The afternoon wore on, dragging out its interminable hours; and with their passing, Colin's anxiety and forebodings increased. He had to wait until twilight for news, since during the daytime signalling was out of the question. A lamp in the Heather Lodge window would have excited suspicion at once.

Hazel reported that food had been left at their door and that no attempt had been made to interfere with them. Someone had shouted a brutal warning against any attempt to escape. Their captors—with the exception of a man patrolling round the house—seemed to have settled down in the lounge and, to judge by sounds which reached the upper storey, they had begun a carouse.

Northfleet frowned when he read off this final message ; and in his reply he ordered Hazel to make the barricade at their door as strong as possible. So long as no one came near them, they were not to worry ; and if anything unusual occurred they were on no account to leave their room.

Reluctantly the two men left the signalling apparatus. The illusion of proximity, which the messages gave, was all that they now had to cheer them. They went downstairs, and Northfleet set to work lashing pairs of bamboo flower-sticks together to form rude crosses. As a preparation for action, this seemed merely ludicrous to Colin, but when he ventured a remark, Northfleet snapped out an angry sentence. Then, in half-apology, he added :

" I don't like the idea of these swine getting drunk. Anything might happen now."

Colin understood only too well. He had his own dire imaginings to occupy him. So far the gunmen had kept the truce. But drunken men might change their minds. And Northfleet had Zelensky's taunts in his memory.

" And now," said Northfleet sardonically, as he finished the last cross, " this seems a suitable time for a few last dying words and deathbed requests. I'm going to Wester Voe by the tunnel, and if I don't get back you'll have to do the best you can without me. A blue lookout, I'm afraid."

" But you're not going alone ? " Colin queried, rather aghast. " You're taking me along, of course ? "

" No use. I've studied the plan of that warren thoroughly. I could find my way about in the dark down there. You'd only be a responsibility, Trent, and I must have my hands free. Sorry. I know how you feel. But it can't be done."

" You're after the rockets ? "

It had been fairly clear, from Northfleet's last directions to Hazel, that he contemplated no immediate rescue.

" We must have them at any cost."

" But you can't fire rockets of that size on the quiet," Colin objected. " These swine are sure to see them if they're fired."

" I suppose they will," Northfleet agreed. " Still, the resources of civilisation are not yet exhausted. Hope for the best, Trent. If I don't turn up in a reasonable time—two hours, say, since I may have to wait my chance at the other end—then block up this end of the tunnel for safety's sake, and do the best you can, after that. By the way, I've locked the door of the lab. Don't put your nose near there at any price. And now I'd better collect my traps and get off."

Some of the articles explained themselves to Colin as Northfleet selected them : his pistol and ammunition, a flash-lamp, a rope, to one end of which Northfleet had spliced a spare grapnel belonging to the pleasure-skiff. But there were others with less obvious uses : a trowel, a lump of chalk, a hammer, a paper parcel containing the contents of two tins of motor-grease, and the bundle of six-foot stakes which Colin had prepared.

" That's the lot, I think," Northfleet said after checking them. " And now for the cellar."

Characteristically enough, he made no demonstration of any sort as he climbed through the aperture Colin had opened in the brickwork. He gathered up his awkward bundle of stakes and, with his flash-lamp in his hand, set off on his subterranean raid without even a farewell. Colin could hear him whistling softly as he went.

Northfleet had a definite scheme in his mind and had no need to waste time in pondering over details. Here and there, as he went through the maze, he chalked deliberately misleading arrows on the walls for the benefit of anyone who pursued him at a later stage. He crossed two of the chasms by the help of his rope and grapnel, hoisting his stakes up by tying them to the end of the rope before he climbed out of the chasm himself and pulling them up when he reached the farther bank.

Just beyond the second pit he set a trap. The stakes were just a shade longer than the breadth of the passage, and by means of the hammer he succeeded in jamming both ends of a pole against the walls so that it formed a barrier across the passage at about a foot above the ground : an arrangement calculated to trip any unwary pursuer and launch him into the chasm as he stumbled to regain his footing. Several other traps of the same type were fixed in the passages at points which Northfleet had already chosen.

On the Wester Voe side of the pit nearest the house his preparations were even more elaborate, for with the trowel he spread a layer of motor-grease over the floor of the passage between the trip-barrier and the lip of the chasm, thus ensuring that a sprawling man would find no purchase to save himself. Between that point and the stairway Northfleet refrained from putting any hindrance in the path of possible pursuers. He left the rope and grapnel in position, so that he could retreat across the pit immediately if necessary ; and at this point he ridded himself of all unnecessary burdens. Then, going with the utmost caution, he made his way to the stair and climbed to the secret door.

Crouching behind it, he listened intently ; but the panel was too thick and well-fitting to permit sounds to penetrate to his hiding-place. With infinite care he operated the catch on his side of the door and slid the panel very slightly in its grooves. Putting his eye to the crack, he could see that the hall was empty. The sound of voices reached him, so clearly that the door of the lounge was evidently open. Northfleet inferred that it had been left so purposely, as through it the foot of the stair could be seen and any attempt of the girls to escape could be detected. The occasional clink of glasses confirmed Hazel's surmise that the gang was passing its time in drinking. Snatches of conversation made it clear that one of the men was already drunk and that some of the others were not altogether sober. An intermittent rattle puzzled Northfleet at first, but he quickly identified it as the throws of dice—poker dice to judge by the accompanying comments. Another group seemed to be playing cards.

If they would only remain as they were Northfleet saw that his task was easy. The lower part of the staircase jutted out into the hall. The door of the lounge was on one side of this projection, the opening into the secret passage on the other ; so that it would be possible to reach the rocket-case without coming within sight of the ruffians in the lounge.

Very cautiously he slid back the panel and crept out into the hall, keeping his ears strained for any sign of interruption from the lounge. He reached the rocket-case and removed from it the code book and seven or eight rockets, congratulating himself that enough remained to conceal the lacunæ caused by his depredation. He rearranged the remaining rockets to make the case seem as full as before. Then, still unsuspected, he retreated behind the panel, which he drew close again.

So far, so good. The whole thing had been so easy that Northfleet wondered at his success. He had expected something much more difficult when he set out. Obviously the first thing to do was to carry the rockets into a place of safety. That was all he had planned originally ; but now a fresh scheme took form in his mind. Once the rockets were safely stowed away, it might be well worth while to come back again to the panel and do some eavesdropping. There would be no harm in listening to the gunmen's talk and trying to get some inkling of what they were thinking about. He could always close the panel, if anyone showed himself.

He picked up the bundle of rockets, descended the steps, and plunged once more into the underground maze. If anything did go wrong, he reflected, he could not afford to burden himself with these things; and he finally carried them to the old Chief's hiding-place, where he deposited them in a corner. If he could not shake off a possible pursuer at that stage in a retreat, luck would be very much against him, after his careful study of the labyrinth.

It was some time before he came back again to the secret panel and slipped it ajar. As he did so, he recognised a change in the talk within the lounge, which he could now hear more plainly since the general babble of voices had been hushed and only one man spoke at a time. The speaker had a high, harsh voice, with something parrot-like in its quality; and he appeared to be making a report.

" . . . gone. I've been an' hunted every-w'ere. Cripes! w'at a night too. 'T ain't there, I tell yer."

" It *mus'* be there," a drunken voice declared in a monotone.

" Shut your jaw, Scarry! You're soused." This was the voice of Hawes's colleague on the deputation to Wester Voe. " If Cockatoo says he can't find it, then it ain't there."

" It *mus'* be there," Scarry repeated, with muzzy obstinacy.

" If I set about you, Scarry—— " the gunman leader warned.

" No, no," protested Zelensky's voice in soothing tones. " All goot friendts here, *nicht wahr ?* No trobble amongst ourselfs till ze work is finished. Ant, after all, zere is no harm donne, really. Zey haff sent somevon off in ze row-boat to get help ? Zat is dopple-faced of zem, after our arranchements. Bot I know ze seas here. Zat little skiff—— "

Evidently a gesture filled out the meaning.

" Mebbe so," Cockatoo's harsh voice objected ; " but now 'ow are we goin' to make a getaway with no boat ? "

" Zat vill be all right," Zelensky explained. " Zere is ze Vester Foe motor-boat vich ze Dinnets vill bring back in a day or so. Zat vill be ready for us. Old Dinnet vill giff no trobble."

" Sounds well," Cockatoo agreed, rather grudgingly.

" Now I haff a little proposition to make," Zelensky continued blandly. " It is dull for us all here. Pleasant company, of course. Nice fellows, all. Still ze time begins to hang heavy. Vot do ve do ? Trink a little, play somm poker. Trink again and play somm more poker. Smoke ze goot zigars ; zis one is first-class. Yet it is razzer dull, after all. Ant opstairs, all zis time, zere are zese two goot little girls who most find it dull also, sitting zere all alone viz nozzing to amuse zem. Vot a pity ! Let's bring zem down,

eh ? A little dance and perhaps ozzer amuse-
ments to follow ? "

Northfleet's hand went to his pocket and
clenched on the butt of his pistol. He waited,
on the rack, for the reception of Zelensky's
broad hint. To his relief, Leo went dead against
the mercenary's suggestion.

" No good," he said sharply. " The gold's
what we're after, and how're we gonna get it if
we meddle with these skirts upstairs ? You tell
me that, mister ; you was there when the bargain
was struck."

But to Northfleet's dismay the tempter had
his plan cut and dried.

" Zat is not very difficult, Leo. Quite simple,
really. You remember ze precise bargain ? Ve
keep ze little girls until zose fellows haff handed
over ze gold. Vonce ve haff got ze gold, ve haff
got it. Zen ve turn ze little girls loose, bot not
before. Zey can tell zeir story after zat—if zey
like—bot zat will not matter. I do not soppose
ve shall giff op ze gold in payment of damages ?
No, not likely."

Northfleet sensed that this cool proposition
had gained the ear of the audience. There was
a stir among the men in the lounge. The leader
was evidently hesitating—not from any moral
scruples, but merely on grounds of expediency.

" It's not for me to say," Leo declared at last.
" You boys must settle it the way—— "

A clamour of drunken approval drowned the
end of his sentence. Northfleet now bitterly
regretted that he had refused to let Colin
accompany him. With two of them, a sudden

attack at this moment might have had a sporting chance of success, since it would have come like a bolt from the blue ; but a single-handed effort was foredoomed. Still, it would have to be made. As his anger rose, he grew cooler and cooler, calculating his best course of action as he crouched at the panel and listened to the brutal jests of the group in the lounge. At last Zelensky's oily voice dominated the rest.

" Komm along, Cockatoo. Ve go opstairs and invite zem down. If zey refuse, ve persuade zem, *nicht wahr ?* Take no denial, efen if zey feel shy."

" I like 'em shy," said Cockatoo's voice, with gusto in its tone.

Northfleet slipped the panel wide open, stepped swiftly through the gap, and sheltered himself behind the projecting end of the staircase. Almost at the same moment at the open door of the lounge appeared a gunman whom Northfleet had not yet seen—Cockatoo, evidently —and behind him was Zelensky, with a leer of anticipation on his broad face.

Northfleet had no intention of taking Cambronne's legendary courtesy as a model. He fired first, and he meant to kill if he could. At that range a miss was impossible. Two shots took effect on Cockatoo, who dropped with a yell of agony. The third, more hastily aimed, hit Zelensky, though evidently it inflicted only a flesh-wound. Then Northfleet in two strides was behind the panel, which he slammed after him.

A general engagement with the gunmen had

been no part of his plans. That could have ended in only one way. What he wanted was to create a diversion which would give the girls a respite ; and, if possible, he hoped to lure the gunmen to follow him into the underground maze. That would occupy time, if he could manage it.

He waited until he heard sounds of blows on the woodwork and then fired again through the panel. The bullet-hole would show them where the passage lay, and he counted on the stoutness of the door to delay them for a few moments while he got into safety.

" Get an axe ! " he heard Zelensky shout, and smiled as he saw that his scheme was working out as he had hoped. Then came more sounds of blows on the panel, and Zelensky's voice :

" You let me go first. I owe him von for zis."

Northfleet had no time to listen further. He sprang down the stairs and continued his flight until he had crossed the first chasm in the maze. He pulled up his rope behind him and ensconced himself on the brink of the pit. For a few moments the blows on the door echoed dully down the passages, then came a final crash as the panel gave way, and Northfleet could hear the eager shouts of his pursuers.

Zelensky's voice raised itself above the tumult, loud enough for Northfleet to catch some of the words. Apparently the stout mercenary had constituted himself the tactician of the party.

" It would be lunatic to go down zere, all togezzer in ze dark, to hunt him out. No goot.

Ve'd be shooting von anozzer by accident. I go down first; and sommbody brings a light, quick. Natorp has a flash-lamp. You get it, Leo."

Evidently this suggestion was adopted. The noise died down. Then, after a pause, Northfleet's straining ears heard stealthy steps in the corridor adjacent to his own. He flashed his lamp against the wall nearest to him, so that only the very faintest diffused illumination could reach the end of the passage where the chasm was. Zelensky's eyes, sensitised by the dark, evidently caught the dim glow on the wall beyond the pit, though it was too feeble to reveal the trip-bar to him.

"Aha! So zat is vere you are, Mr. Norzhfleet?"

"Yes. Just round the corner from you."

He heard another cautious advance made by Zelensky, and calculated that the mercenary must now be close to the trip-bar.

"Nice that I have a light and you've none, Mr. Zelensky. I shall see you as you round the corner."

"Ant so *fery* convenient for me, too, Mr. Norzhfleet. I haff your light to shoot at. So ve are bose pleased, *nicht wahr?*"

Zelensky grinned to himself as he made this suggestion, and his grin widened when he heard the hoped-for answer. On the other side of the partition-wall Northfleet also smiled as he replied:

"Thanks for the hint. I'll switch off."

The dim radiance vanished as he spoke.

This was what Zelensky was hoping for. As

the darkness fell he gathered himself together and sprang forward, pistol in hand. The trip-bar caught his ankle. He stumbled, slid on the grease of the booby-trap, and with a yell of amazement and dismay he shot over the edge into the pit. Northfleet heard the thud of his fall with grim satisfaction.

"Quite comfortable, Mr. Zelensky?" he asked ironically.

The mercenary gasped heavily.

"I zhink my back is broke," he said painfully. "I cannnot mofe my legs at all."

"Ah," Northfleet answered pitilessly. "Like you, I'm a man of few words. I'm damned glad to hear it."

Zelensky made no reply. Evidently he accepted his fate without complaint; and Northfleet might even have found some admiration for this stoicism had his grudge against the mercenary been a lesser one.

A light flashed on the wall in front of him, and he drew back into his corridor as someone turned the corner of the adjacent passage.

"Hello! Zelensky! Zelensky!"

It was Leo's voice. Zelensky did not answer. Northfleet saw that chance had presented him with the very thing he wanted most: the opportunity to talk with the gunman without fear of treachery. Since the man had a flash-lamp there was no likelihood of his being caught in the booby-trap; so Northfleet opened with an apparently well-meant warning.

"Mind the booby-trap, Leo! Zelensky fell into it a minute ago and got his spine snapped.

You can't get at me, and I can't get at you ; so we'd better have a little talk. I'm in the next corridor. Don't trouble to look over the edge of the pit. I've greased the floor and you might fall in."

He switched on his lamp so that the gunman could realise the state of affairs. Leo was evidently taken aback by Northfleet's unantagonistic tone.

" Well, you seem a forgiving sort o' pal," he said, rather wonderingly. " Most people'd bear a grudge."

" I have a use for you, that's all," Northfleet retorted frankly. " You've broken your bargain ; but I'm still ready to deal with you on the same terms. That suit you ? "

" Strewth ! You mean it ? " ejaculated the gunman. " Well, you are a rum 'un, after us double-crossin' you."

" I listened to your little chat upstairs," Northfleet admitted. " You had the right end of the stick. It was Zelensky that queered the pitch."

" Thasso," Leo agreed, readily enough. " He'd fallen for one of the girls—the tall, willowy one. He'd been livin' like a monk on this damned island o' yours for months, an' he let his feelin's get outta hand when he saw a chance to get hold o' her. Silly, lettin' that sorta thing interfere with business. I never do, myself."

" Sound fellow ! " said Northfleet with well-assumed heartiness. " That's the stuff to give us. Now here's how the land lies. The gold's ready. I'll bring it across in an hour : a first instalment, anyhow. Only, this time there must be no monkey business, understand ? No bringing the girls downstairs, or anything of that sort. If you don't keep you word this time you'll never see a trace of gold. I'm speaking as one business man to another," he added flatteringly. " You're not a fool like Zelensky."

" You can kiss the Book on that," the gunman assured him. " What's a skirt, after all ? Once we're rich, we'll buy 'em and give 'em away," he boasted. Then with a note of suspicion : " No kid about all this ? "

" If the lot of you will wait in the lounge upstairs, an hour from now you'll get the first instalment without fail. I don't propose to carry it all over at once ; I'm a bit tired with all this exertion. But there'll be enough to convince you that I mean business. If you're all there when I come, you can share it amongst yourselves on the spot."

" We can't all be there," objected the gunman. " One of us has gotta watch under the girls' window——"

He broke off suddenly as though a deep suspicion had struck root in his mind.

" That ain't your little game, is it, mister ? To get us away from the window an' chuck a rope up to these girls so's they can scoot ? Nothin' doin' in that line."

" Keep your guard under the window," said Northfleet, with an impatience which convinced the gunman. " What do I care ? "

" Jus' a business-like precaution," Leo said,

half-apologetically. " I see you're straight, mister ; but business is business."

" Then that's settled. No bringing the girls down or interfering with them in any way. First instalment of the gold to be delivered in an hour from now. No, say an hour and a half—I've got to get back to Heather Lodge. You'll be in the lounge to receive the gold ; I can't go hunting all over the place for you."

" Right, mister. We'll be ready for you."

" And now," Northfleet went on in a different tone, " just a friendly warning, Leo. I shouldn't push any further along these tunnels, if I were you. There are quite a lot of humorous little booby-traps waiting for inquirers. Another thing. What about Zelensky ? Are you going to pull him out of this hole ? "

" Not me," said Leo callously. " Let him lie. He's not one o' my lot."

CHAPTER XVII

COLIN spent the time of Northfleet's absence in gloomy forebodings. He wandered restlessly hither and thither, unable to find anything useful to do and yet too highly-strung to bear inactivity. Once, entering the sitting-room, he found Leven and the detective in the midst of some talk, of which he caught only a snatch. They broke off when he showed himself. Whatever the topic, it was plainly one which gave Leven little pleasure. He looked as though he had grown years older, and there was a suggestion of numbness even in his attitude, as though he had received a stunning shock from which he was only beginning to recover. Colin, recalling the levity with which he had treated the matter of Hazel and Jean, was quick to infer that this new uneasiness was due to something touching him personally. But Leven's affairs had only the most transitory interest for Colin at that juncture. He dismissed them almost at once from his mind.

Again and again he went down to the mouth of the tunnel and strained his ears for the least whisper of sound. Common sense told him all the while that nothing could reach him from Wester Voe. The numberless reflections from the walls of the labyrinth would deaden any noise. But still he persisted, with growing anxiety as the time passed without bringing Northfleet's return.

At last, almost despairing, he ensconced himself in the bedroom upstairs. From there he could at least see the light shining in the girls' window and give himself the illusion that in some way he was not altogether cut off from Jean. From time to time he put his binoculars to his eyes and gazed at the tiny yellow patch in in the hope of catching a glimpse of his wife's figure moving within the room.

Suddenly his attention was riveted by a swift flickering of the reading-lamp which Hazel used as a transmitter. As he deciphered the message, he felt a chill running down his spine :

"*Shooting downstairs. What's happening? Quick. Answer.*"

Then it recommenced again : "*Shooting. What is it? Shooting. What is it? . . .*" repeated and repeated in frantic efforts to attract attention.

Colin fumbled with the unlit lamp on the floor, keeping his eye on the window in the vain hope of being able to see something without the binoculars. Never had a lamp seemed more difficult to kindle quickly. And as he bungled with the thing in his haste the direst visions thronged through his mind. Northfleet had been detected. And now the gang of scoundrels would want revenge. Colin had a pretty good idea where they would look for it, and he turned icy at the thought.

The lamp was ready in a second or two, though it seemed an age to Colin. He went to

the mirror and signalled, holding up his binoculars with his free hand. The answer did not
relieve his mind much :

> " *Still safe. Shooting stopped. Sounds of
> breaking into somewhere. Who's sending ? Are
> you safe ?* "

To evade the issue, he signalled : " *Colin
sending.*" But the next flickers of the light
demanded : " *Is Cyril safe ?* " and Colin could
get no further news until that imperious question
was answered. He sought for a phrase to
reassure the girls ; but he had no skill in lying,
and was driven to signal : " *Gone out. Back
soon.*" Then, as an afterthought, he added :
" *Tell you whenever he returns.*"

Hazel added one or two additional facts to his
knowledge. The noise below in the hall had
died down, he learned, and no one had come
near the girls' room. With that mite of comfort
he broke off communication lest his flashes
should be observed.

He went down to the sitting-room, where he
gave the detective an outline of affairs. Leven
took no notice of him, but seemed deep in very
uncomfortable thoughts of his own.

Colin found it impossible to sit inactive at
this juncture. He wandered outside the house,
returned to the upper window, fidgeted here and
there, with both his mind and his body a prey
to futile restlessness. At last he made up his
mind to adventure into the tunnel, at least as
far as the beginning of the labyrinth. Northfleet
might be in need of assistance : it was safe to go

there, so long as he kept out of the maze; and anything was better than this aimless time-killing.

In the old Chief's room he found the bundle of rockets which Northfleet had secured; and at first the sight of them raised Colin's spirits. Here, in the last resort, was a means of opening up communication with the mainland. But what had become of Northfleet?

He was puzzling over this when steps sounded faintly in the distance. Careless in his anxiety, Colin stepped out into the passage; and to his immense relief he saw the chemist coming hurriedly along the tunnel from the labyrinth. Colin gave vent to an exclamation of joy. Northfleet, however, seemed to have no time for felicitations, and his first words took Colin by surprise.

"What's the weather like upstairs?"

"Wind's almost died away. It's raining heavily."

"Thank the Lord!" said Northfleet, with more earnestness than seemed called for by the subject. "Come along, Trent. Help me with these rockets."

As they tramped along the tunnel with their bundles, Northfleet gave Colin a concise account of his own adventures; after which Colin summarised Hazel's message.

"You'd better go up at once and tell them you're back," he suggested, as they clambered through the gap in the wall. "I'll bring up the rockets and wait for you in the hall," he added tactfully.

It would hardly be playing the game to read off the messages between Hazel and Northfleet just then, he felt.

In a few minutes Northfleet rejoined him in the hall.

"They're all right so far. No one's gone near them. I've told them to stay quiet now, no matter what happens."

He pulled a note-book from his pocket: the rocket-code, Colin saw. Northfleet studied it for a moment or two, then put it down on the hall table.

"No good. Just as I thought."

"No good? Why?" Colin asked, rather aghast.

"We don't want to send for a doctor, or a nurse, or a packet of matches, or anything of that sort. These are the things in the code. Naturally, there's no signal meaning: 'Send someone to knock out a few gunmen.' If we ask the Stornadale people to send a boat, the men in the boat will be unarmed, won't they? And our friends would just shoot them down and collar the boat. I haven't the nerve to send a signal which would simply mean some decent fellows losing their lives to no purpose."

"Hadn't thought of that," Colin admitted gloomily.

"Leven and the tec are on the premises?" Northfleet asked.

"Yes. Been having a chat. Didn't agree with Leven, by the looks of him. Don't know what it's all about. All I heard was a phrase of the tec's: 'I've seen your letters,' or something like that. And I rather think one of them said 'Extradition.' Anyhow, Leven looks a damned sight sorrier for himself than he was for the girls. Funny, isn't it?"

Northfleet made no comment on this.

"We'll have to hurry up now," he said. "I promised to deliver the first instalment of gold to these swine in an hour and a half, and time's getting on. We need Leven and the tec to help. Rout them out, will you? while I get the stuff."

Colin obeyed, while Northfleet went into the laboratory and returned with something which he carried as though it were fragile.

"You take the lead, Trent. Carry four of these rockets with you. Leven, these bamboo sticks are your share. You follow on Trent's heels. Now you, what's your name? Wenlock? Well, we *could* manage without your help, but——"

"I'd rather not be left out," the detective assured him with a certain eagerness. "It's my left shoulder, and it's really not so bad now. I I can stagger along if you're not going too fast."

"You'll be useful," Northfleet said. "We're short-handed a bit. Now here's the plan of campaign. We make a detour round Wester Voe and come out in the pine spinney beyond the gardens. Once we get there I'll fix the rockets ready for setting off. You, Trent, will make your way through the gardens and round the house until you get into cover somewhere near the girls' window. Your business is to mark the patrolman and knock him out when the first rocket goes off. No matter what happens, you mustn't show yourself until the rocket goes.

We must act absolutely synchronously or the whole affair's a wash-out. Understand that, all of you ? "

" O.K.," Colin acquiesced. " I do nothing till the rocket goes up. After that my job's to knock the sentry out, as quick as possible, eh ? "

" Yes," Northfleet agreed. " Now the next thing. One of you two "—he turned to Leven and the detective—" will have to stay and fire the rockets and join us after that, if he can. The other one comes with me through the gardens towards the house. Whoever comes with me runs the bigger risk."

" I'll come," Leven volunteered in a toneless voice, as though the decision meant nothing to him.

Colin saw the detective give Leven a quick glance, as though not quite sure of something.

" Very well," Northfleet agreed. " You're better able to get about than Wenlock is. Now remember, no matter what happens, no squibbing off your pistols till the first rocket goes. Then each man for himself."

" I've no pistol," Wenlock reminded him.

" It may not come to shooting at all," Northfleet answered. " Still you'd better have one. Get him one, if you have it," he ordered Leven. " And a flash-lamp for each of us, too. You've plenty of them in stock, I suppose. I saw you using them that night the yacht put in here."

Leven went off obediently and procured the things. He seemed indifferent to the events around him, obeying mechanically while wrapped in his own thoughts.

" Don't show the least glimmer of light till the first rocket goes off," Northfleet warned them. " After that nothing matters much."

" Better be a bit clearer, hadn't you ? " Colin suggested. " What's the general idea of the scheme ? "

Northfleet made a gesture of apology.

" The fact is, I've been brooding over it so much in detail that I clean forgot I hadn't explained it to you all. It's simple enough. These swine will be assembled in the lounge—three of them. One of them's so drunk that he'll give us little trouble. I'm going to give them a preliminary shake-up by firing these rockets through the windows, and then Leven and I drop in on them. I don't think we'll have much trouble. Meanwhile, you knock out the sentry. You see why it all has to be synchronised ? And Wenlock here, if he can struggle down after firing the rockets, will act as reinforcement for Leven and me."

" A nifty enough scheme," Colin admitted. " But I think you're expecting too much from the rockets, myself. Tough lot, Master Leo and his pals. A few fireworks will hardly phase them."

" We'll see," said Northfleet curtly. " Now off with you. We've no time to waste."

At the thought of action at last Colin's spirits were rising. He picked up the bundle of rockets and set off cautiously for the gate, stepping carefully to avoid the trip-wires. In his mind he went over the route which promised the best results : along the path to near the lupin field ;

then up to the right through the heather, so as to avoid the house; then west again until they reached the outskirts of the pine spinney beyond the gardens.

" Slower," ordered Northfleet's voice, as Colin set off briskly. " We must keep in touch at any cost, and I can't hurry, with this thing I'm carrying."

Colin slackened his pace and took care not to outrun his companions. The wind had dropped now, and the rain was thinner. Through it, far ahead, glowed the lighted window in Wester Voe, and in his mind's eye he could see the two girls up there in the room, helpless, waiting in agonised suspense for the next turn of events. Well, before long things would be settled one way or another. In some curious way, Northfleet had succeeded in spreading a feeling of optimism. He seemed so certain that things would work out as he had planned. Colin, feeling the heads of the heavy rockets as he tramped along, admitted to himself that they were formidable weapons. One of these things, coming flaming through a window unexpectedly and exploding into stars around one—— Bit of a jar, what ? Last thing one would be looking for. Throw one off one's balance a bit, and give an attacker just the second or two that was needed.

Colin gave a gasp as one of the Ruffa sheep rose at his feet and leapt clumsily out of his path. He realised that he had been thinking too much and not paying sufficient attention to the work in hand.

" No talking after this," Northfleet ordered in a low voice. " We're getting too near to risk anything. Pick your steps and don't make a sound."

They circumambulated Wester Voe at a fair distance and reached the spinney without mishap. Then followed a cautious descent into the gardens, with every precaution against the slightest sound. Colin was inclined to regret the fall in the wind. Its noises might have covered their advance. Then he remembered that wind might have sent the rockets astray. That was why Northfleet had been so relieved to hear that the gale had blown itself out, evidently. He seemed to have thought of everything, Colin reflected in some admiration. And even this minor point served to raise his spirits further.

Now the windows of the lounge were in full view : a broad rectangle of light set in the dark bulk of Wester Voe. The French windows were half-open, but the thin, translucent curtains had been drawn so as to hide the interior. Evidently the gunmen had no intention of sitting visible in a lighted room with potential attackers in the darkness outside.

When the party halted, Colin had fallen back to the rear ; and he could see the figures of his companions in silhouette against the lit-up windows. Northfleet, moving stealthily in the obscurity, began his preparations. Leven surrendered the bamboo crosses, which were to act as rests for the rockets, being easily adjustable to the proper heights when two ends had been planted in the soil. Then Northfleet relieved

Colin of the rockets themselves; but before placing them in their rests he seemed to clip some objects to the rocket-cases. What these things were Colin could not make out. They seemed to be small cylinders, so far as he saw in the faint light, while Northfleet was busy with sighting his battery of rockets and shifting the supports to bring the projectiles to bear on the windows. This done, Wenlock was given some whispered orders, and Colin smelt the tang of a burning slow match. Northfleet had foreseen the risk of using matches to light the rockets, evidently. The flare might have attracted attention had any gunman been on the look-out.

"Now you can start, Trent. Give you fifteen minutes to get to your post. And, look here, mind you keep that wrist-watch of yours under your sleeve. I could see the illuminated dial from yards away."

Colin needed nothing further. He had already decided on his objective : a long clump of bushes just opposite the girls' window and about fifty feet from the house wall. It would give him cover, and by approaching it from the far side he had a good chance of reaching it unperceived. In his Boy Scout days Colin had been the best stalker in his patrol, and some of his old cunning came back to him at this crucial moment. He had a mental map of the gardens to guide him, and he chose a route which gave him cover during most of his transit, so that he was able to move quicker than Northfleet had estimated. With a sigh of relief he gained the shelter of the bushes undetected ; and, crouching there, he cautiously inspected his wrist-watch, to find he was about eight minutes ahead of his allotted time.

Colin, at first, could detect no sign of a watcher ; but within a few seconds steps sounded, and the sentry passed along the face of the house under the girls' window. Apparently he was in high spirits, for he hummed an air as he went. He walked on, still humming ; then, as he turned back at the end of his beat, he broke into full song with an appalling clearness of articulation. It was one of those artless shanties which never by any chance get into print ; and Colin, even in the tenseness of that moment, went hot all over at the thought that every word of it must be reaching the girls through the open window above.

But he had little time to brood over this. A more serious trouble faced him almost immediately. The sentry switched on a flash-lamp and began to examine the face of the wall below the window of Jean's room. His figure was outlined clearly against the illuminated wall, and Colin had no difficulty in recognising the jackal Hawes, still clad in Colin's clothes. The light flickered from point to point on the wall, pausing momentarily here and there on a projecting stone, the thick stem of a creeper, a stretch of waste-pipe, and the window-sill. Colin had no difficulty in guessing what this survey might mean. The creature was searching for the best method of climbing up to the girls' window. Every movement of the jackal was clearly visible ; and Colin could even see him nod approvingly as his light showed a good handhold which would serve his need. Evidently Hawes had absorbed Zelensky's ideas to some purpose.

Colin took his pistol from his pocket and released the safety-catch. Then, as he lifted the weapon, he remembered suddenly that his hands were tied. If he fired now the whole of North-fleet's scheme would collapse. The gunmen in the lounge would hear the report and hurry to the support of their confederate. Except in the last resort he dare not betray himself, but must wait until the rockets went off.

"' *Said Abraham the Sailor !* ' " bawled Hawes, completing one of the infamous verses.

He stowed his pistol in his pocket, switched off his flash-lamp, and Colin heard him spit on his hands. Then he began to climb ; and as he did so, Colin stole silently out of his shelter and approached the house.

In the flurry of the adventure his sense of time had been blunted, and he had no idea whether minutes or seconds still remained before the firing of the rocket. There were only two choices before him. He might shoot Hawes now, when the gunman was at his mercy ; but in that case he would throw the main scheme out of gear and probably assure the triumph of Leo and his confederates. Or he might wait ; in which case the girls would be at the mercy of the armed man in their room.

Above him he could hear the heavy breathing of Hawes as he clambered up the difficult face of the house. Luckily, in the dark he had to grope for hand- and foot-holds, which wasted some of the precious seconds. There came a rustle, as he grasped at the stem of the creeper. Colin knew that his next reach would bring him to the window-sill. And still the rocket did not come.

The gunman's head and shoulders were just visible now in the diffused light from the window. Colin saw him put out his right hand and grasp the sill. Another effort and he would have his knee up. Colin put his thumb on the button of his flash-lamp and lifted his pistol.

Then came a sound like some giant drawing his breath through his teeth. The rocket! But the explosion which followed was far more formidable than any rocket ever made. Then, in quick succession, swish! swish! swish! the other rockets followed, and the reports of the explosions shook the house. Something fell with a thud like a giant hammer-stroke, and glass tinkled like an harmonica.

Colin switched on his lamp and revealed Hawes, clinging to the house-side like some grotesque and gigantic insect : one hand on the sill, the other clutching the creeper. As the glare fell on him, he turned his head, saw Colin, loosed his hand from the sill, made an effort to pull out his pistol. But as he did so his whole weight came on the creeper ; the tendrils gave way, and Hawes pitched backwards on to the ground. Colin darted forward, but one glance in the light of the flash-lamp showed him that he need do nothing. It required no experience in first aid to diagnose the cause of that curious wryness in the attitude of the body. Hawes had pitched on his head, and his neck was broken.

The window was thrown up and Colin saw Hazel leaning out.

"Who's there?" she cried tensely. Then, as her eyes caught the picture in the circle of the flash-lamp's glare: "It's you? Are you safe?" She turned back into the room as he nodded: "Jean! Here's Colin, dear." Then, as Jean ran to her side: "Where's Cyril? Is he all right?"

"Yes," said Colin at a venture. "Back in a minute."

He tore himself away reluctantly and raced round the house to assist the others. With some idea of taking the gunmen in the rear, he dashed through the front door and made for the lounge. It was only afterwards that he discovered he had been using his flash-light. At the moment he was so keyed up that he failed to notice that no lamps were alight in the hall.

As he reached the open door of the lounge a flash-lamp glared in his eyes. Northfleet's voice reassured him.

"Oh, it's you, Trent? What luck?"

"Hawes broke his neck. The girls are all right," said Colin breathlessly. Then at the sight of the lounge he gasped in surprise. "What the devil has happened?"

"I must have misgauged my fireworks a trifle," said Northfleet with a sinister grin. "The ceiling came down on top of our friends and saved us trouble. Leo's dead, Natorp's just passing in his checks, and this drunken lout—Scarry, I believe—has got concussion and some other damage which will probably rid us of him for good. We hadn't to fire a shot ; just walked in and took away their guns."

He broke off and turned to Leven, who was stooping over Scarry.

"There are fire-extinguishers in the hall. Get 'em, and put these curtains out, or we'll have the place ablaze over our heads."

Colin now noticed that here the electric lights were out and the curtains afire, evidently set alight by sparks from the rockets. The air was filled with dust and smoke. Colin smelt the tang of exploded fireworks in his nostrils. Huge slabs of broken plaster littered the floor, partly concealing the bodies of the gunmen who had been overwhelmned when the ceiling gave way.

"No rockets ever did that ! " Colin exclaimed. "What was it ? "

"The alchemists called it *aurum fulminans*," Northfleet answered. "I promised these swine they'd get enough gold to satisfy them. I guess I've kept my word. And I don't think they'll come back to ask for more now."

"Oh ! " ejaculated Colin, suddenly enlightened. "So that was what you meant all the time.

"Yes," said Northfleet impatiently. "I've no time to explain just now. I must see Hazel. Are you coming ? "

He hurried up the stair, with Colin at his heels.

CHAPTER XVIII

WHEN Northfleet and Colin returned to the
lounge they found the detective standing by
what had once been the fireplace, examining
imperturbably the wreckage which cumbered the
room.

" Well, Mr. Northfleet, you seem to have given
them a house-warming of sorts," he commented
ironically.

" One does one's best. What happened to
you ? "

" Oh, I hobbled up as quick as I could ; but
when I got to the window it didn't take much
penetration to see that you needed no help here.
So I went round to lend Mr. Trent a hand in case
of accidents. But all I found was someone with
his neck out of joint ; so I came back here and
found you gone. Professor Leven explained
matters, more or less. The young ladies are all
right, I hope ? "

" A bit shaken up by the crackers, naturally,"
said Northfleet briefly. " Otherwise they're all
right. They're staying upstairs till we get some
of this mess cleared up. No place for them just
now. Then we're going to take them over to
Heather Lodge."

The detective nodded with tacit approval.

" By the way, there are four of these fellows
here," he pointed out. " The last of them died a
minute or two before you came down. The one
outside makes five. But there were six altogether,

weren't there ? If the sixth man's got away he may give trouble."

Northfleet suddenly remembered that his own earlier doings at Wester Voe were still unknown to Wenlock. The fourth body in the room was Cockatoo's. If the detective chose to imagine that he had died with the others, there was no harm done.

"The sixth man's down in a subterranean tunnel. His back's broken, he says. He won't give any trouble. It's Zelensky : the one who ratted at Heather Lodge."

Wenlock made a non-committal gesture.

"If he's alive, shouldn't we get him out ? "

"I'm not keen," Northfleet admitted frankly. "In Zelensky's case I feel less like a good Samaritan than almost anything you can think of."

"I'm not keen, either," Colin declared. "Still —it doesn't look well to leave him, does it ? "

"Not good form, eh ? " Northfleet translated with a rather ugly smile.

Leven surprised them by offering to help.

"Oh, then, I go with the majority," Northfleet conceded. "Get a ladder, will you, Trent ? We'll need it. And some ropes too."

The detective with his disabled arm was useless for any work of the kind. Leven went ahead with a flash-lamp, while Colin and Northfleet carried the ladder down into the subterranean passage. Leven reached the trap while they were still manœuvring the ladder round the right-angled turn before the pit.

Northfleet saw him step over the trip-bar cautiously and test the greasy surface beyond. Evidently he found a foothold on it—a clear spot which Northfleet had left on purpose for his own retreat—and he stepped to the edge of the pit and bent over.

" Ha ! Zelensky," he said in a taunting tone, " quite comfortable, I hope ? No regrets ? Still, between ourselves, I think you'd have done better not to change sides."

Zelensky did not seem to resent Leven s tone.

" Vell, vell," he answered faintly, yet with something of his old genial tone. " Ve all make mistakes, efen ze clefferest of us, *nicht wahr ?* Perhaps I did blonder zat time. Bot zen zere vas your niece, ze beautiful Hazel. A goot old sober-sided fellow like you, Leven, you cannot appreciate ze strong appeal zat female beauty makes to onscientific people like me. You are moch too dry ant ascetic for soch zhings, eh ? So you make your own little mistakes—in my case, for instance."

Colin saw the irony and wondered at Zelensky's insolence in alienating his possible rescuers. That speech was meant to irritate both Leven and Northfleet.

" Ant, after all," Zelensky went on philosophi- cally, " I haff always managed to keep my own name. It most be curious to lose one's name : to be called Leven yesterday, ant to-day to be called Arrow, and to-morrow to be called Nom- ber So-ant-So, viz no name at all. A curious experience."

"Shut your mouth!" Leven exclaimed sharply.

"A dying man is priffeleged," Zelensky pleaded, not without a certain dignity. "Bot if you do not like it, I say no more. I haff somzhing important to tell you—somzhing that will get you out of zhis little trouble of yours."

He seemed to find difficulty in speaking.

"Bendt down, please. I cannot raise my voice."

Leven stooped over the edge of the pit to catch the faint tones, and as he did so Zelensky raised his concealed pistol and shot him through the head.

As the body fell into the pit Colin made a movement to dash forward, but luckily Northfleet restrained him.

"Anybody else care to komm forwardt?" Zelensky's voice inquired with some of the old jocosity. "Each ant all, I giff zem ze same velcome. It is ze only amusement I haff, down here, viz a broken back. Mr. Norzhfleet? You care to step forwardt?"

"No, thanks," Northfleet said, dryly. "I believe you mean it. And as I haven't much taste for your choice in last words we'll leave you, I think. Come along, Trent. There's nothing for us to do here."

Colin recognised the futility of persisting. Zelensky meant what he said; he preferred to die where he was, and wanted no interference. And one of his utterances had given Colin food for thought, which he resolved to put to the test as soon as he saw Wenlock.

The detective was waiting for them at the head of the stairs.

" Where's Zelensky ? " he asked, seeing that they were alone. " And Leven, have you left him down there? "

" Yes," said Colin, with a slightly hysterical laugh, " he's down there. Zelensky put a bullet through his head. You were trying to net him, weren't you, Wenlock ? Well, there's a hole in the fence."

" Shot him ? " Wenlock was evidently unsympathetic. " H'm, there's a hole in the fence, as you say."

Something in the phrase seemed to catch Northfleet's attention.

" Your brand of humour verges on the macabre, Wenlock," he commented.

But that sentence completed Colin's illumination. Things fitted together in his mind, and at last he saw the whole mystery of Ruffa in its true perspective.

" Well, I'm ——," he exclaimed, as the light broke on him.

But Northfleet had no intention of wasting time. His main idea was to get the two girls away from a place which must be loathsome to them after the strain through which they had gone. He went across to the case and extracted some rockets of a particular pattern.

" These ones are a sort of S O S in the code," he explained. " It's no time of night to attract attention, but some of the fishing-fleet may be at work round about here, and they might see them. No harm in trying, anyhow. Take them

outside and set them up, will you, Wenlock?
The rocket-stand's in the case there. Come on,
Trent. We'll bring the girls down now, touch
off the rockets and then go over to Heather
Lodge. I don't think any of us want to linger
about here just now."

CHAPTER XIX

JEAN and Hazel had not dared to sleep during their captivity ; and when they reached Heather Lodge there was little difficulty in persuading them to go to bed at once. They were so worn out by their ordeal that they had no energy left to feel curious about recent events. Jean's eyes, in which terror lingered even yet, betrayed that she was on the verge of collapse ; while Hazel, now that she was in safety, seemed to be paying the price of her coolness during the long hours of ceaseless strain.

The three men had no inclination to sleep just then. The excitement of that last hour, when it seemed touch and go in their conflict with the gunmen, had strung them up to a pitch which made immediate relaxation impossible. By tacit consent they went into the sitting-room. The detective stretched himself on a sofa, Colin collapsed into an arm-chair with a sigh of relief, and Northfleet chose Leven's seat beside the hearth. The dog Peter settled himself on the rug and, content with human beings around him, fell asleep.

Northfleet pulled out the characteristic pipe of the practical chemist, with its bowl heavily charred on one side by constant rekindling at the flames of Bunsen burners. He filled and lighted it mechanically, and for a time seemed lost in not unpleasant reflections. Colin bore the silence as long as he could, and then broke into Northfleet's reverie.

" About time I heard the whole story of this affair, isn't it ? A bit unusual, these late proceedings. Apt to give rise to comment when they leak out. I see something of the business, but the details are beyond me. Better put me wise now, while the girls are out of the way. I want to know just where we stand."

Northfleet nodded assent and took his pipe from his lips.

" I can give you some of it ; I rather owe you that, Trent. And perhaps Wenlock may see his way to give us the rest of it."

The detective made a non-committal gesture, but sat up to listen.

" Starting at bed-rock," Northfleet began, " there are three ways of setting up in business like Leven. You might make gold, *à la* Emmens ; or you might strike on some treasure-trove and dispose of it under the pretence of alchemy ; or you might set up as a receiver of stolen goods— a fence, in fact."

" I guessed that was the meaning of the joke about ' the hole in the fence '," said Colin, throwing a slightly disapproving glance in the detective's direction. " Bit callous, that, Wenlock, if you don't mind my saying so."

" Not at all," Wenlock assured him, without any marked signs of contrition. " I don't care for puns either ; but I couldn't resist that one."

Colin thought it best not to labour the point. He turned to Northfleet with a gesture which requested him to continue.

" There's no need to explain how I came into the affair myself," Northfleet went on. " I've

pointed out already to you the sort of people likely
to be interested in gold-making. Some of them
asked me to look into Leven's business, on the
quiet. I'm not going to give them away."

Peter whimpered in his dreams, and Northfleet
stooped to pat him soothingly.

" I got a sample of Leven's gold," he went on,
as the dog stretched itself out and fell asleep
again. "You saw the results of my analysis.
The gold was all right, but the impurities
interested me. You may remember what they
were : a lot of silver, a fair amount of copper, and
small quantities of iron, platinum, and zinc.
Now, you're a store of odd information, Trent.
Aren't silver and copper present in jewellers'
alloys of gold ? And in one alloy—blue gold,
they call it—there's a lot of iron."

Colin's face showed his chagrin.

" I never thought of that," he confessed
vexedly, "and yet it does stare one straight in
the face, once it's pointed out. You mean that
Leven's gold was just old jewellery melted
down ? "

" Well, it looked like it. That's as far as I
cared to go. I'm not keen on leaping to conclusions. But if Leven was melting down old
gold settings they weren't prehistoric stuff. Some
of the jewellery must have been quite modern."

" Don't follow that," Colin admitted. " Where
is your evidence ? "

" The platinum impurity," Northfleet explained. " Platinum settings are a fairly recent
craze."

" That's so," Colin had to admit.

"There was another bit of evidence that pointed in the same direction," Northfleet continued. "I told you that Leven's sales of gold were intermittent. That looked as though he had no steady source of supply such as he would have had if he'd really been making gold. But that spasmodic series of sales fitted in neatly with the idea that he was a fence, buying the proceeds of robberies at odd times and getting rid of the stuff almost as quickly as it came into his hands."

"I ought to have thought of that. And, of course, if he had been selling treasure-trove he could have made steady sales."

"Another point. I told you that after a time he hired Natorp and Zelensky as guards. Why? If it was merely burglary that he was afraid of, insurance would have covered that risk. Obviously there was something else to be guarded against. And if you assume that he was a fence, it's plain enough what he was afraid of. A burglar might get away with some of his purchases before they were melted down; and then, if that burglar were caught by chance, Leven would have had a troublesome bit of explanation before him to account for the stuff being in his possession. Or, even without that, the burglar might spot the game and blackmail him. You must remember that his whole business depended on his reputation as an eminent chemist."

"But how did he get hold of the stuff at all?" Colin demanded.

"I told you he was in the swim with a lot of queer fish," Northfleet reminded him. "And he was a clever devil, or else the police would have got on his trail earlier."

"He was one of the smartest," Wenlock agreed. "He never made a false move, so far as I know."

"What brought him to Ruffa, if he was doing so well in London?" Colin inquired.

"That's what I asked myself," Northfleet returned. "Put yourself in his place, and see what you make of it."

"Oh, yes," said Colin, enlightened by a recollection of the yacht's visit. "In London he'd be tied down to the proceeds of English burglaries. Up here, away from the Customs, he could get stuff from the Continent as well."

"That was what I inferred myself," Northfleet confirmed. "If you think of the life he was leading in London, it implied that he must have an extremely strong inducement to bury himself up here. I expect that one motive was a desire to launch out as an international fence : buy the stuff abroad, where there was less chance of it being traced to him and where he had the whole of the Continent to draw on after a time. Of course the expenses were pretty big. He had to share with those fellows on the yacht, who brought him stuff ; and he had to pay those other men who ran his motor-boat. But with his wider range he could probably drive a bigger trade, and he must have made it pay. Besides, it was a far safer game, run from up here in the wilds, compared with working in London with a policeman at every street corner ready to note anything queer going on."

"I see now," Colin broke in. "They must have brought the stuff across, hidden in the yacht's sand-ballast bags. Puzzled me, that night, when I saw a beggar pitching handfuls of some powder over the yacht's side. Emptying out the sand, evidently, to get at the gold down below in the bag. And that explains Leven's short-wave advice to keep clear of the Fisheries gunboat. Afraid of them reporting the yacht to the Customs, probably."

"Obviously," Northfleet agreed. "And on the same basis you can account for that muffle furnace in Leven's lab. here and for his installing a benzene-gas plant in the house. He melted down the gold and cast it into ingots; and then the motor-boat called for these and transported them to the buyers."

He paused for a moment or two before recommencing.

"We've got a bit ahead of the course of events," he pointed out. "I had my suspicions, but I hadn't anything in the way of real proof. I dare say we could have employed a private inquiry agent to come up here and watch Leven's doings; but quite likely nothing would have come of it. A non-technical watcher might have overlooked something that would be plain enough to a chemist. And there was another possibility, though it wasn't probable: Leven *might* have discovered gold on Ruffa. The impurities in his gold were, after all, natural impurities. Even platinum occurs in some samples of natural gold.

"I decided to come up here myself and have

a look round. As I meant to hunt for the hypo-
thetical alluvial deposit, just to make sure, it
would hardly be sound policy to come as a
geologist. That would have put Leven on the
scent. So I chose to call myself a bird-watcher ;
and if people laughed at me, so much the better."

He gave Colin a bland smile as he explained this.

" Well, I arrived. I saw the yacht and the
motor-boat. I found there was no gold. The
thing was as plain as print. And yet I was
no nearer proof than before. And there were
unexpected complications, too."

Colin guessed that Hazel had furnished these ;
but the subject was one which it was needless to
discuss before Wenlock. He contented himself
with an understanding gesture.

" The presence of these two armed scoundrels
on the premises was a puzzle to me for a time.
Ruffa wasn't the place where the burglary risk
is high. Then I had a glimmering of an idea.
Somebody might have got wind of Leven's
private affairs—somebody dangerous. He might
have given himself away to a woman, as the
cleverest men do at times, and covered up his
real doings by this bluff of gold-making. And she
might have let that slip to someone else who could
take a hint. There are very rum ramifications
in that underworld. It's all pure guesswork, this.

" Then came your revelations, Trent, and my
ideas grew much clearer. That reference to
Nipasgal in the code message was pretty sound
proof that someone was on Leven's track,
although he'd done his best to cover that when
he came to Ruffa—changed his name and so

forth. And the fact that he was being forced to land his gold consignments at unexpected ports was a plain hint that the people he was up against wouldn't scruple to try a hold-up game if they could get their hands on the gold. Still, I must admit I didn't take the business quite seriously at that stage.

"So far as my own investigations were concerned I was no nearer proof than when I came up here. Everything pointed to Leven being a fence ; but if I'd been asked for clear evidence I couldn't have produced it. I'm fairly honest, so I sat down and wrote to my employers saying that I thought I was wasting my time."

"Oh, that was it ? " Wenlock interjected unexpectedly.

Northfleet laughed unaffectedly.

"I suppose you charitably assumed, when you saw that letter, that I'd decided to rat to Leven's side, where money was obviously to be had ? Well, well. No, I wanted to resign for quite other reasons. My position between Leven and Miss Arrow was hardly to my taste."

"You puzzled Jean and me for a while with your methods," Colin confessed. "We couldn't understand what you were playing at."

Northfleet evidently had no relish for a discussion of his intimate affairs.

"You can't spy on a man and make love to his niece at the same time," he said curtly. "But that's a mere side-issue. The point is that somebody had swallowed Leven's lies about gold-making completely, however they got hold of the yarn. It wasn't from the newspaper stunt—that was dead and forgotten long ago. It must have been something on the lines I sketched a minute or two back. Perhaps you know who they were, Wenlock ? "

" Leo and his gang ? " the detective answered. " We suspected them of several bank hold-ups, but we couldn't prove it up to the hilt. They weren't the harmless brand of criminal. Regular bad hats, all of them ; and most of them had done time."

" And what brought you yourself up here so opportunely ? "

" Suspicion, merely. I've no official status up here. We've had our eye on Leven for a long while, but we could prove nothing against him. Take this international dealing that he'd been doing. Suppose the proceeds of a French robbery came to his hands. If the French wanted to extradite him, there was nothing doing. We don't surrender our nationals to be tried in French courts, especially for a crime committed outside French jurisdiction. What we could have done was to put him on trial for receiving—under the Larceny Act 1916. But you've got to prove that the receiver *knows* that the goods were stolen property ; and he'd beaten us there. Besides, that charge would involve getting a lot of evidence from the French side ; it would have been expensive ; and it couldn't be risked unless there was a clear case. We had to prove that he *knew* what he was doing."

" I see," said Colin, rather dazed by the vistas of legal procedure which opened up in his imagination. " Difficult job, no doubt. So you came up here hoping to try some psychoanalysis on him and lay bare his soul—or words to that effect ? "

" Or words to that effect," Wenlock retorted gravely. " As it chanced, I got what I wanted."

" You did ? How ? "

" Well," Wenlock admitted, " since there'll be no case now, I don't mind confessing that I went a shade over the score. One has to, from time to time. I had no search-warrant, of course ; but that night the gunmen shot me I was left in charge here, you remember, while Leven was snoring upstairs. I went through his papers. He hadn't bothered to keep them in a safe or anything like that. I read his correspondence with his friends abroad. Some of the letters established guilty knowledge beyond any possible denial."

" By Jove ! " Colin's admiration was unstinted. " And you did that when you'd just been shot and were expecting to have your throat cut any minute."

" That was the business I came here for," said Wenlock stolidly. " Of course I did it. I might never have had another chance."

" And you talked to him about it the next afternoon, didn't you ? " Colin demanded. " I overheard something about ' letters ' and ' extradition.' "

" I explained the state of affairs to him," Wenlock admitted candidly. " Of course I had no warrant to arrest him. I'm off my own ground. But that didn't amount to a row of pins, once we got out of here. I could easily have got the necessary authority to work. It seemed only fair to warn him. It crumpled him up," the detective added thoughtfully. "Seven years is the maximum, and his was a bad case. Seven years—at his age——"

An expressive gesture filled in the sense.

"Not so young as he was, and not much chance of making a living when he got out again," Northfleet interpreted. "He looked a bit dazed, I remember. Now I begin to understand why he chose the risky job at Wester Voe. H'm! That explains why he began to taunt Zelensky at the last. Hadn't the pluck to suicide, but let the gunman do the job for him instead. There's going to be a lot to explain about when we've got to tell our tale to the police."

"Luckily there's no coroner in Scotland," said Wenlock in a tone which suggested that he did not approve of coroners. "The procurator-fiscal deals with the case of deaths where there's any hanky-panky suspected. If he's satisfied that's the end of the matter."

"Leven's dead, so the case is closed," Northfleet pointed out. "No point in digging up Leven's career, is there? I don't want a scandal for Miss Arrow's sake."

"I think it might be got round," Wenlock hazarded in a tone which went far to reassure Northfleet.

"Thanks," said Northfleet, answering the spirit rather than the words. Then, leaving a painful subject, he turned to Colin.

"Craigmore will be a bit disgusted when he sees what's happened to his house. I don't mind paying—cheap at the price, I think."

"Halves," Colin amended. "And that reminds me. What was that patent thunderbolt of yours?"

"Fulminating gold."

"Gold fulminate, you mean?"

"No, I don't. I hadn't the stuffs for making that. I dare say we could have turned out some gun-cotton if we'd tried; but there was the bother of a detonator for that. So fulminating gold was the only thing we could make. It's easy to prepare. Dissolve gold in *aqua regia* and then treat the gold chloride with ammonia, and there you are. What scared me stiff was the chance of it going off prematurely. I dare say I was a bit snappy with you when you came bustling into the lab., Trent, but I was afraid of even a slight shock sending it off. It's not been worked on much, and my recollections of its properties, beyond its explosiveness on shock, are very vague. So I was a bit on edge while I was working with it."

"You were a bit crusty, but that's all right."

Northfleet nodded absently in acknowledgment.

"You're a mine of miscellaneous information, Trent," he said at last. "Know anything about the marriage laws in Scotland?"

"No," Colin admitted. "But there's a *Whitaker's Almanack* over at Wester Voe. You'll get all the information in it."

"Thanks," said Northfleet.

THE END

》》》 If you've enjoyed this book and would like to discover more great vintage crime and thriller titles, as well as the most exciting crime and thriller authors writing today, visit: 》》》

The Murder Room
Where Criminal Minds Meet

themurderroom.com